SUDDEN HUNGER

He walked out of the water towards her, taking steady, deliberate steps. The long strands of his hair dripped down his chest and arms and back. In a catlike move, he shook his head, sending water droplets through the air.

He approached her, closer. She could feel the naked heat of his golden skin. There was no mistaking the sudden hunger that radiated from him.

With just the tip of his finger, he lifted her chin. Silken hair slid forward to brush against her shoulders, a hushed caress. Slowly, he lowered his lips until his mouth—that incredible, sensual mouth—was just a hairsbreadth from her own. Warm, clean breath drifted across her lips like a sultry breeze which heralds thunder.

Jenise paled. "I—I said I do not want—"

"Let me tell you something, my creamcat; I do not have a tendency to heed words that are so patently false."

"What does that mean?"

"It means," he drawled in a husky purr, "that my senses have already told me that you do *want* me very much."

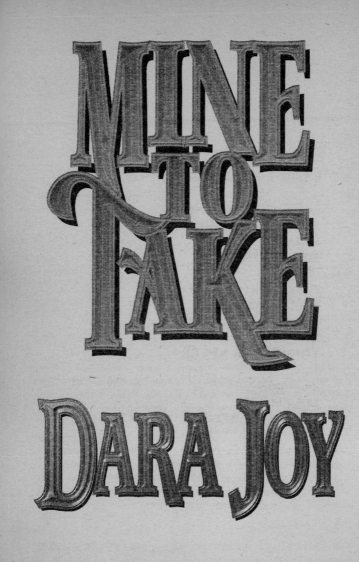

MINE TO TAKE

DARA JOY

LEISURE BOOKS NEW YORK CITY

A LEISURE BOOK®

November 1998

Published by

Dorchester Publishing Co., Inc.
276 Fifth Avenue
New York, NY 10001

ISBN 0-8439-4446-3

For My Mother
A Daughter's Love Lasts Forever

"THE CAT KNOWS WHOSE LIPS HE LICKS."
—Ancient proverb

Prologue

There are those who say that of all the mysteries in the universe, it is power which is most curious.

Is it force or is it ability? Is it illusion or is it a reflection of nature? Is it seized or is it bestowed? Birthright or destiny?

Or perhaps its elusive essence rises from other sources, nebulous and arcane.

Over time, numerous sages have inquired into the esoteric nature of power, for by its essence it is a catalyst of forces, nations, and beings.

It can enslave and it can liberate.

It can come from darkness and from light.

And by either its presence or absence, it rules us all.

There are those who spend their entire existence seeking it; while there other others to whom it simply comes. Those few who understand and respect

11

its nature, never questioning its presence, become its source.

For what is known positively about power is that it writes history.

And the pages of its story, for good or ill, are written by the hand that wields it best.

Thus say the Mystics of the Charl.

Chapter One

He was an absolutely stunning creature.

The Observer peered through the tiny viewing aperture at the delicious male specimen chained to the wall.

He was uniquely beautiful. In every way.

Like all Familiars, he walked in two forms, that of man and cat.

In their human form, Familiars often had a tendency to be mysterious, independent, and, on occasion, extremely playful.

Except when captured.

Cornered, they became fearsome adversaries; difficult to ensnare, let alone contain. This bold trait only added to their value, and they were highly sought after in certain sectors—sectors that were ungoverned by civilized law.

Some said they were priceless.

It was their very nature that put them at risk. For the Familiar were a highly sensual people. In fact, the males of the species lived for the sensuous. Reveled in it. Lost themselves in it.

It was claimed that the Familiar's erotic magnetism was difficult, if not impossible, to resist. His ability to entice was only surpassed by his legendary skills in the art of pleasure-giving. Some of these skills were cloaked in mystery, and rumors abounded as impossible tales circulated of the Familiars' extraordinary prowess in all things sensual.

Looking at this specimen, the Observer could believe that every rumor was true.

Silky, with a sheen all its own, the man's hair was extraordinary. *But then, no one had hair quite like a Familiar's.* It was said that the glossy strands felt better than the finest *krilli* cloth and that it flowed smoothly through the fingers (if one had fingers) with the texture of spun crystal.

Smooth and lustrous, the overall color was a burnished, dark gold accented with deep strands of gilded bronze. Individual gleaming strands of black also wove through the supple mane, which hung resplendently to the middle of his back. *Devastating!*

And his eyes . . . !

All Familiars had remarkable dual-colored eyes, but the Observer had never seen one with his combination before—had never even heard of it.

The captive was stunning, of course.

Like all of his kind.

The wretched thought made the Observer fume silently.

This one seemed even more glorious than the others. *All the more reason to revel in his capture!*

Yes, he would do quite nicely. Not like that other one . . .

Pity the soldiers got to that one before Karpon did. It appeared the Observer was not the only one to resent Familiar beauty. The other one had not fared very well. In fact, he was quite a mess by the time they arrived. He hadn't lasted long either. Karpon had him tossed out onto the refuse heap behind the keep as he drew his last breaths.

The Observer shuddered at the delicious memory.

Besides, after examining this superior specimen, who needed the other?

"He i*sss* a vibrant animal in the peak of hi*sss* manhood—we have *ss*een but one marking on him," the Observer murmured approvingly in its sibilant voice.

It was often noted that Familiars sometimes displayed one or several thin, tiny lines on the insides of their upper thighs. They were no longer than a human eyelash. It was not known what significance these small bands had, except that those who had few or none seemed to live longer than those who had many.

The Observer smiled slightly. At least it appeared to be a smile. "Thi*sss* one will do what you need, Karpon and then *ss*ome. *Ss*tories have it that the male*sss* can physically *enhance* the act

15

of *s*sexual love." A dry chuckle issued forth.

It seemed to irritate the Observer's companion.

"Really. Do you have any idea how many of my guards he took down before we were finally able to subdue him? He is dangerous."

"What do you expect, Karpon?" The Observer sneered. "The more difficult the capture, the better the champion. He i*sss* a premier catch—with a long, u*sss*eful life ahead of him. Hi*sss* longevity will make the trouble of hi*ss* capture worthwhile."

"*Longevity?*" The man named Karpon spat. "When he has done that which he has been captured for, he dies!"

The Observer looked askance at the foolish man. "A wa*sss*te of good raw material."

Karpon shuddered with distaste, both at his companion and at the suggestive remark. He knew it best to think of his erstwhile accomplice as "it." To think of such a being in any other way was to *invite* it in.

He quickly pushed the terrible thought away lest it gain substance. Horror had many masks.

"We under*sss*stand *ss*uch *ss*entiments." It rustled as it moved closer to him. "Did you know that the male Familiar can *ss*ense his mate? Too bad we do not have *ss*uch abilitie*sss*. We can only choo*sss*e to whom we give our love."

Karpon shivered inwardly. He did not want to think of such a macabre gift. Or the poor unfortunate on whom it would be bestowed.

A long black nail stroked teasingly down his cheek. He tried not to flinch.

"We feel your jealousssy . . . we admire it."

Karpon raised a cynical eyebrow, stepping back. The last thing he wanted was its admiration.

As if it understood his actions, it smiled knowingly. Chills skittered down Karpon's back.

"Are you sure he will get the deed done; what if he cannot—"

A dry crackling sound issued forth. Karpon assumed it was a laugh; although what its sense of humor might be was anyone's guess.

"He isss a Familiar; we asssure you he will get the job done."

Karpon fumed silently, grinding his teeth. Just the thought of the Familiar animal touching . . . ! He was not happy with this; Karpon was not a man who shared *anything* he deemed his. However, in this case, it was the only way to get all that he ultimately wanted.

"I don't want her cringing from my touch afterwards. If he frightens her—"

The Observer seemed highly entertained by his inference. "If she cringes from your touch it will not be from what he hasss done, but from what you have not. He isss a fitting choice for your future consssort."

Unthinking, Karpon pulled out a curved blade and held it to his companion's throat. "I could kill you for that."

"You could losssse your ssanity and attempt it."

It was fortunate for Karpon that he was a man

whose passion for power overrode his passion for other . . . things. He quickly withdrew the blade. What did words matter now? When it was over, he would have it all: Jenise and her kingdom.

"Yesss, yesss," it hissed, understanding more than it should about his nature. "I believe my work here isss done."

"Not yet. Where is the drug? You promised it to me in exchange for—"

"And we keep our promisssesss." It reached inside a hidden sac, pulling out a small vial of amber liquid.

Karpon took the vial gingerly, not wanting to touch it, yet knowing he must. He viewed the limited contents in disbelief. "Where is the rest of it? There is not enough here!"

It rustled again. "My dear Karpon, we asssure you there isss enough there to render helplesss the entire Familiar race."

Surprised, he asked, "How?"

"One drop isss all it takesss . . . jusst one drop. The Familiar who leaves their homeworld will be delivered unto you. All you need do isss find the ssecond Tunnel and you have the ressst." It reached up and closed the small viewing panel with a snap.

Karpon smiled evilly. With the Familiar available to him to sell to the highest bidders, he was assured of an unending supply of wealth. Yes, he would have it all.

"My work here isss done. If you do not mind,

we *ss*hall bow out of your little drama." It was not a request.

For a moment Karpon forgot himself. His cruel eyes narrowed. "And if I do mind?"

Once again, the long black nail ran teasingly down his cheek. "Watch your*sss*elf, he who would be ruler. That i*sss* the *ss*econd time. Be glad we have a fondne*ss* for you."

Karpon immediately realized his mistake. He stepped back and nodded.

"You have what you need now. We have *sss*e-cured your kingdom for you. The Familiar are almo*sss*t in the palm of your hand. Remember u*sss* . . ."

It left him standing there thinking about all the power that would soon be his.

He could not believe he had been taken.
Not him.
Not Gian Ren.

He was Guardian of the Mist! In the language of his people, the Familiar, Gian Ren was a name given to him in the time-old tradition of naming a newborn babe by using the special senses inherent in their race. It was a name sacred to his people and it carried with it many meanings.

The designation paid homage to his spectacular ability to blend into mist as if shadow. To watch. To track. To hunt. *To protect*.

When he pursued, he was cunning, clever, and silent. His innate tactical ability resided on levels most could not even hope to follow—even amongst his own kind. *Never* did he deliberate. His methodology was lightning-fast thought process, followed instantly by the appropriate physical response. These reactions were always based upon the superior instincts with which he had been born.

And yet, he had been taken.

Even now, days later, the effects on the drug they had originally given him still dulled his senses; although not as much as he was leading them to believe. It was not the usual drug that Oberion slavers used to capture Familiars. That drug would not have affected him to such a degree. He had been trained to fight that drug.

This drug, however, was something else. Something different. Something *dangerous*.

This drug interfered with his innate senses— not just by diffusing their focus, as the Oberion drug had done. When first administered, this drug blocked out his special senses entirely.

Gian did not want to even remember what *that* had felt like. Had he not been so centered within himself, he might truly have gone mad from the sensory deprivation.

It had been days before he realized that the effect was temporary. By that time, he was being given regular doses of the Oberion drug. Even so, he might be able to attempt transformation soon . . . provided they did not drug him again.

That was highly unlikely, he admitted to himself. The affects of the present dose were starting to wear off, but they had been very careful about keeping him controlled.

They kept him naked on a raised pallet, his back against a stone wall. Occasionally, they let him exercise. When they wanted him back in this position, they simply pulled taut the chains from the other side of the wall. It was very effective way to control him, for he never got close enough to anyone to cause any real damage.

Although he had tried.

Once a day, he was brought food and water. The food had been sufficient; apparently they were not trying to starve him. The water was fresh and they usually gave him enough to cleanse himself as well as drink. At those times and for brief periods in between, the chains loosened and he was allowed to get up and exercise.

During those interludes, he paced and prowled the cell, looking for a way out.

So far, he hadn't been able to find one.

When he had been taken, he had not been adventuring; he had gone out in search of his blood relative, Dariq, who was missing. The trail had led to this unknown, barely civilized planet on the Far Rim.

Dariq was young and had been on his first adventure. Gian was not surprised to see he had ventured so far afield. Younger males often did such things, forgetting to come home in light of the fun they were having. However, Dariq had been gone too long. His family was worried and rightly so.

He had gone after Dariq himself. Much to the objections of his mother's brother.

He was almost sure of the fate that had befallen Dariq—for his trail led close to this very keep. He was also reasonably sure that Dariq was no longer living, for he had not been able to sense his life signs.

Gian exhaled sadly. The young Familiar would not have been able to endure the new drug nor its torture. He prayed he was wrong.

Sickened by the injustice, Gian once again tested the chains that bound his powerful wrists to the stone wall. He did not expect them to be any looser but it never hurt to continually test one's enemy. Sometimes, mistakes were made. Familiars knew how to take advantage of mistakes.

He was not surprised when the chains did not give.

He had been testing them for days with the same result. Nonetheless, he would try again later. Gian was a contained predator and all the more deadly because of it. Unlike Dariq, he was not an inexperienced Familiar out on his first adventure.

He was a most dangerous adversary in his prime.

Through his dulled senses, a frisson of awareness suddenly tracked down his spine. *Someone was watching him . . .*

Immediately, his long, silken hair slid forward as he lowered his head, hiding his too-alert expression.

Keeping his head lowered, he surreptitiously watched through the thick veil of his lashes. There was a very small aperture in the wall facing him. He caught a glimpse of a malevolent eye staring at him. Another chill raced down his spine. His senses were trying to return.

If only he could prevent them from redrugging him . . .

His normally super-acute hearing picked up muffled sounds. A sibilant voice. Whoever was behind that wall was not alone. Barely he made out words. " . . . *the Familiar who leave their homeworld . . . delivered unto you . . . find the second Tunnel and you have the rest . . .* "

The blood froze in his veins.

How did they know about the second Tunnel? There was only one known entrance to his homeworld of M'yan and that was through Aviara. It was carefully guarded by the High Mystics of the Charl.

No one knew about the second Tunnel except the High Guild of Aviara and—

It seemed his enemies had plans.

He had to reach Aviara quickly!

Just before the viewing aperture was snapped shut, he caught a faint glimpse of an orange ring. Familiar eyesight being what it was, he was able to make out a portion of an unusual design.

It was not much. But it was something.

Often in the past, Gian Ren, Guardian of the Mist, had been known to do much damage to his enemies when he had even less to go on.

With a regal toss of his head, he flung back his mane of hair, leaning his head against the cold stone. He closed his eyes as he gathered his strength to him.

His eyes . . .

They would not know the special significance of the color of his eyes.

And because of that, and that alone, the corners of his lips curved upward slightly. No, they would not know.

Foolish of his adversaries to think they had taken him. Familiars, like their counterpart the cat, could never be subdued under the lash.

These beings had no true *power* over him. They only thought they did.

Methodically, he tested the chains again.

Power. She did not care about power!

Jenise walked over to the tower window and looked out at the courtyard below, quickly switching her gaze as she always did, to the meadows and fields beyond. Since it was night, she could make out only the outline of a hill on the horizon. Just two of the lesser moons were visible tonight. It made for a darker eve but she was glad of it.

The darkness would aid her plan.

A tear trickled down her resolute features. How oft in the past had she gazed out over this similar scene wondering when or if she would ever be free of this place, this life?

She sighed. *Too many times.* She had been so young when they came here; she hardly remembered her other life at all. Only her mother's stories and songs had kept that other life alive for her.

Tonight, if she had her way, everything would change, but not in the way that odious Karpon intended! A small, secret smile curled her lips as she remembered how he had come up to her chambers earlier in the day, full of misplaced confidence in his own power to succeed. He had outlined in very precise terms what he expected of her.

Jenise had been expecting this visit for some time.

What she had not been expecting was the depths to which the man would stoop to acquire what he deemed to be rightfully his.

Up to that point, Jenise had not really believed that his interest in her was genuine. She had never considered herself anywhere near as attractive as her mother; therefore his obsessive interest in her was puzzling.

Suddenly, she remembered her mother telling her that her magnetic ability would come late, and would, therefore, be very powerful.

There was that word again. *Power.* Jenise flinched.

At the time, she had laughed and teased that her mother was simply being a mother, wanting only the best for her fair daughter. Now she wondered if . . .

She glanced at her reflection in the window.

She frowned. Her image was the same as it had always been. *I do not see anything unusual.* Certainly nothing to have inspired Karpon's obsessive interest. Jenise concluded that the odd proclivities of men were very much a mystery to her.

But then, nothing had been the same since her mother's mate had died.

She closed her eyes wearily, leaning her forehead against the cool stone encasement, her mind running over the conversation that had taken place not long ago in this very room.

"I will rule this kingdom," Karpon had bluntly stated. He was the brother of her mother's consort, the man who had ruled this often barbaric land.

Jenise had shrugged. "Then rule it." She certainly had no desire to do so. Indeed, it was the last thing she would ever want. She longed to be free! Free like her mother's people, the nomadic Frensi. Free to live and laugh and love as she desired; free to explore and travel and learn. Not be bound by the conventions of this harsh and unforgiving land which stifled the spirit!

"Thank you for your vote of confidence, but there is a small problem." He walked over to her, his hand reaching out to grasp her chin, forcing her to look up at him.

"What is it?" she asked, even though she knew what he was going to say.

"*You* are the problem. The people will not recognize me as leader because they look to you. Your gentle disposition, your kindness, and your gift of laughter have reached them. They want only you."

Jenise shielded her eyes, hiding the effect his words had on her. "There is nothing I can do about that. I have told you I have no desire to rule. Ever."

His gaze fell to her full, lush lips and stayed

there. "So you say . . . *now*. You will always be a threat to me."

"No."

His cold finger slid down her cheek, causing her to shudder. "In more ways than one."

Jenise broke free of him and his hateful touch. Better to be dead than endure that touch! "Then kill me and be done with it."

"I think not; for I have a desire for the kingdom and you."

That jolted her. She quickly regained her composure. "You cannot have both, as well you know!"

"Not true."

The two words sent a chill down her spine. "What mean you by such words?" Karpon knew that should he take her as consort, she would automatically ascend to rule. It was the one thing that had protected her this long, for Karpon did not want *her* to rule—he wanted the power for himself. Surely he hadn't forgotten that?

He smiled slowly, wickedly. "There is a way, my sweet Jenise."

The smile unnerved her. Karpon looked much too confident. Her hand went to her throat. "Wh-what nonsense do you speak?"

He said three words. "Your maiden state."

Jenise blanched. She was still a maiden—not by choice, but because of the laws of this savage land. Had she been free to live her life as she chose, she might have been able to explore what it meant to love. "What of it?"

"As you know, it is a condition to your ascendance. Without it . . ." He let the thought linger, leaving her to draw her own conclusions.

Realizing what he was implying, Jenise blanched. However, she quickly recovered. She would not allow this creature to think he had shaken her.

"So, that is what this is all about?" Tossing her waist-length hair back, she forced herself to laugh in his smirking face, knowing it would infuriate him. "Then do it—if you dare."

His dark eyes flashed in anger, but he held himself in check. "I would, never doubt it. Unfortunately, it is not that simple."

Now Jenise did quake inside. He meant to kill her. Despite her resolve not to give him the satisfaction of seeing that he had shaken her, she flinched slightly.

Her reaction did not go unnoticed by the wretched *zorph*.

He snickered softly. "Do not worry, Jenise, I have something much better in store for you. For both of us," he whispered.

She did not want to ask. She had to ask. "What?"

"I have contained a Familiar for you."

A Familiar? What did . . . ? Jenise swallowed as his devious plan suddenly became clear to her. Familiars were known for their sexual appetites. He was mad!

"You will be given to him tomorrow. The two of you will be discovered—too late."

Controlling herself in order to learn what other horrors he might have planned for her, she asked, "And after?"

"Why, it will be my duty to tell the people what has befallen you. They will be beside themselves. Naturally, the rule shall fall to me, as I am next in line. I shall then execute the Familiar; publicly, of course."

"They won't demand that," Jenise quickly interjected, already feeling sympathy for the poor unfortunate Familiar who had landed himself in such a predicament.

Karpon's cruel eyes flashed. "*I* will demand it. When he touches you, his fate is sealed."

"But you will leave him no choice!"

"That is the price he pays for knowing you."

Sick at heart, Jenise turned away.

"After he has been killed and all is set to right, I will tell the people that I have decided to take you as my consort. So you see, Jenise, I will have the kingdom and you."

He placed his rough hands on her shoulders, squeezing her none too gently. "A perfect plan, would you not agree?"

Jenise would not answer him. She was too busy trying to think of a way, any way, to foil him. She would never tolerate his touch upon her. "You do not have to do this, Karpon. I am not a direct descendant. It should never have come to this! I understand how you feel cheated; you can declare yourself—"

"No. Though he was not your true father, my brother claimed you."

"Something my mother never wished him to do!" she reminded him.

His thin nostrils flared. It was well known that

29

Jenise's mother stubbornly clung to the ways of the Frensi and resisted the dominating love of his brother. Fool that his brother was, he had chosen to ignore that, taking the woman even as he conquered her.

Karpon shrugged. She had liked him well enough toward the end, he reminded himself. "It is too late for that. We both know that my brother did everything he could to please her, including claiming you."

"He did what he *thought* would please her. He never asked her," she said softly.

Karpon's temper rose. "Enough! Prepare yourself and let it be done on the morrow! For I warn you, Jenise, if you do not go to him willingly, I will have you brought to him." He hesitated a beat. "I can assure you he has been well primed for your visit. We have kept the beast alone for some time. And they do so like . . . their female company. You might even come to thank me," he goaded.

Everything inside her rebelled at his callous attitude. She did not know why, but Jenise felt a need to defend this unknown Familiar captive, the victim of such cruelty. "He is not an animal, Karpon; he is a man."

He sneered. "You will find out, I am sure."

Karpon turned to leave, then stopped, saying briskly, "Just do not become too used to his ways, for mine are quite different."

With that ominous pronouncement, he left.

Jenise sagged to the floor. Even though that conversation had taken place earlier in the day, she could still feel the remnants of Karpon's evil presence in her chambers. What was she to do? Karpon had laid out his plans in a neat, precise, frightening way.

As if she would just fall in with his machinations!

Did he think she would have no choice? There was always an alternative; she simply had to explore the options.

Karpon's brother had thought to control her mother and so had placed her in a comfortable cage. But it never really worked. Though her mother did come to care for him, she had always longed to be free. Like Jenise, she cared nothing for the trappings of power.

Jenise knew that Karpon's plans for her future would kill her spirit. And if she did not agree to his plans, he would probably truly kill her. Or force his will upon her. Such was his way.

So what could she do? If she went ahead with it, then—

Wait. Maybe there was a choice. . . .

She inhaled sharply. *Yes! It might work.*

Her shoulders straightened and a bittersweet smile tinged her lovely mouth. She would follow Karpon's plans, only on her *own* terms. Not tomorrow. *Tonight.*

The foolish Karpon did not realize that he had provided the answer to her dilemma! The Familiar could set her free! If he took her first and they then escaped . . .

The glimmer of freedom tantalized her. And she would never again have to worry about having to rule Ganakari. That possibility would be destroyed along with her maiden's shield.

Even if they were recaptured (and the odds were high that they would be), she would never let Karpon forget that *she* had gone to the Familiar on her own terms and that the Familiar had been her first and *best*. She knew Karpon. Over time that knowledge would slowly destroy him.

Although not to her liking, the plan was her best option. She did not want to live a life of revenge, but if forced to, she would.

Resolved in what she must do, Jenise turned from the window to make herself ready for him. She did not know too much about male Familiars, but she did know that they had a wild hunger for women.

She prayed the captive would temporarily find this one to his taste.

She did not expect him to be so breathtaking.

Adjusting the hood of her cloak to cover her face from view, Jenise entered the dank stone chamber, closing the heavy wooden door behind her. Her gaze went immediately to the man chained on the bed, his back leaning against the stone wall.

He was a comely creature, she'd give him that.

His head was bowed forward as if he had fallen asleep; his long hair concealed his face from her view. She could not help staring at his form.

He was exquisite! Positively magnificent.

Jenise had never seen a Familiar before, but if this was any indication of the species, she could well understand their astounding reputation. Even chained, there was a potent aura of sensuality encloaking him.

The man did not look up or give any other indication that he was aware of her presence in the room. Nonetheless, Jenise wasn't fooled. She knew that he knew she was there; she had heard that much about Familiars—they were almost impossible to take unawares.

Suddenly she wondered how Karpon had managed to capture him.

In a confrontation, the males were said to be fearless. When cornered, they would often fight to the death—usually of their opponents—rather than be taken. By his sheer size and musculature, this one appeared especially capable of defending himself.

So his capture was all the more puzzling.

Since he did not deign to acknowledge her presence, Jenise took the opportunity to study him further. He was soon to be her first lover, so her interest in him was more than simple curiosity.

He was naked. Had he been captured that way or . . . ?

She didn't want to think about that.

Jenise abhorred violence of any kind and her heart went out to the Familiar for what he had probably already suffered in the name of Karpon's greed.

His tawny golden skin was smooth all over, its

Dara Joy

texture so evenly sleek that she almost found herself reaching out to touch him. He manifested a sensuous warmth.

And he was perfectly formed.

His expansive chest was athletic, masculine, sculpted. Muscles bulged in his upper arms; the veins in his forearms were prominent as his sturdy wrists pulled taut against the manacles that bound him in place.

Her gaze moved lower.

The chain looped around his midsection, riding low on his lean hips. The links slid against the golden skin of his hipbones as he breathed steadily.

As expected, his stomach was flat and rippled with muscle, while his . . .

Apprehensively, Jenise swallowed again.

She immediately shifted her focus down to his powerful thighs, which were also incredibly firm and tautly muscled. Even though he was half-reclining, she could tell he was a very tall man.

She had always heard the Familiar were an exceptionally beautiful people, but she couldn't imagine any more beautiful or more intrepid than this one.

Jenise remembered something else she had heard—that their skill in the art of lovemaking surpassed what their appearances promised. Tales constantly circulated about their legendary prowess.

Looking at this one, she could understand how some women could come to crave the Familiar so.

Well, she was not interested in his special skills.

There was only one thing she wanted of him. And it was not pleasure.

Jenise exhaled, trying to gather her strength of purpose. He seemed a bit too much to handle! Was there any kindness in him? she wondered.

Convulsively, she swallowed the knot in her throat as she thought about what she had to do. A small price to pay, she kept telling herself, to gain her freedom and her life.

Furthermore, it was going to be on her terms. Not Karpon's.

Silently, she approached the side of the bed. At closer range he was even more impressive, and she wondered again how Karpon had ever managed to contain him. She voiced her thoughts aloud.

"How did they come to capture you?" she asked him softly.

At first he did not respond to her in any way. Then he slowly raised his head. He did not answer her.

Which was just as well.

For when Jenise caught sight of his exquisite face she was momentarily speechless. He was terrifyingly beautiful.

He had the kind of masculine features women were prone to dream about. Strong, fierce, unyieldingly sensual.

Yet in a face so arresting for its masculine perfection, it was his eyes that commanded the most attention. *They were two different colors.*

One was clear green; the other fiery gold. She noticed that the green eye had three tiny gold flecks in it. Very curious.

And very captivating.

The lambent eyes were rimmed by thick black lashes. Potent affirmation of his sensual nature was reflected in that green-on-gold stare. When he leveled that measured gaze on her, Jenise noted that those incredibly seductive eyes seemed to offer up everything while giving away absolutely nothing.

She also noted that they were dilated. Was he being drugged?

As she studied him, his firm lips curved secretively.

His mouth was nothing less than bewitching; there was no other way to describe it. There was a certain mischievous tilt to those firm, masculine lips that—

Jenise pulled herself back.

She had no intention of allowing herself to fall prey to the Familiar's considerable charms! She needed to make a pact with him, and quickly, if her plan was to work.

"Will you not speak to me?" Her voice was gentle. "I had nothing to do with your capture, I assure you."

"Then why do you hide from me beneath that cowled cloak?" His voice, like his skin, was smooth, even, and rich. It flowed over her like a lover's caress. Jenise began to believe all the rumors she had heard about the Familiar male . . .

the stories that they could make themselves ir-
resistible to women.

She mentally shook herself.

Hypnotized by that commanding, lush tone,
she tried to find her own voice. "I am not hiding
from you. I wish to speak with you on a matter
that may be beneficial to both of us. If you agree
with what I have to say, then I will reveal myself
to you. If not, then I will leave."

Gian could not credit what his drugged Familiar senses were telling him. He had noticed
her from the instant the door opened. There was
no way he could not notice her. He had thought
they were coming to dose him again.

His eyes narrowed. She was strong. But then
she would have to be. His lips curved enigmatically.

Of all things, he had never expected this intriguing development.

His glance fell to her hands. Small and white,
they gave no clue as to who she might actually
be. Even though Gian was still feeling the effects
of the strange drug they had given him, his
senses were alive and humming as to who she
was to *him*.

Nothing could dull that particular perception.
It was accurate and clear.

Which could only mean one thing. Or so he
thought.

Consequently, he spoke to her in the secret Familiar tongue. *"K'mar keana latarq shinteera?"*
How did you find me? *"L'mee tuan doenn?"* Who
else is with you?

"I—I don't understand you."

Gian's mouth parted very slightly, his only outward show of surprise as his mind took in what his Familiar senses had already ascertained. "You are not a Familiar woman?" He was soft-voiced.

"No, why would you think that?" She sounded confused.

Why, indeed.

Most unexpected. He blinked, ramifications and complexities dancing around his head as he accepted this curious fact.

Gian watched her carefully. That she was non-Familiar was highly unusual and somewhat disturbing but, like all his kind, Gian did not waste too much time pondering reasons. Theirs was a reactive race. They accepted what was, then dealt with what could be.

However, this could be a very unpredictable situation. He almost smiled. He adored such complexities; they made life interesting.

Gian had the distinct impression that his life was about to get positively fascinating.

He already knew she was telling the truth about his capture; she had had nothing to do with it. His abilities told him that much. He decided to hear what she had come to say.

If he didn't like it, he could always seduce her.

Her words might alter his method, but not his objective. Gian Ren, Guardian of the Mist, was already mapping out his strategy for a very special hunt.

He tossed his hair back and viewed her

through half-lowered eyes. The eyes of the ultimate pursuer. Secretive, disciplined, and sexual. His voice was a low, rumbling purr.

"Then speak."

Chapter Two

Jenise swallowed. The concept had seemed more *reasonable* in the privacy of her own chambers.

Things were somewhat different, she discovered, when one had to look into the face of commanding reality—*he*, who was calmly waiting for her to rationally lay out her plans.

As if she was there to do his bidding!

He was a much more compelling subject than she would have preferred. There was a majestic air to him that was disquieting. Jenise shivered.

However, there was no choice. He was it.

She was just going to have to look into those enigmatic green/gold eyes and tell him what she wanted of him. And what she was willing to give him in return.

After all, the initial risk was entirely hers;

what did he have to lose by such a bargain?

"I want you to take me."

The pupils of his dual-colored eyes momentarily flared. It was then that Jenise remembered what Karpon had said—that the Familiar had been well primed for her. What had he meant by that exactly?

A small muscle worked in his firm jaw. His eyes narrowed. For some reason, he did not seem overly pleased. Or overly surprised.

Nonetheless, pleased or not, he was obviously not stupid.

Gian watched her carefully. Coming to some decision, he shook his chained wrists. "Very well. Then release me."

Jenise wondered how often these Familiars made such bargains. She had no way of knowing that the answer to that was *never*. Familiars only did what they chose to do.

She laughed at his directive. Did he think her so foolish? Even the guards had warned her only to loosen his chains if necessary but under *no* circumstances to release him. They had even tried to talk her out of visiting the dangerous captive.

"Do I seem like a fool to you?"

His nostrils flared in annoyance. He was in no mood to play. "On the contrary," he said precisely, "you seem desperate."

Jenise's shoulders sagged beneath the voluminous cloak. If she were not desperate, would she even consider this? "Yes, I am."

Gian sensed the woman's spirits plummet. Instantly, he realized that he had inadvertently hit upon the truth. This was not as he had first thought. There was more to this than sexual curiosity. Relieved, his attitude changed to one of concern.

"Explain why you want this from me," he said evenly, his voice low and coaxing.

"The man who captured you is named Karpon; he is the brother of the deceased ruler of this land."

"Go on."

"My mother was his mate—unwillingly." She explained their relationship to him. Gian gestured for her to continue. "So you see, Karpon wishes to rule. In order to do that, he must—"

"Eliminate you," Gian finished for her.

"Not exactly . . . you see, I have no desire to rule."

Gian viewed her curiously. Already, she was beginning to lure him. The sound of her melodious voice caressed his senses. And her scent! Like the meadows on M'yan right after a warm rain shower.

It had been too long for him. Much too long. He shifted on the pallet. "Why do you not want to rule?"

"Because I detest the trappings of power. It is not the life I seek."

Gian studied her from beneath veiled eyes. She was an interesting conundrum in so many ways. And the riddle was becoming more complex by the moment. He said nothing for several moments. "If Karpon knows this, what is the problem?"

"He wants me as well."

There was a pause. "I see."

"But if he takes me, he can only become *my* consort, as I will ascend to rule—something he does not want."

Gian was beginning to understand the scope of her problem. And his as well. "So what has this paragon Karpon concocted, hmmm? Why do I think my capture is part of it?" He glanced shrewdly over at her.

It was the first indication Jenise had of his intelligence and his cunning. She made a mental note never to underestimate him.

"Yes; he has sent me here to you."

His lips curved enigmatically. "He sent you to me . . . now that is curious. What does he hope to gain from that?"

"In this land, in order for me to ascend to rule, I must either have taken a consort or—" She hesitated, embarrassed. She did not wish him to know the entire story. The maiden state was extremely awkward. Women naturally sought their pleasures.

He lifted a dark brow. "Or?" he prodded.

She did not directly answer him. "That is not important. What is important is that I have thought up a way to thwart Karpon."

"I still do not understand what significance—"

She quickly interrupted him. "You see, I wish to leave here. With your help, my dream can finally become a reality."

Her words stopped Gian. Now she was getting to what was of paramount interest to him. "You wish me to help you escape."

"Not exactly. *I* will help *you* escape if you do what I have asked of you."

He grinned broadly at the absurd idea of someone bargaining to get a Familiar to do the one thing he loved to do most. "With pleasure, my hooded mystery. After we leave here, I will show you everything I—"

"No, it must be now."

He frowned. "Do not be foolish! This is neither the time nor the place to—"

"You do not understand. Those are my terms."

"You are right; I am at a loss to understand such reasoning. Are you saying that if I take you, you will not be able to rule this land?"

"Yes."

"Is that not what he wishes?"

"Not exactly. You see, if you agree to this, I will help you to escape as well. We will make a pact to aid each other until we leave this land. If we succeed, it will drive Karpon mad to know that not only did you have me, but he lost me forever as well. With my disappearance, I may be able to help these people by delaying *him* from taking complete rule of the land. They will have to wait a standard Alliance year to see what has befallen me before a new ruler is actually named. Who knows? In that time, mayhap someone will aid me and let the assemblage know about Karpon's evil nature."

Her words disturbed him. Familiars did not

believe in using loveplay as a means to an end; in their view loveplay *was* the end most worth achieving. And some part of her story seemed to be missing.

"You would do such a thing strictly to avoid taking your rightful place?"

"Yes, I would; for it is a place I do not desire."

Gian sighed. He would not do what she asked. "I must refuse then."

It was Jenise's turn to be shocked. "*What?* You cannot refuse!"

A dimple curved his cheek at the sound of outrage in her sweet voice. "I just did."

Since Jenise could not imagine a Familiar turning down a chance to explore his sensuality, she took Gian to mean that he would take her, but would not escape with her. "B-but—do you not wish to escape? I assure you, Karpon will kill you regardless once you . . . well, do you not wish to bargain?"

"I do not have to bargain."

Jenise bristled. No one had ever mentioned how difficult a Familiar could be! Or how unpredictable. "I can get what I want from you without releasing you," she stated bluntly.

"You think so?" He leveled a meaningful look at her.

Perhaps not. What did he want? Exasperated, she threw her hands up in the air. "Why would you not bargain? Need I remind you that you are at a disadvantage? *You* are the captured one. You are mine to take!"

"Appearances can be deceiving," he intoned softly.

Jenise shivered. What exactly did he mean by that? He was too confident. It was almost as if there was a hidden knowledge in those dual-colored eyes of his. It unnerved her.

Perhaps she would be better off not playing with such fire. He was not one to control. Jenise was having second thoughts about the wisdom of tangling with him, no matter how desperate her need.

"How did they capture you?" she whispered once again.

"I was drugged," he answered flatly. "Something that was very powerful. It overcame me quickly, before I could compensate."

"Does the drug affect you in *that* way?" She gave him a meaningful look.

Gian gaped at her incredulously. "*Nothing* affects us in that way."

She let out a sigh of relief. "At least you weren't harmed. I have heard terrible rumors about what Karpon does to some prisoners."

He snorted. "Not harmed. Do you know anything about this drug they used?"

She shook her head.

"It deadens our special senses."

"What does that mean?"

"We have many more senses than you. Imagine, if you will, suddenly losing your sight, your hearing, your ability to speak, your sense of touch and smell *all at once.* Now magnify that a hundredfold."

How horrible. Her hand came to her mouth. "I—I did not know. Is it still affecting you?"

He was careful how he answered her. Regardless of what he knew about her, she could still be a danger to him. And herself. "Some" was all he would say.

He was fencing with her and she was tired of it. He either trusted her or he didn't.

Apparently he didn't.

"I have changed my mind." Jenise turned to leave, adding poignantly over her shoulder. "You have suffered enough already. Perhaps one of the guards will help me—"

[Stop.]

For some reason, his voice made her do just that. She turned slowly back to him, having no idea he had sent her a telepathic command. "Yes?"

He could not let her go to anyone else. "I have changed my mind as well. I will do as you ask."

He could feel her victorious smile even though he couldn't see it. So . . . she had played him, had she? He almost purred. He rather liked that.

"Fine. We will do it like this, with you chained. Afterward, I will—"

"I think not. You will have received what you came for and I will still be chained. You see the flaw to that."

Jenise was indignant. "I have given you my word!"

"You will not think too badly of me if I say that the word of one of your kind—a people who enslaves another—is not sufficient for me." Besides his stated objection, Gian had a very important reason for needing to be released before performing. He intended to take her in a most traditional Familiar way. Something he could not do in his present position.

"I only have *your* word, Familiar."

"Familiars always mean what they say." He did not add that often their words could be interpreted many different ways. The Familiar was a master of subtlety, yet always truthful.

"In any event, you have the option of calling out to the guards, do you not?" Gian did not say that once he was released, she would never have time to utter a sound before he moved. She really knew very little about his kind. The thought was not a comfort to him.

"I suppose one of us must trust the other." Jenise worried her lip as she thought it over.

"Mmmm. It is your choice."

She took a deep breath. "Very well, in the interest of expediting matters, I will release you."

Gian waited, not moving a muscle lest she change her mind and take flight. Slowly, Jenise leaned over him, keys dangling in her hand.

She placed the key in the first lock on the manacle at his wrist. *Yes*, Gian urged silently. *Keep going . . .*

She stopped.

He looked up at her out of the corners of his enigmatic eyes; his expression was one of wary expectation combined with thoughtful contemplation.

"Remember, you promised," she reminded him.

He nodded curtly once.

Clink. The first manacle fell off.

She never got to the second.

In the blink of an eye he was off the bed, the keys already in his hand, and his second wrist was free.

Jenise had never seen anything move that fast. Perhaps she had made a mistake. The Familiar was much more imposing standing before her, unchained!

He was even taller than she'd surmised. *And bigger.* Nervously, she began to back up.

He advanced on her, rubbing the soreness out of his wrists. "Now we are shy?" A deep, languorous laugh exited his perfectly formed lips.

"We—we have a pact!" She backed skittishly up against a wall.

"Yes, we do." He expertly cornered her. His large hands reached under her hood, tossing it back.

Freed from the protective folds of material, she stared up at him, not at all sure what to do next.

He studied her intently.

At first glance, she was not beautiful.

But she was captivating.

Gian could not pull his gaze from her. There was something about the way the light danced on the contours of her features, the spark of true intelligence in her eyes. She radiated vibrancy and mystery.

Inside her heart there was a kindness he could not overlook.

Her hair was a pale, creamy shade and it hung straight and thick to her waist. If Gian were in any other circumstances, he might have gloated, for it was a shade he was particularly partial to. Had this woman been a Familiar female, she probably would have turned into a cream-colored cat.

A dainty, hissing little cat.

He smiled at the image that provoked.

In every situation, one must look at the positive aspects.

Her lovely eyes were a rare shade of aquamarine and reminded him of the Placid Lagoon on his home world of M'yan. They were surrounded by long, light brown lashes which were tipped with gold.

A tremor of desire shook him. He wanted to run his lips across those lashes . . . feel the golden tips against his mouth . . .

He could not stop staring at her. Her pull on him was almost magnetic!

Gian immediately revised his initial impression of her to one of utter beauty. He knew exactly why this Karpon was intent to have her. She was wrong if she thought he would let her go so easily.

A man might just risk a kingdom for her.

Gian smiled mysteriously in appreciation of the games of destiny.

He reevaluated his appreciation of destiny in the next moment. Now that he had full sight of her, his special senses were able to discern much more about her. All amusement fled as he stared at her with a stony expression.

Misinterpreting his look for one of dissatisfaction, Jenise quickly said, "It is just this one time; you need not—"

"You are untouched." He spoke tonelessly.

As if he had just discovered that she had committed an unspeakable crime!

Jenise frowned. She had hoped to keep that truth from him. "How do you know that?"

At that point Gian was thinking that he had been captured, chained to a wall, drugged, deprived of female company for days on end, and now this! *A maiden.*

He exhaled noisily, slapping the palms of his hands against the wall behind her with a dull thud.

Jenise peeked up at him through her gold-tipped lashes. "Is there something wrong?"

His eyes kindled. He slammed the wall again. "No . . . no . . . why would you think that?" He glared down at her.

She bit her lip. "A guess?"

"Do you know anything about Familiars?"

Jenise dropped her eyes, slightly embarrassed. What she had heard couldn't possibly be true. "Some," she answered evasively.

He raised a disbelieving eyebrow.

"Very well . . . little."

"Fine. Then I will tell you something about the males. We—how shall I phrase this?" His tone was sarcastic. "We prefer to engage in intense loveplay."

Jenise listened closely, nodding her head slightly. Yes, that was what she had heard. What was his problem?

"*Prolonged* loveplay," he stressed, since she didn't seem to be understanding him.

"Well, that is not possible. We must make haste to depart—"

"Exactly."

"—as soon as you are done. It should not take long. You misunderstand me if you think I am interested in pleasure. I am not."

"I understand you think the first time will not be pleasurable; but I assure you I can make it so for you if—"

"No."

"*No?*"

She lifted her chin. "I simply want this done and done quickly."

Gian's sharp gaze ran over her determined features. A hissing little cat. His hand cupped her face. "Listen to me, Creamcat. You do not know what you are asking. It would be better for us both if we—"

She shook her head. "No. We had a pact, Familiar, you promised."

Gian ran his finger down her pert nose, his expression contemplative. He seemed to be weighing his alternatives. And the consequences of those alternatives.

As always, it did not take Guardian of the Mist very long to come to a decision.

"Turn and face the wall."

"Wh-what?"

"There is not much time; do as I say."

Gingerly, she turned.

"Drop your cloak." She did as he asked. A pastel pink diaphanous gown clung to her curves. "Unclasp the gown."

With a shaking hand, she undid the broach near her shoulder which held the garment up. It slithered to the stone floor.

A deep, growling sound of hunger issued from the male throat behind her.

Jenise closed her eyes, trying to still her shaking. Rumor said these Familiars were half-wild when they made love.

A hoarse, rumbling voice spoke from behind her, near her ear, sending tremors down her exposed throat. "I ask you one last time. Wait until a better moment."

Jenise opened her eyes, turning to gape at him over her shoulder. "Why would I wait? What purpose would there be in that? The whole point is to get this over with to—"

She gasped, for he had wrapped her hair around his powerful wrist, tugging her head back so their lips almost but not quite touched. His expressive eyes burned as he looked down at her.

Then he spoke in words she could not understand. Familiar tongue?

"Gian Ren K'tea . . .
Ei mahana ne Tuan

53

Gian Ren K'mea sut la.
Ei re Tuan
Taj Gian Ren litna K'shintauk rehan.
A jhan vri re Tuan."

Jenise furrowed her brow at the strange words. Although it was not visible to the eye, she had an Aviaran translator device implanted in her temple. Apparently it did not work on this dialect.

Was this recital something all Familiars did before they engaged in sexual relations? It was an odd ritual; for truly the words sounded ritualistic.

She didn't have time to think further about the strange phrases, for it was then she noticed that an exotic, enthralling scent was beginning to encloak her. It took her a moment to realize it was the Familiar's sexual scent!

She had heard of this as well; of how their scents could entangle a woman and bring her to offer herself up to him. *Offer anything he desired . . .*

Briefly, she closed her eyes, inhaling the luscious aroma. The essence reminded her of rare *krinang* spice, evocative of nights on the high desert plains. Dry, hot breezes and sultry, tropical storms. Crisp, tantalizing dreams.

It was a scent that provoked feminine sexual surrender. Compelling, commanding, promising . . .

The aroma hinted of his luscious flavor.

Jenise moaned, trying not to fall prey to his

overwhelming allure. How would she ever forget this scent? Would she dream of it in future? Be cursed to want him whenever a touch of its elusive essence teased her memory?

Curiously, she noted that his mysterious eyes were dilating yet more. That was odd, considering that it had been a while since he had been drugged and the dilation should be lessening, not increasing.

Jenise did not think this dilation was the result of the drugs. It seemed to be some prelude to—

He captured her in his hypnotic gaze and she could not seem to look away! Green and gold depths, sensual and lambent, became her entire universe. She found herself looking into the man's soul of passion.

There was a wildness to him that would never be controlled.

He was feral at heart.

Jenise shivered again. He was more alien than she had initially thought. What was more, she realized that rumors rarely circulated without having some basis in fact. And some of those stories! Even if only a quarter of them were true . . .

She had made a mistake! A grievous mistake.

She was no match for him; he would consume her with his ravenous Familiar appetite! Jenise tried to pull back, but it was too late.

His mouth descended firmly to claim hers.

Velvet lips parting slightly, he captured her in

a taking that seared her with animalistic passion. He tasted of the untamed.

Panicked, she struggled under his mouth, trying to break the overwhelming contact.

The Familiar held her fast to him.

He inhaled her rapid exhalation deep into his lungs as if he were taking her very life into himself. Jenise blinked. She could not breathe!

Frantic, she tried to turn all the way in his arms but he held her immobile. The room began to swirl around her as she grew faint; she wondered if she had been a fool to trust him, after all. What did she know about his capabilities? Could these Familiars kill by stealing one's breath?

A sound of despair flowed from her mouth into his.

Once again, he surprised her.

With a surge of force he respired into her mouth, giving her back her breath, which was now mingled with his own spicy scent. At least, she assumed it was partly her breath.

Greedily, she inhaled this rush of warm life, clinging to his tenacious lips. At her action, he *pur-r-red* deeply into her mouth.

He lifted his lips from hers. His white teeth captured her bottom lip, which he then released gradually as he pulled back from her. Murmuring something resonant and sultry, he turned her completely away from him so that she faced the wall again.

"Place your hands against the stone." He breathed huskily in her ear, his mouth skirting around the lobe, his tongue swirling its delicate folds.

With her hair still tightly wrapped around his wrist, he continued to hold her fast. Tangled in the strands, his strong fingers splayed against her scalp. A muscular arm came around her waist to pull her back taut against him.

The length of him was hard and hot.

Jenise couldn't seem to stop her trembling. "Please," she whispered, willing him to finish and be done with it. He gave her one final chance.

"Tell me to stop," he growled. Short, hot gusts of his breath skittered along her shoulder blade.

As much as the confines of his strict hold on her would allow, she shook her head no.

A snarl escaped his lips, a cross between anger and satisfaction. With no hesitation whatsoever, his teeth clamped down on the back of her neck to grasp her sharply in their grip.

Jenise cried out in alarm. *What was he doing?* Frightened, she tried to writhe free but could not.

Decisively, he thrust forward.

In one swift movement, he pierced her maiden's membrane with a powerful stroke. Jenise's knees buckled as shock and pain hit her.

The Familiar released her hair to clasp her hands in his. He steadied her against the wall, still deeply embedded in her.

Jenise gulped in air, trying to find her breath against this terrible invasion. She felt him above her and behind her and in her as he, too, fought for his breath and, perhaps, his control.

They seemed to stay like that for an eternity, yet in actuality it could only have been a few moments. It was curious but Jenise noticed that they were starting to breathe together. In and out, in and out, their breaths were the only thing moving between them, like waves flowing together. . . .

Her tense muscles gradually began to relax, liquefying into him. It occurred to her that he might be deliberately calming her with his even pacing. His rugged chest rose and fell against her back; his compelling scent gently lulled her now.

Jenise closed her eyes, leaning back into him.

A murmur of approval rolled from his chest. His large, skilled hands dropped to the curve of her hips. The tips of his fingernails scraped up over her hipbones. Simultaneously the edges of his clean teeth grazed up the sensitive side of her neck.

It was an incredibly erotic ploy.

Jenise shivered, but not from fear. The arousing action had whetted her interest in what was to come.

Which was as Gian intended. There was a pulling friction as he abruptly withdrew from her.

Shocked, she stared at him over her shoulder.

He released her, stepping back, away. "There is not much time, *taja*. We must leave now."

Jenise was stunned. "But you . . . that is . . . you have not . . ."

Strong fingers cupped her chin. He smiled faintly. "No, I have not."

A small line of puzzlement furrowed between her brows. "Why?"

"Because you have said you do not want pleasure and so I cannot take mine either."

Jenise flushed. She hadn't meant that he should not find his own satisfaction! It would have been too cruel to expect that of any man. "Surely you did not think I meant you!"

Gian grinned. He couldn't help himself. How little she knew about his kind.

Well, that would change soon.

This creamcat was very engaging and the journey to Aviara would be most entertaining. Not to mention enlightening. For both of them.

He bent over to whisper against her mouth, "I thank you for being so considerate of *my* welfare." His lips brushed hers teasingly. He sipped the pink skin delicately. Just a hint of touch. "But I never said I was *finished*."

It took a moment for the meaning of his words to sink in; Jenise was drowning in the expert touch of that succulent male mouth.

She blinked as her sanity returned. "Unfortunately, Familiar, you *are* finished. You have done what I asked and now I will honor the rest of our agreement. We will attempt to make Tunnel point together. As for anything else between us, that is over."

Gian gave her an amused, knowing look which calmly refuted the statement. In the past, he had often told his younger blood relative Rejar that a Familiar was never finished until he was *good* and finished. Gian was far from good and finished.

In fact, he had not yet begun.

"I will be glad to explore this unique interpretation with you later; now, am I to assume one of these keys opens the door?" He held up the key chain, dangling it from his fingers.

The man made such a splendid picture standing there—sleekly muscled and completely nude, with tawny golden skin and magnificent hair, which was slightly tousled—she was inclined to let his assumption rest until she had a chance to clarify her position.

Jenise smiled slowly. At least she would have the pleasure of looking at him during this portion of her adventure, especially if he continued to go about without clothes on.

Her eyes traveled the length of him. He was, to say the least, extraordinary. A surge of unbidden desire startled her. Was it because of what they had just done or *not* done?

She gathered her wits about her. "No, they do not open the door. I am supposed to call to the guards." Retrieving her garment and cloak, she quickly donned them. A lingering tremor assailed her; she would think about what had occurred in this room at a later, safer time. For now they must focus on escape.

Gian's green/gold eyes flashed in secret knowledge. He knew exactly how she had been looking at him. And *why*. "How many guards are out there?"

"Three."

"Good." He placed himself behind the door. "Now scream, woman who seeks no pleasure."

He was going to be difficult, of that she was certain. Jenise rolled her eyes and screamed as loudly as she could.

The guards came rushing in.

In the blink of an eye the Familiar took all three down. He moved so fast, she couldn't even distinguish the individual motions. Never had she seen anyone move in such a way, with deadly accuracy and feline grace.

Impressed, she raised an eyebrow as she caught his eye.

Nonchalantly, he held the door open for her. As if he hadn't just rendered three highly trained men unconscious without ruffling a hair on his gorgeous head!

As she strolled through the door, Gian took the opportunity to run his palm over her cloaked backside.

Stopping short, Jenise gasped. Up until a short time ago, she was the heir apparent. Men did not do such things to women who had that kind of power.

He gave her an innocent look. "I never said I would not seduce you."

Jenise snorted. "You certainly can *try*, Familiar."

A roguish dimple curved his cheek. "Same thing."

Chuckling at her outraged expression, he took her hand and led her through a maze of corridors, his innate tracking ability serving him well. Nothing felt as good as the taste of freedom! He looked over at his companion. Well, almost nothing.

"How do you know the way out?"

"I am a Familiar." He glanced down at her out of the corner of his eye. "You had best remember that, *taja*."

She was too excited by the prospect of finally gaining her freedom to be annoyed with the arrogant thing.

"Quickly, this way." He pulled her into an alcove just as a contingent of guards passed.

"I did not even hear them approaching! I cannot believe—"

His mouth seized hers in a sizzling kiss. "I am Gian," he purred against her lips. "Remember that, too, Creamcat."

Before she could respond, he grabbed her hand once more and darted down another hidden corridor.

Chapter Three

The Familiar stopped so abruptly that Jenise bumped into him. His arm came out to steady her as he pulled her back against the wall of the corridor.

"What is it?" she asked worriedly. "Why have we stopped?"

He placed a tapered finger against her lips, warning her to be silent. Then he cocked his head to one side, listening for something Jenise could not hear.

"There is a male guard up ahead, around this corner. He is alone . . . not so tall as I am, but of a size. I may be able to utilize his garments." His voice was very, very focused. "I will take him down."

"How do you know all of this?" she whispered back.

"My senses tell me. By his footfall I can ascertain his size. . . . He is not very alert at the moment—that I can tell by the rate of his breathing. He is relaxed, almost bored."

"That is amazing; I am impressed, Familiar."

He gave her a crooked grin. "You have not yet seen how I can impress you, Creamcat."

Jenise flushed as his meaning became clear. He laughed quietly at her telltale reaction.

"You may keep such impressions to yourself!" she hissed indignantly. "That is *not* part of our bargain."

The firm lips twitched beguilingly. The tip of his finger stroked the side of her face. "It will be your choice," he purred.

Jenise stiffened, pulling away from his touch. "Yes, it will be my choice."

A flash of white teeth gleamed in the darkened corridor—a hint of amusement. The Familiar lifted her chin with the same finger, bringing her face up to his.

"Exactly," he whispered, brushing her mouth with his own.

Before Jenise could respond, he was already gone.

A few moments later she heard a brief scuffle, followed by the sound of a body falling to the floor.

His hand signaled to her that it was safe to come forward.

When she rounded the corner, he was already stripping the man's black leather breeches off.

"Is—is he dead?" Jenise nodded in the direction of the fallen guard.

The Familiar seemed affronted. "Of course not. We only kill when we are forced to—unlike Karpon."

He pulled the thigh-hugging *tracas* on over his own lean hips, fastening up the rawhide laces in front. Jenise watched him, for some reason fascinated by the effortless action.

The Familiar glanced up slowly, catching her in his glinting regard. There was a very knowing look in those dark green and gold eyes. It was the first time Jenise got a true sense of just how experienced the man was . . . in everything.

She began to wonder about this captive she had released. Who was he? Did all Familiars have such a compelling presence or was it he alone? Already, she'd had glimpses of his control, his mastery, and his resourcefulness. Perhaps he was more than what she imagined?

He did not seem to be one who would allow himself to be persuaded into anything unless it was his desire to do so. And yet he had repeatedly told her that it would all be her choice; that she would be the one in control. At least, it *seemed* he meant that.

Jenise decided to take the Familiar at his word—for the time being. So far, he was living up to his side of their bargain. However, if he proved himself difficult, they would be parting company very rapidly.

Gian bent over the prone guard, lifting his foot to pull the man's boots off. He stopped suddenly.

Dropping the man's foot abruptly, he jumped up, grabbing Jenise's hand. "Hurry; there are many coming! They seek us—our escape is already known."

No sooner had he said this than a contingent of Karpon's men came into view yelling for them to stop.

Bare feet slapping against the stone floor, Gian swiftly pulled her along, turning into a room on an upper level. He threw the bolt on the door to gain them a few precious moments.

Jenise scanned the room in dismay. No other door led from this chamber. "There is no way out!"

But the Familiar was already racing to the single small window in the corner. Pushing open the hinged panel, he glanced down to the courtyard below. Far below. The distance was too high for any man to jump without breaking several bones. Or worse.

Nonetheless, Gian was not any man; he was Guardian of the Mist.

"Listen to me, *taja,* for we do not have time to debate this."

"Debate what?" she asked nervously. Jenise was well aware how high up they were; surely he was not thinking of jumping that distance? He would fall to his death!

"I am going to jump."

She gasped aloud. "You cannot! You will be killed!"

He smiled faintly, moved that the creamcat cared. "Hopefully not. I will transform into my other self; it will aid my landing. Listen carefully; after I touch ground, I will metamorphose back into my human form. You must jump to me then. Do not be afraid; I will catch you."

"Are you mad? What if you miss? It is too risky!"

He gazed at her evenly. "It is your choice."

Jenise bit her lip. Already the guards were pounding on the door. If she didn't try . . .

"Are you sure you can catch me?"

"If I survive the jump, yes."

Jenise wasn't sure she'd heard him correctly. *"What?"*

"I have not jumped from such a distance before."

Jenise threw her arms up in the air. That settled the issue for her. She would not have his broken body on her conscience. "No, I cannot allow it!"

Gian raised a dark eyebrow. Whoever heard of a woman proclaiming she would *allow* a male Familiar to do anything? He would have grinned if the situation wasn't so serious.

Jenise read his expression very well. It was a universal male look, which said clearly, *oh, really.*

"It is too dangerous," she emphatically stated.

"Ah, but that is *my* choice, Creamcat. And I choose to escape. I will wait for you below." He slid out of the leather breeches and tossed them out the window.

He started to turn from her, then hesitated. "You are about to see what few outside our own people have witnessed: the transformation of a Familiar. It is an experience we do not share with many."

"I understand. You may trust me."

Satisfaction brightened his eyes. His palm cupped her cheek, then fell to his side. "What is your name?" he inquired, an unexpected tenderness lacing his smooth voice.

"Jenise."

He nodded as if he liked the sound of it. "If I fail, Jenise, then you will remember this Gian Ren . . ."

It seemed as though he wanted to say more, but his words trailed off as a glowing light began to pulsate from him. Streams of photons flowed around him, gaining in number and strength. His entire body began to shimmer, seeming to melt into light itself.

Jenise had never seen anything so beautiful.

In the next instant, a large, multi-colored cat was standing before her. There was a majesty about him that invited awe and respect. Broad areas of vibrant bronze and black and gold formed patches in the long silken fur. The animal's stunning eyes were two different colors. Deep green and lambent gold.

Gian!

Tossing his head in an action she had seen the Familiar make in human form, the proud feline gave her a haughty stare.

It was nothing less than Jenise expected.

The powerful cat jumped onto the windowsill.

Looking over its shoulder at her one last time, he leapt bravely into thin air.

Jenise ran to the window, afraid to look out but knowing she must. The great cat had landed far below in the stone courtyard. He lay there, not moving.

The pounding on the door grew louder. Was he simply stunned or . . . ?

A slight movement alerted Jenise. He was alive!

Somewhat dazed, the beast awkwardly got to his feet. In the moonlight, Jenise could discern the odd angle of one of his paws. She winced. He had broken a leg. A hind leg.

Not only must he be in terrible pain but he would never he able to catch her. Her spirits plummeted.

She turned away, missing the flash of light from the courtyard below.

Just then the door to the chamber crashed in and Karpon's men filled the doorway, led by Karpon himself. His thin nostrils flared as he viewed her. Clearly he was furious at her rebellion.

Mayhap he would even kill her. She glanced out of the window, thinking she might be able to signal to Gian to go on without her. At least he might be able to save himself.

She was shocked to discover that he had already donned the *tracas* and was motioning for her to jump. Not only that, but he was standing perfectly on two legs. Jenise's hopes lifted; somehow the Familiar had repaired his injury when he had changed his form. A handy ability, indeed.

Unfortunately, while she was watching him, Jenise's mind registered exactly how far the fall was. Her fingers clutched the sill. How could she find the courage to make that kind of jump?

Below in the courtyard, Gian sensed her indecision, her fear. He willed her to meet his eyes as he inhaled a deep, calming breath. *{Come to me, taja. I am here for you.}*

Jenise's hand went to her forehead. Surely she could not hear him from this distance? She took a deep breath. It seemed to calm her. She made her decision. Better to die in the attempt at freedom than be caged with Karpon!

Guessing what she was about to do, Karpon hissed, "Do not, Jenise! You will be killed!"

Throwing her leg over the sill, she turned back to Karpon to give him a last insolent sneer before she jumped.

As she fell through the air two things crossed her mind at once; the sound of Karpon yelling "nooooo" and the hope that this Gian would truly be there to catch her. She had put all of her faith in him, a man she barely knew.

He caught her and held her fast.

The impact of the fall brought him to his knees but he held her securely in his arms. Jenise burrowed her face into his warm throat. She hugged him tightly in response.

Against the innocent press of her lips, she felt the vibration of his strong heartbeat. The steady, sure beat comforted her in a way no words could. She thought his lips grazed her hair in answer.

"Come, we do not have much time." The deep, smooth voice spoke gently in her ear. She nodded against him.

As they ran from the courtyard behind the keep, Jenise glanced up at the window she had jumped from. Moonlight silhouetted Karpon's harsh features as he watched them flee.

Even from this distance she could see the look of fury stamped on his cruel face. It spoke of revenge.

Two pathways opened up before them. One led around the left side of the keep; the other straight into the fields. Had Gian's senses not been partially dulled by the drugs they had given him, he might have discerned a faint, barely audible moan coming from a heap of flesh that had once been a vibrant young Familiar.

It came from just around the corner of the keep, not thirty paces away.

But fate, being the capricious riddle that it is, decided that Gian Ren would go on his way, unknowing. He guided Jenise not to the left but to the path that led straight through the meadows.

And so a page turned and one young man's life was forever altered.

"We may rest here shortly."

The Familiar finally released her hand. He had refused to do so numerous times as they raced across the countryside, Karpon's men in close pursuit.

Taking in great gulps of air as she tried to regain her normal respiration, Jenise sank down wearily onto a boulder by the edge of a stream. "Did we lose them?" she panted.

Gian smiled inwardly at the use of the term "we." It appeared the creamcat had linked her fate with his somewhere along the way. Still, she had much to learn of him. And he of her.

"For the time being." He, who was aptly named Guardian of the Mist, had led the pursuers on a false *circle hunt*, the likes of which he was sure they had never seen. Gian chuckled to himself. "It will take them some time to reorient themselves. You may rest awhile here."

Jenise watched him in wonder as he squatted in front of a nearby stream, cupping cold water in his palms. He was not even winded, while she could barely catch her breath.

He stood in the moonlight, walking towards her. Truly, he was breathtaking.

The silvery light illuminated his burnished golden hair; the sculpted masculine features; the perfectly delineated physique. Even barefoot and shirtless—wearing nothing more than the black breeches which molded to his muscular thighs—there was an aura of uncommon sleekness to him. In everything he did, the man moved with an elegant feline grace.

He knelt before her, offering her a drink of cool water from his hands.

Jenise was touched by his attentive gesture. Cupping her hands over his, she greedily drank the sweet offering.

Gian waited until she had drunk her fill before he partook of his own refreshment. It did not go unnoticed by Jenise that despite his own thirst, he had seen to her comfort first. The revealing action said much to her.

He looked intently into her eyes before speaking. "There may be some *systale* gourds on the bed of the stream. I believe it is important for us to carry some water with us, for we do not know if we will have the time or the opportunity to stop later. They will have already sent word out; it will not be safe for us to go into any villages until we are ready to leave this place or until we have no alternative but to do so."

She nodded agreement.

Gian walked downstream a ways as he searched for the telltale yellow filaments of the *systale* plant.

Known to have saved many a traveler's life, the *systale* was a gourd plant that grew underwater. The bulb-shaped fruit was filled with a unique healing mixture of water and minerals. No one was sure where it had originated. Found on many planets, presumably carried by travelers through the Tunnels, the plant was able to propagate itself from the discarded husks.

While Gian searched for the gourds, Jenise sat back on the rock, wincing slightly at the soreness between her legs. Even now, she could hardly believe what she had done. Oh, she had no regrets . . . yet she had been raised in a culture that put much value on her purity.

There was a slight stickiness between her inner thighs.

Untying her cloak, she let it drop onto the rocks behind her. The breeze would feel good against her heated flesh.

She lifted the edge of her dress. Traces of blood stained her legs. Evidence of what *he* had done. What they had done.

Despite her acceptance of what had happened, her hand shook as her fingers partially covered the vulnerable spot.

"You are injured?"

Stunned, Jenise glanced up into the tawny gold and green eyes. She had not even heard him approach. Embarrassed to be caught in such an intimate moment, she looked away from him.

Silently, she shook her head.

His steady hand covered her fingers. Gently, he removed her hand from her thigh, revealing the dried bloodstains.

He said nothing, but he did not move for several moments. Then he picked up one of the gourds he had found, breaking the lip of it open with his teeth. He poured the *systale* water in the cup of his hand and carefully began washing her with it.

Jenise's mouth parted, shocked at the intimate gesture. Her hand came over his to stay him.

He disregarded it, going on with what he was doing.

"You should not be doing this, Gian."

The long black lashes—which, at the moment, hid his mesmerizing eyes from her view—

flickered at the mention of his name. It was the first time she had used it.

"Why not, *taja?*" he murmured as he worked.

"Be-because it is too intimate."

"Too intimate . . ." He paused to capture her with his eyes. A dimple curved his cheek. "How is that possible?" he whispered.

Color instantly heightened Jenise's cheekbones. She looked down again, unwilling to let him see how he affected her.

What should she have expected? It was well known that the Familiar were entirely sensual. She had simply never realized *how* sensual. It was in the way he moved, the words he spoke, the purring tone of his voice, and the intent, hidden messages in his fiery eyes.

"I was only supposed to share that with my mate." Her voice was very faint.

He stopped to stare at her. "Do not worry about such things, Jenise. Your mate may understand more than you credit him." He resumed his work.

"You misunderstand; I shall have no mate."

He hesitated in his ministrations briefly. "You think not?" he murmured dryly. He rinsed the area a final time and stood.

She nodded seriously. "I must be free. I can never mate."

"What has the one to do with the other?" He began unlacing his *tracas*.

"I need to feel free. A mate would bind me, keep me from what I seek."

"How do you know that?" He finished unlacing the breeches.

She explained to him the situation in which she had grown up; the stifling atmosphere around Karpon and his brother.

"Your mother's people—the Frensi—they mate, do they not?" He dropped the *tracas*, stepping out of them.

"Yes, of course they do—but that is different. In any case, I seek to explore life, not become caged by it."

Nude, he stood before her and moved his hands through the air above and around her.

"What are you doing?"

"I see no cage here."

She snorted, grinning slightly. "Very amusing."

His raised an eyebrow, placing a warm palm over her heart. "It is here, I think."

"What do you mean?"

"When you unlock this, you will be free."

"I do not think so, Gian. What you speak of *is* the cage."

"No. It is the wind which will carry you."

He turned from her and entered the stream, dunking under the water when he reached the middle. Jenise wondered if he was symbolically washing away the feel of the prison chains.

When his burnished head broke the surface, he flung the wet and dripping strands out of his face. Dual-colored eyes gleamed with a predatory light as he intently marked her under the silvery shine of two moons.

Jenise's breath stilled in her throat.

He was beauty and he was fire.

He walked out of the water towards her, taking steady, deliberate steps. The long strands of his hair dripped down his chest and arms and back.

In a catlike move, he shook his head, sending water droplets through the air, their scattered pattern crystallized by the dual moons.

There was no mistaking the sudden hunger that radiated from him. Feral hunger.

Jenise paled. "I—I said I do not want—"

He approached her, closer. She could feel the searing heat of his golden skin. Hot moisture and *krinang* spice.

With just the tip of his finger, he lifted her chin.

Slowly, he lowered his lips until his mouth—that incredible, sensual mouth—was just a hairsbreadth away from her own. His silken hair slid forward to brush against her shoulders, a hushed caress.

On so lightly, he grazed his bottom lip over hers. His warm, sweet breath drifted across her lips like a sultry breeze which heralds thunder.

Let me tell you something about me, my creamcat . . . I do not heed words that are so patently false."

Jenise's eyes widened. His other hand grasped her upper arm, holding her to him.

"You see . . . I come from a people who rely on instinct."

"And what does that mean?" She tried to pull away from him. He drew her closer.

"It means," he drawled in a husky purr, "that my senses have already told me that you do *want* me very much."

The shock of his accurate revelation caused her to release a pent-up breath of dismay as well as hidden desire.

Gian inhaled the breath as he gazed down upon her. His eyes dilated with the rich sensory perception he received from her. He knew what she wanted.

Jenise stared at him, astonished.

"Exactly."

Before she could question him, his mouth firmly came down over hers. It was a hot taking. He singed her nerve endings. Worse still, the man seemed to claim everything as he kissed. *Everything*.

Stunned senseless, Jenise was immobilized under the skilled onslaught. It was yet another side of the Familiar she had never heard about before—this need to capture. In fact, Jenise had heard that they were always very casual in their alliances, enjoying their partners as their partners more than enjoyed them.

She wondered if this behavior was usual for a Familiar . . . or simply a personal trait of Gian Ren. For if it was—

She could no longer think.

Gian had expertly slid his rogue tongue between her lips and he was *licking* the inside of her mouth!

Quivering, she moaned at the exquisite, delicate flicks that could only be called torture.

His hands cupped her shoulders and he slowly drew away from her. Dazed, Jenise blinked up at him. The corners of his mouth curled upward enigmatically as he released her.

Stretching sinuously, he reached for the breeches on the ground, stepping into them and sliding them much too languidly—bit by bit—up over his hips. He began lacing them up, but the Familiar wasn't watching what he was doing; he was intently watching her.

His potent kiss had rocked her. Jenise felt dizzy and muddled. She did not like the way he was looking at her either. As if she were something edible. She coughed.

He chuckled knowingly. Low and husky.

Uneasy, Jenise decided to ignore what had happened. She cleared her throat and straightened the folds of her gown. "What about you?" she blurted out.

"What about me?" he asked, still watching her.

"Do the Familiar mate?"

He laughed. The rich, deep sound nestled in her like a snug cuddle. Shivering, she suddenly imagined what that laugh would feel like resonating against her own lips as he . . .

Instantly, she banished the erotic image, wondering what was coming over her. She was never one to fantasize over such matters.

"Yes, we mate, Creamcat." The teasing dimples were back.

Appalled at her question, which he undoubtedly misinterpreted in a typical male way, she clarified, "I meant a *permanent*, singular bonding."

He grinned broadly. "I know what you meant."

She snorted.

He sat behind her on the boulder. His clean scent was mingled with fresh water and the night. And just a hint of that special scent of his. The scent that was beginning to make her go weak with desire.

Jenise tried not to inhale.

"Most often we mate among ourselves," he offered in explanation, speaking from behind her shoulder. There were many reasons the male Familiar mated only among his own kind. It was not simply his intense desire, for desire could be taught. There were reasons of a deeper nature.

When she didn't comment, he added, "There have been a few exceptions, but only amongst the females."

"Why is that?" She did not turn to look at him, choosing instead to rearrange the folds of her dress. Again.

"Most often such alliances have not born issue. When they have, a Familiar child has been a rarity. In fact there has been only one child born of mixed blood who inherited the Familiar abilities." He thought of his blood relative Rejar, wondering if Yaniff had yet located him in the Tunnels. "He is most uncommon," Gian murmured thoughtfully.

"Do you continue your ways of pleasure after you mate?"

"Of course we do."

Shocked, she gaped at him over her shoulder. His eyes sparkled teasingly. "With our mates."

"Oh."

"Once mated we are strictly bound to each other. Only each other."

"Then you are not mated."

He paused. "Why do you say that?"

"Because we—well—" Her heart sank as she thought of something terrible. "Did—did I force you to break your bond so you could escape?" Her eyes filled with tears. "I would feel truly terrible if such were the—"

His thumb wiped a tear from under her eye. "I would never break my bond, *taja*. Not to escape; not even for my life. It is not our way."

Relieved not to have caused him any personal grief, she exhaled a breath.

He inhaled it.

An *ollyn* screeched in the night, its plaintive wail a customary cry to its mate. Gian lifted a front lock of Jenise's hair and placed it behind her back. Then he leaned over and rubbed his chin back and forth on the exposed skin of her shoulder. A low, humming purr followed.

Jenise shivered.

"We must leave shortly." He spoke in a distracted, hushed tone.

She nodded.

In the darkness of night, outside of the keep, a rickety cart pulled by an equally rickety *safir* beast made its way slowly around the perimeter of the imposing structure. The old woman who was steering the cart urged the stubborn *safir* beast to hurry. She did not like coming near the keep. The guards were cruel and anything might happen, especially at this time of night.

The old woman had only ventured out because she knew this was the day the servants cleaned the storerooms. Often in the past, she had found useful things that had been discarded in the refuse pile behind the stone wall. When one had so little to live on, one did not mind taking certain risks.

She sighed heavily, her ancient bones creaking. So far she had found nothing. Her back hurt from fighting the reins and she was ready to turn the cart toward her home in the Silver Forest. At the moment a nice cup of hot *mir* by her fire sounded better than the finest of clarified stones.

Yes, that was it. As soon as she passed this next bend, she would turn and head back. Away from the darkling Karpon and his barbarous guards.

She had just about completed her circuit when she discerned a slight movement on a heap of offal. A *riat*, she thought; they liked to burrow through such refuse. Nothing more.

A faint moan traveled the night wind.

The sound was agony on the lips of something barely living.

The old woman paused. There was something out there that the guards had tossed out for dead. Immediately she turned the cart in the direction of the sound.

Karpon was dangerous, but she was not concerned about Karpon. Something or someone needed her out here in this offal pile. Spying a heap of rags and wounded flesh, she pulled the cart up short.

Jumping down, she hobbled over to the broken mass. Whether it was man or beast, she could not tell, for it was so badly mangled. She bent down slowly in deference to the soreness in her back and pushed the bundle onto its side.

A terrible groan of pain rattled from its chest.

By the two moons' light she could see that it once had been a man.

He was in a very bad way. From a cursory glance it looked as if he had been beaten and tortured . . . and maybe worse. There was no telling what he had looked like originally—not that such a thing would concern him anymore. Whatever comeliness he had once possessed was gone forever.

Not that it mattered. He probably wouldn't live long.

But she would try to help him anyway.

She put her face close to his ear so he might hear what she was saying and focus upon it despite his pain. "I do not know if you can hear me, but if you wish to live then you must help me. I am too old to lift you by myself. There is a cart here . . . if you can aid me, I will attempt to get you into it. You must try not to call out, no matter the pain; Karpon's guards are near."

Compassionately, she took his hand in hers. She didn't expect a response; the man was too far gone. A few moments passed while she debated what to do.

The hand weakly squeezed hers. He was attempting to tell her that he had heard her and wanted to live!

The old woman's eyes gleamed. Mayhap she could save this one from being another of Karpon's victims. "Yes, I understand, my poor friend. We will try." Placing his arm around her shoulders, she told him she was going to stand.

It was difficult and for a moment they almost toppled over together, but she was able to steady him. His entire body shuddered but he did not cry out. He was brave, she realized, saddened that he had been so unlucky as to fall into the hands of Karpon's guards.

The cart was right next to them, and somehow she managed to shove and push and pull his mangled body into the back. He twisted and convulsed from his pain, but he still did not cry out.

Finally she had him in the cart. Covering him with a worn blanket, she scrambled back to the front seat and slapped the reins.

She was going to help him fight to live. The idea brought new energy to her tired body.

It wasn't until they were far away in the Silver Forest, where no one could hear him, that he let out his agony. A wrenching cry of utter pain came from the depths of his soul.

It was a sound she would never forget.

Chapter Four

For most of the night, Gian led them across the extensive meadows and glades that surrounded the keep. Karpon's family estate was vast, covering a massive territory, and it took them most of the night simply to leave his land.

They paused at a crossroad in a field on the edge of Karpon's territory. Before them the land dipped slightly; to their right lay another pathway.

Gian looked up at the night sky. "There are three Tunnel points on this world."

"Yes. Do you know where they are?"

"Not exactly. I can sense them and know what general direction they lie, but I cannot tell how far away they are."

The Tunnels connected worlds and were strictly controlled by the High Guild of Aviara.

The Guild employed knights of the Charl to protect both the Alliance of planets and the structural integrity of the Tunnels. Within the High Guild itself, the Tunnels were under the absolute domain of the revered House of Sages.

Since this world was an outlying one and not a member of the Alliance, the Tunnel points were limited in their connections to sponsoring worlds who wished to open trade and commerce.

Familiars could sense the presence of Tunnels, but they could not call them forth. Only certain mystics of the Charl could do that. On this non-Alliance world, the portals would not be maintained by the Gatekeepers of the Charl. Most likely the Tunnel points would be left open in stasis, as was the one Gian had used to enter this world.

Often on barbaric worlds such as this, Tunnel points were initially kept closed until further exploration could be made by a Familiar. The Familiar, who were naturally inquisitive and had a zest for adventure, were the perfect candidates for such tasks. In exchange for such services, the Guild rewarded the Familiar with certain privileges and protection.

However, Guardian of the Mist had not come to this world as a seeker for the House of Sages or the High Guild. He had come as a hunter for Dariq.

In any event, it would be a long and dangerous journey back to Aviara. They would have to travel world by world until they reached Alliance

space. From there all Tunnels connected to Aviara.

"The closest and most active one is in the royal
village, a day's journey from here. Over this hillock is a pathway that should lead us directly to
the Traveler's Path. It will take us straight to the
center of the village where the Tunnel lies."

That was the Tunnel that Gian had used to
enter this world. "No, Jenise. Karpon will expect
us to go there and will have both the path and
the Tunnel entrance heavily guarded. We must
try for another of the Tunnels. How far is the
next one?"

"It is about five days' journey from here." A
day on this planet was slightly shorter than a
standard Alliance day. Gian noted that his step
here was slightly lighter as well.

"And the other?"

"Fifteen days' journey."

Gian speculated a moment, weighing his alternatives. "We will attempt the one that is five
days' journey. Karpon will be expecting this as
well, but the risk of staying on this planet longer
outweighs the danger of the choice."

"That Tunnel lies in this direction, but we
must circumnavigate those hills in the distance."
Jenise pointed to some hills far ahead.

Gian's innate tracking ability told him different. "It would be quicker to travel in this direction." He indicated a route that would take them
right through the valley between the far hills.

"Quicker if it could be done. We cannot go
that way."

"Why not?"

"Because the *valdt* will kill us."

"What is the *valdt*?"

"Do you see the vines covering the entire valley before us?"

"Yes; the plants continue as far as I can see across the vale."

She nodded. "Well, they are not plants."

His brow furrowed. "What do you mean?"

"That is the *valdt*. It is a flesh-eating plant that crisscrosses the terrain for miles."

Gian said hesitantly, "What do you mean by *flesh-eating*?"

"Just that. It is carnivorous, Gian."

He paused. "I sense no danger from it." He frowned in puzzlement. "How can that be?"

"No one is sure what it is—plant or animal; or a combination of the two. Perhaps that is why you cannot sense the threat?"

That, or the residual drug in his system was still affecting him.

"What else do you know of it?" He listened to her intently.

"It sleeps by day but awakens at night. See the spines?" She pointed.

He nodded.

"They are deadly poison. The vines entangle its prey, the poison spines immobilize it. The *valdt* gains nourishment by slowly absorbing its still-living victim."

Gian's narrowed eyes scanned the *valdt*, his clever mind working. A scream sounded in the distance and he caught the faintest blur of a vine snapping through the air, snagging a low-flying winged creature. Whatever this thing was, it was extraordinarily fast.

Jenise shuddered.

"What about the spaces in between?" Gian pointed to the small patches between the intersecting vines. "Is it possible to travel through these spaces during the day as it sleeps?"

"It has been done on rare occasions by young men on a foolish dare from here"—she indicated a short span of space—"to say, here. But to cross its entire expanse in one day, before nightfall, is impossible."

Gian looked out over the vine-covered vale, his mind occupied with dangerous possibilities. "Exactly how far is the distance to the other side?"

"Almost a two-day journey—if it could be walked with no impediment."

"I see . . . and if it could be done, how much time would we save on the five-day journey to the Tunnel?"

She frowned. "Approximately three days, but—"

Gian calculated in his head. "It may be possible."

"You cannot walk that distance in a day!"

"No . . . but I may be able to *run* it."

"*What?* Are you mad? The spines are still poisonous during the day and the poison is long-lasting. If you even scratch your leg or foot, you will be immobilized until nightfall. There are places where the branches grow thick and high. It cannot be done!"

Gian observed her steadily. "That is not certain. What *is* certain is that Karpon waits for us if we follow this path." He gestured to the path that led to the royal village. "Here we have a chance."

"We?" She scoffed. "*I* cannot run that distance."

"Of course not. I would not allow it."

Her nostrils flared at *that* remark.

Before Jenise could begin berating the arrogant man, he continued, "I will carry you upon my back."

There was silence for a moment. Then the arguing ensued.

"That is the most ridiculous thing I have ever heard!" Jenise's aqua eyes flashed fire, while the Familiar's eyes sparkled with something akin to amusement.

It was a fact that Familiars loved to rile up females. Although Gian had not intentionally set out to do that, he saw no reason not to enjoy her reaction just the same. He crossed his arms over his chest and leaned on one hip; it was a stance he knew was sure to add to her irritation.

He was not disappointed.

"I will not entertain this insanity!" She threw her hands up in the air. "If you wish to commit suicide, then you must go on by yourself. I will make my way around the hills."

He tossed his bronze-gold hair back over his shoulders. "We have a pact to stay together—"

"Just until we enter the Tunnels." He looked at her in that unnerving, silent way he had. Jenise swallowed.

"As I was saying, you will not be able to outdistance Karpon's men if you go the other way. You will be taken, Jenise. Or you can come with me. It is your choice."

He waited for her to make a decision.

She bit her lip as she thought it over. Karpon might very well kill her for defying him and fleeing. "You think you can do it?"

"It will be a challenge."

A challenge? That was an understatement if she ever heard one. A worried look crossed her expressive features.

"Every moment of time will be needed if I am to succeed. We will leave as the first rays of light touch the far horizon and the *valdt* begins its slumber."

"But that is only in a short time!" Jenise protested for his sake. The Familiar had not slept yet this night.

"We must go today or we will lose our advantage."

"You have not had any rest and—"

"Jenise"—he cupped her chin, staring straight into her eyes—"we cannot rest now. Not if we wish to leave this place."

Jenise inhaled a shaky breath, nodding when she realized he was right. Gian brushed her mouth in a quick sliding motion before he released her. He picked up the *systale* gourds and slung them over his shoulders.

"The water is too heavy—you will not be able to run with it," she said quietly.

"I will not be able to run all day without it."

Holding up a gourd to his mouth, he took a long drink of the *systale* water, replugging the lip of the gourd with its own heavy fibers when he finished. For some reason the sight of the muscular column of his throat going up and down as he swallowed fascinated her.

Jenise quickly looked away when she realized he was done.

Gian smiled slightly. He knew exactly when she was looking at him and how. "You must not speak to me during the run, Creamcat, as I will need to focus my concentration to keep up my pace."

"I understand."

"I will tell you what to do to aid me . . . " *[like this].* He spoke in her mind, causing her to jump.

She had heard of this telepathic ability of the Familiar; that they could send their thoughts but not receive the thoughts of others. At the time, she'd dismissed the tale as rumor. She inhaled a breath. It seemed most of the rumors were proving true! What else had she heard? Something about their sexual ability to—

Gian distracted her. "Come, the time grows short."

Gingerly Jenise approached him, trying not to think of what they were about to attempt. A wave of nausea went through her. She did not want to be food for the *valdt.*

Gian faced away from her and knelt down,

motioning for her to put her arms around his neck and her legs around his waist. When she had done so, his hands clasped the underside of her knees at his waist. He stood, shifting her weight from side to side, getting his balance.

"Am I too heavy?" she asked in his ear.

He grinned at her over his shoulder. "No, *taja*, you are perfect." That said, he purposely grunted loudly.

Jenise nipped his earlobe. He chuckled.

"I cannot stop once I start—do you understand what I am saying?"

"Yes."

"Good. Do you wish to get down for a moment or are we ready to go?"

Jenise smiled behind his back. He really was very gallant. "I am ready to go, Gian." Her warm breath brushed his ear.

Gian almost caught himself purring, but stopped short. Now was not the time to be distracted. He needed to focus fully in order to get them both out of this alive.

He handed her a small rock. "Throw this at the vines when I tell you."

"Excellent idea."

His green/gold eyes scanned the horizon as he flexed his legs, readying himself to begin what was sure to be the feat of a lifetime. He began breathing deeply, preparing his body for the challenge.

The first rays of light crested the horizon.

"Throw the rock, *taja*." Jenise did as he said,

aiming at a thick, entangled segment. The *valdt* lay perfectly still. It was sleeping.

"It is sle—"

But Gian had already begun his run.

And he was moving fast.

He ducked, he moved, he surged, he twisted, without getting a scratch on his bare feet.

Jenise had never seen anything like it. He seemed to know just where he must step between the vines. When to change speed. What path to take across the impossible skein of vines. How fast to move and what angle to move in.

The ability was called kinesthetic sense and it was just one of the many special senses Familiars possessed.

Throughout the run, he instructed her telepathically, sending his thoughts moments before he made the actual maneuver: *{Lean to my right}; {Shift to the left}; {I need some water}; {Stay awake, Jenise!}*; the latter when the constant rocking movement began to lull her to sleep.

Her legs were cramped from staying in the same position, but she held on to him tightly. As the sun began its downward descent, Jenise marveled that the man could still run. His breathing became very labored and he was sweating—something Familiars did not do unless they were under extreme duress.

The light was waning. Worried, Jenise looked over his shoulder to see the distance remaining.

It was too far! They were not going to make it!

A tear slid down her cheek and she prepared

herself for the worst. "Gian," she whispered shakily, speaking for the first time since he began.

The last ray of light crested the peak of the hill, hovering for an instant as if giving them a moment extra of life before it disappeared behind the rocky wall.

The *valdt* began to stir.

Instantly, Gian's arm came crosswise around her back to the right side of her waist. In one strong move, he plucked her around to his front, shielding her in his arms. Jenise burrowed into his warm chest, tears in her eyes at his courageous action. Surely he was trying to shield her with his own body!

"You cannot save me," she cried out.

Gian gathered his remaining strength. With one last valiant effort, he *leapt* the remaining distance.

They landed with a crash on the ground. Gian, even then, protected her from the impact, rolling with her secured in his arms.

A vine slapped down not a hairsbreadth from their entwined bodies.

He quickly rolled them out of its hideous reach.

When she didn't feel the expected sting of the vine, Jenise slowly opened her eyes. *He had done it.* Somehow, the Familiar had done it!

Her lips pressed against the moist skin of his throat. For an instant he hugged her tightly in response, then rolled off her, still gasping for breath.

Jenise scrambled to sit up.

Ignoring the pain in her cramped legs, she cradled his head in her lap. Taking one of the gourds that still hung from his neck—although most of the *systale* water was gone now—she poured some water between his lips. He drank greedily.

Wearily, he tried to focus up at her, his phenomenal eyes already glazing over with exhaustion. "Do not . . . do not let me sleep too—"

He didn't finish. The gentle rise of his chest told her he was already in spent slumber. Amazing how he could simply fall off to sleep like that, she marveled. How utterly . . . *catlike.*

Jenise gazed down at him; at that handsome, strong face now softened in repose. He had defeated the *valdt.* She reflected on the incredible triumph of skill and endurance she had witnessed.

Not even a Familiar should have been able to do what he had done.

She looked up at the stars.

Who was he?

When he opened his eyes, the third moon was beginning to rise in the sky. The other two moons were almost half-full, so their light was brighter tonight. He had slept longer than he'd intended.

Gian switched his focus from the night sky to Jenise.

She was bowing over him, dozing as she sat up, still cradling his head in her lap. The long strands of her pale golden hair had fallen forward, draping them both as she sat sentry.

A tender expression crossed his handsome features. It was an expression he was not ready to show her when she was awake.

Her gold-tipped lashes made crescents on her smooth cheeks. He reached up with two fingers and lightly stroked them, his touch so gentle that her sleep was not disturbed. Not many, even among his own kind, would have been able to endure what she had without a sigh of complaint. She had been brave that day.

She had trusted him.

Yes, he was beginning to understand. And more. He desired her.

Deeply.

It was getting stronger moment by moment.

Even though he'd expected this to happen after what they had shared, he was nonetheless surprised by the depth of his wanting. Soon, he promised himself. When their position was more secure. Then he would show her what true pleasure was.

Gian Ren could not wait to see the reflection of such pleasure portrayed on her open face as he took her. Again and again. He would bring her along slowly, he decided. *Each time he would give her more*.

He wanted to reveal himself to her. To share so many things he kept hidden. In time he would open himself to her, he knew. Already, he knew.

His knuckles brushed her cheekbone lightly. The feathery touch was designed to waken her gently. The gold-tipped lashes fluttered before she gradually opened her eyes and gazed down at him in her lap.

She smiled softly until her focus sharpened. When that happened, Gian knew she was truly awake. Her protective barriers were in place.

"How are you feeling?" she asked gently.

He gave her a crooked grin. "I am alive and lying in the lap of a beautiful woman; how do you think I am feeling?"

She snorted. "Seriously, Gian, are you all right?"

He nodded.

Her hand smoothed the tousled hair from his forehead in an unconscious gesture. Gian purred softly. Like most Familiars, he loved to have his hair stroked.

Not that Gian would ever admit to it.

There were many spots that could render a male Familiar vulnerable to the female. In addition to the usual areas, each Familiar had his own individual places of sensitivity. Places he would never openly reveal.

It was up to the female to discover them—if she could.

"I cannot believe what you have done, Gian. Crossing the *valdt*—" She stopped, at a loss for words. She would never forget the way he had tried to protect her at the end, shielding her with his own body.

"It is all right, you do not have to say anything." His hand reached behind her neck and pulled her down to him. To his lips. "Just kiss me, woman who seeks no pleasure, and I will know what you mean."

She smiled against his mouth, causing him to smile.

He kissed her thoroughly, bringing her sweet mouth over his. *The Familiar licked her lips.* She tingled all over.

"Mmmm," she murmured, surprised.

"Mmmm," he acknowledged, teasingly. He slipped his tongue inside her mouth to carefully stroke and lap. *{You taste so good, Creamcat.}*

She twitched slightly, not expecting to hear his masculine voice in her mind while he kissed her. It was a very useful talent, she acknowledged. Especially when a sensual voice like his could be used to heighten the erotic experience he was giving her.

Jenise sighed into his plundering mouth. Gian purred louder.

He took the offering of her breath and inhaled it, his commanding hand behind her neck making sure she stayed just where she was—lowered to him. By the time she realized that the Familiar had her exactly where he wanted her, it was too late. Already, his spell was enveloping her, along with that wondrous scent.

Jenise closed her eyes and moaned aloud at the expert touch.

{Tell me} he coaxed her, his tongue sliding against hers in a measured, languorous stroke. Jenise shivered, a small sound coming from her throat.

{Yesss, speak to me, my creamcat.} He with-

drew his tongue to nip delicately at the edges of her lips with his teeth. Then he captured her upper lip between his own and suckled on it.

Jenise began to quiver at the incredible sensations. She did not know that some Familiars had the ability to bring a woman to peak by their kiss alone. However, she was about to find that out; for Gian had decided to begin by introducing her to this little talent of his.

Jenise had no idea what was happening to her except that it felt good. Incredibly good.

His other hand came around her. The tips of his skilled fingers played along the rim of her ear in a feathering caress. He slipped within her mouth once more to rhythmically surge inside. Her entire body began to throb with his heated laving. Jenise was not even aware she was making rapid sounds of pleasure, so caught up was she in his feral passion.

{More, taja . . . more . . . } He built sensation upon sensation. Her body was thrumming and hot, pulsing to the wild rhythm he set.

Gian opened his mouth upon her then and gave her her first peak by purring in a deep, resonant rumble. A strong vibration sliced through her as he prolonged the low, exciting sound.

{Sing for me, Jenise.}

She cried out at the exquisite, pulsating sensation trickling inside her. Gian felt her tremors against his mouth.

{Ah, yessss . . . } He swallowed her beautiful, innocent cries of first passion.

Jenise sagged limply over him, trying to catch

her ragged breath. Her entire body was still vibrating. "Wh-what did you do to me?" The thready, breathy voice did not sound anything like her own.

The Familiar looked up at her in the moonlight and smiled very slowly. It was the smile of a satisfied cat.

Jenise dumped him off her lap and stood up, brushing her dress off. "Do not do that again!"

He folded his hands behind his head and grinned up at her. "How will I stop myself?"

Jenise exhaled a gust of air. The Familiar took what he wanted, she realized, then he went for more. He was dangerous. She narrowed her eyes at him. "Do not give me that innocent look! I know very well what you attempted to do."

"Attempted?" An aggrieved dimple popped into his cheek.

Jenise blushed. "Just do not do it again. I was half asleep—you took me unawares." As an excuse, it was rather lame. They both knew she had been wide awake.

Gian raised an eyebrow. "I see."

"And do not raise that eyebrow at me either."

His lips twitched. "You sound like a queen, Jenise. Are you sure you do not wish to be one?"

That she would not even respond to. She turned her back on him and began walking over the hillock. To the *valdt* with him!

Gian's sultry voice caught up with her. "Ah, *taja,* you do wish to go to the Tunnel point, do you not?"

101

"Of course I do!" she spat over her shoulder as she marched along.

"Well . . . you are headed the wrong way."

Her step faltered. Silence ensued as she thought of how she could correct this without losing face.

"Turn around and go to the opposite hill," he called out helpfully.

Her shoulders scrunched. Resolutely, she marched herself around in a semicircle—just to make it seem she was not following his directions—before she followed his directions.

Gian roared with laughter.

Jenise ignored him. Familiars had the oddest sense of humor.

The next thing she knew he was strolling beside her. She hadn't even heard him come up from behind, which was highly irritating.

"Will you forgive me?" he implored sweetly. Too sweetly.

Despite herself, her mouth twitched. He was unpredictable and a scamp besides. There was no denying the fact. "Well, if you apologize nicely."

"Please forgive me," he begged teasingly, clutching his heart. Not meaning a word.

Jenise arched a delicate brow. "Very well, since you have asked so sincerely."

A gleam came into his dual-colored eyes. "My thanks to you—woman who seeks *no* pleasure."

She slapped him with the *systale* gourd.

He chuckled, taking her hand as he led her into the moonlit night.

Chapter Five

Crouched down behind some large bales of produce, Gian scanned the tiny outlying village for any signs of Karpon's men.

They appeared to be safe for the time being.

He turned to Jenise, who was kneeling beside him. "Either word of our escape has not reached here, or Karpon's men have not yet arrived," he whispered to her. "They have not even posted a sentry near the Tunnel entrance." He pointed to the unguarded maw of flashing lights which stood directly in the center of the square. It was the Tunnel that led to the next world.

As Gian had suspected, it was unmanned, left in continual stasis. He surmised that the small hamlet had sprung up around the Tunnel point.

Jenise also scanned the village. Karpon could be very tricky, and even though they had shortened the journey here by crossing the *valdt*, she was still wary. In either case, the Familiar was sure to draw attention. Besides his exceptional looks, the man was half-naked, wearing only the *tracas* he had stolen from the guard. Barefoot and shirtless, he was sure to be stared at.

"Should we—"

He seemed to know what she was thinking. "No. It is too risky. The longer we remain here, the less our chances of escape. Once we pass through the portal, our path will be more difficult to trace. I think we should leave now and worry about my attire later."

Jenise's brow furrowed as she thought the situation over. "What if it is a trap?"

"It may be . . . but I have no sense of it."

So far, the Familiar's instincts had proven remarkably accurate. He had led them unerringly to this point.

After Gian had awakened, they had traveled the road to the south for the rest of the night. Near daybreak, he had led them off the pathway into a rolling field. There he had covered them in leaves and brush, effectively camouflaging them from anyone who might be passing by.

The tip of Jenise's ears turned pink as she recalled that he had taken her in his arms under that blanket of leaves, telling her to sleep in that low, purring voice of his. Surprisingly, she had done just that, his body warmth and gentle caress soothing her into much needed slumber.

She had awoken to his hot, sweet breath brushing the side of her neck, under her ear, where he had burrowed that beautiful face while he slept. His arms and legs were tangled protectively around her.

She had whispered his name to see if he was awake.

He had sleepily murmured something incoherent before nipping his way up the side of her throat. The tips of his fingernails scored her hipbones. She was beginning to suspect this sexy maneuver was a favorite habit of his. Together, the grazing strokes seemed to awaken myriad sensations in her all at once.

Gian smiled slowly at her. "What are you thinking?"

"Wh-what?" she stammered, caught off guard.

A grin curved a line next to his mouth. "The tips of your ears are pink." He tweaked one with his finger. Jenise brushed his hand away, irritated.

"What nonsense are you talking, Familiar?"

"I have noticed that every time you seem to be thinking about a certain subject, the tips of your ears turn pink." He crossed his arms over his chest and arched a provoking brow. "I wonder what it could be?"

Jenise's nostrils flared. These Familiars were far too observant when it came to women! As if it was his concern what she was thinking about! "It is probably an adverse reaction to my proximity to you!" she shot back, annoyed.

His white teeth flashed in a quick grin. "I thought it might be . . . but thank you for confirming it."

Jenise stared at him disgustedly. "You know you should really work on that humble attitude of yours—your lack of confidence is starting to get on my nerves."

He bit his lip, grinning. "Now where have you ever heard of a Familiar that was any different, Creamcat? We are a humble people to be sure."

"Gallingly humble, if you ask me." She covered her pink-tipped ears with her hair. Gian's eyes gleamed in amusement.

"Perhaps, but we never deliver less than promised, *taja*." There was a wealth of meaning in the heated glance he gave her.

She could feel her ears getting pinker.

Impishly, the Familiar bent over and uncovered them, nodding to himself when he viewed the results.

Exasperated, Jenise exhaled loud and long. "I do not know how you can make sport at a time like this! We are in grave danger and yet you—"

He captured her chin, forcing her to meet his eyes. "Never mistake—I take the danger and you very seriously. It is the Familiar nature, however, to enjoy the moment whenever possible. Life, we believe, is a passage whose complexity is comprised of individual moments. Therefore I choose to enjoy *you* in this moment, Jenise. Surely you would not fault me for that? If you are captured, I would remember my last enjoyment . . . shared with you, *taja*."

"If *I* am captured—you mean *we*, do you not?"

He shook his head. "They will not take me

again, Jenise. A Familiar's true strength is that he can never be owned."

She gasped as his meaning sank in. "Surely you would not—"

"I would prefer to go down fighting. It is as simple as that. I will not give Karpon the pleasure of my execution."

His brave words made sense. "Then I will do the same," she stated courageously.

Gian cupped her chin. "No, *taja*, if it comes to that, you must promise me to stay alive to fight him another day. For both of us."

An unbidden tear fell out of the corner of her eye. "I do not wish to stay with him."

He wiped the tear away with his thumb. "I know. Nor do I wish it for you," he said softly. "But do not worry overmuch; you see, I have faced much more powerful enemies than he in the past and am here to tell the tale. Besides, I have no intention of leaving you to him."

Puzzled, she looked up at him.

"The principle of the thing," he whispered enigmatically, brushing her mouth with his lips.

"Come." He stood, taking her hand. "It is time for you to begin a new life, Creamcat. Let us see what awaits us beyond this Tunnel." With that, he led her through the throng of people selling their wares in the open marketplace that had sprung up in front of the Tunnel.

Gian shook his head, thinking to himself how similar tradesmen were the universe over. These, like most, hoped to catch the travelers coming into this world as well as the ones leaving. They displayed inferior goods at outrageous prices. Haggling was expected. He chuckled at the almost comedic nature of the scene.

Unfortunately for the merchants, this Tunnel point did not seem to be very active. During the time he had been observing it, no one had entered or exited the portal, which meant that the trade route was not a heavily traveled one.

Although this would make their escape easier, he wondered exactly what terrain lay on the other side of the Tunnel. From the lack of travelers he could surmise that whatever was on the other side was probably nothing more than a remote place that served as a way station between two planets. It very well might be uninhabited, serving simply as a link to yet another world.

One thing was certain—whoever was on the other side would not be an Alliance member. The two of them might well be stepping into a barbaric world worse than this one. Especially since this was not the primary Tunnel point on this world. His protective grip on Jenise's hand tightened.

She looked at the tall Familiar questioningly.

"You must stay by me at all times, Jenise. I know not what danger lies on the other side."

"Yes but we—" She bit her lip, hesitating to continue. Their special agreement only lasted until they got off this world.

For a moment her eyes watered. In the short time they had been together, she had come to rely on the man. Jenise suddenly realized how much she *liked* the proud Familiar. For all his arrogance, there was an imposing strength of character to him. And he had been her first. . . .

She would miss him, she was sure.

He squeezed her hand lightly, misinterpreting her hesitation. "Do not worry; I will protect you."

Moved by his gallant words, she nodded, keeping her sentiments to herself.

In no time at all they were standing before the maw of the Tunnel. Its bright, flashing lights swirled and pulsated. Curious, Jenise peered into the portal, hardly believing she was about to take a step that would change her life forever. Finally she would be free of this place! Though she had been birthed here, this place had never been her home.

Someone exited the Tunnel, quickly hobbling past them.

Gian turned to smile at her, then stopped suddenly, his back straightening in a wary stance.

"What is it?" she asked him, worried.

He did not answer her. Slowly he turned, his gold and green eyes scanning the crowd of merchants in the marketplace. *Someone was observing him intently*.

His eyes shifted back to the Tunnel entrance and rested on the dwarfish alien who had just exited the Tunnel. The alien was leaning heavily against a small, crooked staff. His wrinkled features and long snout gave him a curious appearance.

As the being rested a moment, his bumpy head pivoted. Small dark eyes, lost in multitudinous folds of skin, peered at them intently.

Gian returned the scrutinizing stare if for no other reason than he was a Familiar who would not be intimidated. For an instant he thought he saw surprise in the alien's eyes. It was as if the alien hadn't expected to see a Familiar there; although why that should be was a mystery.

Under Gian's masterful, piercing look, the odd alien rapidly turned from him, hurrying on its way.

"It is nothing to be concerned about, *taja;* simply a vagabond traveler."

She smiled at him, relieved.

And in that moment it struck Gian how beautiful her smile was, how pure and sweet and genuine. He smiled softly back at her and led her into the turbulent cosmic miasma known as the Matrix.

They exited the Tunnel onto a flat plain, an unending vista of brown.

The dry, mostly barren plateau was dotted occasionally by sparse vegetation—also brown. On this world, the binary suns were setting; already night sounds of wild fauna echoed across the expanse.

Gian's acute senses immediately scanned the area, alert for any danger. His grip on Jenise's hand remained secure.

"Gian . . ." Jenise spoke faintly at his side. "I feel . . ." She swayed, unexpectedly dizzy.

The Familiar swiftly caught her in his arms before she toppled over. He swung her up in his embrace. "Jenise, was this your first time in the Tunnels?" He was astounded.

"Y-yes. What is wrong with me? Why do I . . . feel . . . so disoriented?"

"It is the effect of the phasing on the first passage. You should have told me before we entered. There is an elixir we might have been able to obtain in the marketplace to ease your displacement symptoms. Although the effect is temporary, you will feel quite ill for a while, Creamcat."

Jenise viewed him through eyes that were bleary and frightened. "You—you won't leave me while I am like this, will you, Gian?"

"Leave you?" He frowned down at her for the ridiculous statement. He had carried her across a death pit on his back for an entire day! And had almost died doing so. *Now she thinks I will leave her because she is a little dizzy?*

No wonder Familiars adored women so! Who knew how their convoluted minds worked?

"Yes . . . our agreement . . . just until we entered the Tunnel . . ."

Now he understood.

He gave her a tender look, stroking her cheek with one finger as he held her. *"Taja,* I would never—"

But she didn't hear him; she had already passed out from the vertigo caused by the transplacement through space.

Night was falling fast on this unknown world. Gian thought it wise not to take any chances.

Carrying her, he walked along the plain until

he spotted a lone *nanyat* tree. He had seen this kind of tree on other worlds. Symmetrical in shape, the flat branches were just wide enough to lie upon for shelter. The thick, dark fronds would shield them from view from anyone on the ground while the height would protect them from unknown predators.

Making his decision, he slung the unconscious Jenise—who had almost been the sovereign ruler of a planet—over his broad shoulder, much like a sack of grain. He then proceeded to climb the tree with her swinging over his back. Familiars were never ones for protocol.

When he found the branch he wanted right near the middle, night stars were already dotting the sky. A meteor shower soon created a dazzling display.

Jenise opened her eyes to streaking lights whizzing in and out of swaying fronds. Her brow furrowed. How could that be?

Something warm and comfortable was wrapped around her.

She blinked and tried in vain to stretch.

Apparently whatever was keeping her warm was also preventing her from stretching. A masculine leg was thrown over her thighs. Strong muscular arms were wrapped securely around her waist.

She sighed. It was the Familiar. He hadn't left her. She sighed again.

"Mmmm?" His teeth grazed her throat.

She waited for . . .

His nails pressed and scraped teasingly at an angle over her hips. She smiled to herself. "Why are you holding me so tightly?"

"So you do not fall out of this *nanyat*," said the husky voice next to her ear.

"Nanyat?" Her palm felt along under her until the support seemed to just fall away. Carefully, she peeked over the edge of the branch they were on. It was a long way down. She was astonished. "Gian, how did you get us up here?"

She felt him smile against her neck. "Very carefully," he murmured.

"Can we get down?"

"Yes," he chuckled, nuzzling his chin against her shoulder. "How are you feeling?"

Jenise rubbed her forehead. "Not too bad, most of the ill effects seem to be gone." She bit her lip and glanced at him over her shoulder. "You stayed." She spoke in a cautious voice.

The tip of his tongue began to tease her ear. "Did you really think I would leave you?"

"I was not sure." She sucked in her breath as that wicked tongue delicately probed at the canal. The stimulating action sent shivers down her spine.

"How can I make you sure?" he whispered hotly in her ear.

"What do you mean?"

"Nothing . . ." His Familiar touch skipped along her heated skin. "Nothing . . ." His Familiar mouth captured hers. Hotly, fiercely.

She groaned something, whether denial or encouragement she had no idea. With his skilled mouth drawing on her, he made her lose every thought in her head save the feel of him.

{Open for me, Jenise.} The telepathic command was accentuated by a sexy little nip he gave to her bottom lip.

"I—"

His tongue stroked inside her mouth. A damp, sensitizing invasion. Warm puffs of breath escaped her lungs, going into his mouth. Gian growled softly.

The Familiar kissed as if he loved the taste of her. Deep and passionate, he laved her lips, her tongue, the inner recesses of her mouth. Jenise kissed him back, enjoying his expertise in this simple act.

Only with him it was not so simple an act.

She wondered if he was going to do what he had done the last time—gift her with that exquisite torture that made her . . .

Surely there was no name for it!

Remembering how he had opened his sensual mouth over hers to purr directly into her throat, Jenise moaned and squirmed against him in anticipation. She shouldn't be thinking of such things or even inviting them, but it had felt so incredibly good.

Gian smiled faintly as he licked a molten path along the delectable fullness of her lips. He knew exactly what she was remembering.

He intended to add to those memories in a most notable way.

Gian had no intention of bringing her to peak

with his kiss as he had the last time. He only wanted her to think he might.

As he was forced to pace himself during this journey to Aviara, so too, he must pace himself on this other, sensual journey with his creamcat. The time had come for him to begin to introduce her to the real pleasure that existed between a man and a woman.

This non-Familiar woman was about to learn a lot about the Familiar male. Best he teach her carefully about their special desires. Carefully and gently. *At first.*

So Guardian of the Mist quickly made up his mind, as was his nature on two matters: the first, that he *was* going to take her now; the second, that his touch upon her would be a slow and easy hand.

Her anticipation would lead her unknowingly to follow him as he led her deeper into her own sensuality.

In all ways, Gian was true to his feline self. He was sometimes mischievous. He could be tricky. He was often protective. But he was always smart.

In all ways, he was a master strategist.

Regardless of the parameters of the match, Guardian of the Mist played to win. He was a powerful Familiar in his prime and, like most Familiars, he was at his most dangerous when his intent was sexual.

Jenise, who had just begun her life of adventure, had no idea how serious a Familiar could be when it came to certain matters.

As he continued to kiss and nip and lave at her mouth, using a highly expert technique, Gian carefully untied the thick black ribbon that held her cloak together. With a master's light touch, he spread the cloak out, letting the sides drape over the *nanyat* limb.

A light breeze caught at the heavy material, flapping it gently in the sporadic wind. He liked the sound of it.

His clever fingers threaded into her long hair, letting the pale strands sift gradually through his hand as he examined its lovely sheen. The back of his other hand brushed against the creamy skin of her collarbone, in a feathery touch.

All the while, his creative mouth and tongue promised her nothing but pleasure.

Jenise clung to those talented lips, unaware of the skill he was using on her. She arched up as male fingers whispered a sensitizing pattern down the side of her breast, over the loose material of her gown.

Gian's open mouth teased along her jawline, his tongue flicking and darting as he went. The same hand that just skirted her breast continued its descent in a gradual exploration, lightly massaging to heighten her awareness of his touch. His other hand tangled in her hair, gently tugging.

Calmly, he licked across her collarbone, his tranquil movements enervating her. Then at the base of her throat, just above her collarbone, he suckled delicately. There was a tiny *sting*.

Jenise gasped, her hands sinking into his hair.

The sensitive spot was a pleasure center well known to male Familiars. Gian drew carefully on the tender skin, purposely leaving his signature bite—a tiny love mark.

Now, he would see it every time he looked upon her. See it and remember the incredible feminine taste of her.

Remember this first time of true pleasure.

A roll of satisfaction soughed from the back of his throat.

His palm press-rubbed the length of her thigh and calf, gathering the material of her gown in his grip as he reached her slender ankle.

Lifting the material, he let the tips of his fingers stroke up the satiny side of her leg in an easy, meandering path. Before she realized his intent, he inserted his muscular thigh between her now-exposed legs and rubbed against the soft inner skin.

Jenise blinked. What was he doing? It was certainly more than kissing. More than she had intended. "Gian," she croaked, "perhaps we should—"

He was not listening to her.

His white teeth captured the peak of her breast right through the fabric of her gown! She could feel that damp, burning mouth as if no cloth at all lay between them. Jenise wriggled on his thigh to get his attention, but the movement only seemed to make matters worse.

Or better, depending on one's point of view.

Mortified, she could feel herself becoming damp. She opened her mouth to say something.

Taking Jenise's squirming as encouragement, Gian pulled her thigh up closer around his hip and rocked enticingly against her. Still gripping the tip of her breast between his teeth, he began to draw strongly on the throbbing nub.

Jenise forgot what she had been about to say.

The man was making her feel things she had never felt before! And all of the sensations were pleasureable. Perhaps she should explore this further and see what transpired?

He unclasped her gown at the shoulders, tugging it down to her waist. His mouth truly captured her now and if she thought that what he was doing to her before could not be improved upon, then she was highly mistaken. His broad palm cupped her breast, holding it up to his lips.

A rough tongue scraped the swollen tip in a long, slow lick.

Taking soft nibbles along the underside of her breast, he nuzzled his chin along the plump globe, purring contentedly into the satiny valley of her chest. The erotic vibrations skittered over her like pulsating waterfalls.

Jenise's arms encircled his neck, drawing him closer to her as she decided that she definitely liked what he was doing. She had already known this man; had felt him inside her in the most intimate way possible. Now her body seemed to be humming for him, reaching toward him in a way that was not simply physical. Perhaps it was because of what they had shared in the cell where he was held captive?

Absently, she stroked his nape as he purred roughly against her.

By now she knew his scent.

It covered her, exciting her. She also knew what that alluring scent promised.

When her hand grazed the *krilli*-textured strands of his burnished golden hair, Jenise realized that rumors about the exquisite feel of Familiar hair were also true. She had never felt anything like it. . . . Stroking it was addictive.

At her petting touch, Gian encouraged her by murmuring huskily.

She smiled faintly, pressing her lips against his smooth brow. He liked her touching his hair, she discovered, surprised.

If she only knew what else he liked.

His tongue traced a meandering route down the valley of her chest; its languid flicking relaxing her yet stimulating her at the same time. When he reached her navel, he circled the perimeter of the small indentation, then teasingly poked at it with the tip of his tongue.

In a very unsovereignlike action, she giggled at the ticklish sensation.

Gian chuckled at her innocent response, wondering if she was aware that the area was alive with nerve endings perfect for certain stimulation. *Friction* being the first that came to his mind.

She would be feeling that particular stimulation very soon now.

He grinned to himself as he expertly plied his sensual arts upon her.

Nudging the draping material of her gown lower with his nose, he subtly bit the rounded curve of her lower belly. It was one of several special Familiar bites that he would be introducing her to. This one was an airy graze using a gentle combination of teeth and pressure. Named *the Kitten's Kiss*, the bite was designed to entice but not devastate.

Gian was not aiming for devastation.

Yet.

As far as he was concerned, this was her first real experience with lovemaking. He had no intention of overwhelming her with his Familiar appetite.

Unless she asked him to.

Then he would be most happy to oblige her.

Jenise shivered from the erotic sting. Once again, she began to have doubts about the wisdom of engaging a Familiar in such activities. His tastes seemed far too sophisticated for her. Her touch became noticeably hesitant upon him.

Guardian of the Mist did not give her time to become any more hesitant.

Moving up on her once again, he covered her mouth in a fiery possession, driving every concern out of her head. As he lingered upon her, kissing her senseless, his hand surreptitiously went to the lacings on his breeches. Familiar dexterity being what it was, he unlaced the *tracas* in no time at all.

Then he purposely sent her a very heated thought.

{I want to be inside you, Jenise. Like I was before . . . only this time, I want to show you what it is supposed to be. . . . } He rubbed his shaft against the delicate folds of her femininity.

As he'd expected, she was very wet. He had taken great care that she would be.

Jenise moaned at the thick surge between her legs. The Familiar slid back and forth along her nether lips, his mouth coaxing, his body pressing her down as he spoke in her mind, erotic messages, asking her to let him *in*.

{Do you know what you felt like to me . . . ?} His tongue stroked hers. She cried out against him, caught in his spell.

{You are sweet fire and spicy cream, taja *. . . I have never felt anything like it. . . . }* He rotated his hips against her, the broad head of his shaft pressing heavily against her dewy moisture.

A whimpering sound of desire came from her.

It was good, but Gian wanted her more than ready for him. He held off even as she opened her thighs for him. His arms encircled her, one hand sliding up under her hairline at the nape of her neck. The other hand reached down to cup her bottom, bringing her tightly to him.

He twitched against her.

Jenise thrashed in the intimate embrace, wanting him now with an intensity she never knew existed between a man and a woman. She whimpered against his lips, begging him in guttural sounds to appease this longing he had created.

{Yes, I will, Creamcat, but when I stroke inside

you, I want to hear who it is you are feeling . . . }

He released her mouth to slide fast into her. As deep as he could go.

"Gian!" She screamed out his name.

He groaned a feral response before sharply biting her shoulder.

There was no getting around the fact that he was a cat at heart. Wild, intense, untamable.

But he could also be very loving.

His silken lips sipped on her jawline; then he let his mouth brush tantalizingly across the tips of her eyelashes as if he had longed to do so forever. A low moan of gratification hummed from him.

Cognizant of her untried state, he moved carefully within her, using long, slow thrusts designed to acclimate her to him. The even rocking motion built and built until Jenise thought she would die of it.

"What—what do you do to me?" she panted raggedly.

{Put your other leg around my hip, Jenise, and I will show you . . . }

Jenise did as he asked, wrapping him completely in her embrace, wondering what more he could possibly do? Surely nothing could be more pleasurable than what he was doing now?

She was soon to discover how wrong that assumption was.

Guardian of the Mist truly came to her then. Powerfully. Consummately. He thrust into her with a steady rhythm that made her tremble all over.

A wild pressure built between her thighs where he moved. More and more. *Too much!* She tried to tell him. "I . . . something . . ."

"Yes, *something*," he drawled out loud before capturing her breast to draw upon it strongly, his hips rotating once again.

Jenise came apart.

She reared up as rapid explosions vibrated through her. The sensations radiated from the place where they joined, intensifying moment by moment. Again she called his name, only this time on a wave of satisfaction.

Gian covered her lips to experience her cries of passion as he, too, found release. A perfect release of their first completion. He sagged against her before lifting himself on his elbows to stare down at her.

Jenise gazed up at him in awe.

Tossing his silken hair back, he gave her a crooked grin. "So, woman who seeks no pleasure, now what do you think?"

Her palm cupped his cheek. "I think from this day forward I shall be known as 'woman who *seeks* pleasure.'"

He laughed huskily, winking at her. Since they were still joined, she could feel his deep laugh move through him and her. Curling his large hand over hers, he turned his head to kiss the center of her palm.

A puff of air escaped her lips at the warmhearted gesture. He could be so . . . so . . . *unpredictable*. But then, Familiars—

Her brow knitted as she suddenly remembered that other rumor she had heard. The one regarding their sexual skills. Her expressive aqua eyes opened wide.

"Gian . . . they say that Familiars have the special ability to—to 'enhance' during the sexual act. What does this mean?"

He didn't answer her; he simply gave her a very sexy, very mischievous smile.

Then, while still joined to her, he gave her a very nonverbal explanation. *He enhanced.*

Her cries of ecstasy echoed across the plains for a long, long time.

Chapter Six

Planet Aviara, House of Sages, High Guild

"We must send someone! And quickly! Gian Ren has been missing too long!"

"Perhaps we should wait a little longer? What if we send someone and he is angry that we interfered?"

Yaniff, the most revered mystic in the House of Sages, closed his eyes and groaned. This debate had been going on in the High Guild for days upon days and still nothing had been decided. He thought of the old saying that two wizards in a room usually resulted in three different opinions. It certainly seemed to be true here.

Let me see, he ruminated whimsically to himself, with twelve mystics in the chamber, that was about . . . eighteen opinions.

An *arghhh* of acute pain sounded a lengthy note in his head. It was time he stepped into the fracas.

"Interfered?" Yaniff snorted in disdain. "Interfered!" He pierced each member with a disgusted look. Since they were all sitting at the long debate table and he was standing off to the far right side, Yaniff felt he had a pretty good advantage.

As one, they all turned to stare at him, identical expressions of surprise on their faces.

It was not often that Yaniff voiced such a vehement sentiment. Usually the old wizard's opinions were shrouded in the mysterious verbiage universally adored by high-level mystics. Verbiage designed to send lesser wizards and scholars into a frenzy of interpretation. Indeed, it was often remarked that the more obscure the pronouncement, the more accurate the insight.

The wizard named Gelfan was the first to recover from the shock of the bold statement.

This did not surprise Yaniff. Of all the members in the High Guild, it was Gelfan who had to be watched most carefully. The man was shrewd, powerful, and not prone to leniency. He was a high sixth-level mystic who wore his immense power like a proud cloak.

Yaniff had never been impressed by him.

"You have something to say to us, Yaniff?"

Yaniff came forward, leaning on his tall wizard's staff, his long white hair flowing behind him. A small crystal point flashed in his ear, as it did from every member of the House of Sages.

They were all members of the Charl; an elite group of warrior mystics whose special skills were revered throughout the Alliance.

In addition to the crystal mark of the Charl, Yaniff wore the crimson-magenta robes adorned with the golden symbols of a high seventh-level mystic. In all of Aviara there was none greater than he.

As usual, Bojo, his winged companion, sat squarely on his shoulder.

He captured each and every member in his penetrating regard as he shifted his focus down the long table. It was well noted that Yaniff's eyes were darker than the darkest night, their depths were always unfathomable.

Bojo captured the Sages in the same black-eyed stare. The overall effect was daunting, to say the least.

"Yes, I have something to say. We have wasted too much time with these infernal, endless debates! It is time for action. *Taj* Gian is missing; of that there is no doubt. There is great unrest on M'yan, the homeworld of the Familiar people. We have an enduring, binding covenant with them and even if we did not, we personally owe such action to Guardian of the Mist. We must send a knight after him. *Now.*"

Gelfan's mouth pursed in annoyance. "No one is disputing our loyalty to the Familiar people, Yaniff. You need not hold our special alliance with them before our faces as if we are unaware of it."

"No? Then what is taking you so long to act?"

Ernak, a kindly old wizard who could never make up his mind on any issue because he talked himself in circles, stroked his face thoughtfully. "We must debate such issues, Yaniff. Otherwise, how would we know we were proceeding on the proper course?"

"True, true," several voices chimed in.

"But on the other hand," Ernak continued, "perhaps we do need to come to a decision. . . ."

Yaniff stared at Ernak with a flat expression. *There Ernak goes.* He winced. *Round and round.*

"True, true," the same voices concurred. It was all Yaniff could do to contain himself.

"I say this!" Wolthanth suddenly stood up, pointing his forefinger straight up in the air. Everyone silenced to hear what momentous thing the man had to say.

Unfortunately, in the time it took for Wolthanth to stand and deliver that uprised finger, he had already forgotten what it was he wished to say.

Such an occurrence was a regular one and seemed to go along with the general age factor in the room. To be a member in the House of Sages one had to be a Sage, and to be a Sage one had to be *around* for quite some time. Yaniff shook his head, muttering under his breath. It was business as usual in the High Guild.

Oh, how he would love to hurl a rapid power bolt at the wall just to silence them all! Lamentably, the use of magic within the sacred halls was strictly forbidden.

He took a deep breath instead. It was not as if he hadn't been putting up with this for ages upon ages.

Gelfan surprised him, however, by suddenly switching his viewpoint and coming to Yaniff's aid. Or so it seemed.

"Perhaps Yaniff is right—we need to stop this bickering and make a decision. I call for a vote. Those in favor of sending a knight out to search for Gian, raise your hands.

Seven hands rose. Eight if you counted Ernak's, which was raised, lowered, and then raised again. Apparently the eternal struggle to debate never ceased in some philosophers. It mattered not. With seven votes, they had a decision. A knight would be sent.

Already anticipating the next round of torture, Yaniff waited patiently.

Gelfan started it by saying, "Unfortunately most of our high-level knights are already on quests for the Charl. We will have to send Lorgin."

Yaniff was ready for this. And he also knew where Gelfan was headed. "No. Lorgin cannot go." As Lorgin's mentor, Yaniff's words would carry much weight.

"Why not?" Gelfan asked slyly. "He is here and available. He also happens to be one of our best knights."

Yaniff knew Gelfan's methods; the man was seeking information. Consequently, he was very careful about what he said and what he did not say. "This may prove a dangerous mission. Lorgin cannot be the one."

Gelfan was not about to accept that. "I fail to see why not—he is highly trained and a fourth-level Charl."

"Heed me when I say he must remain here with his mate."

Several eyebrows rose at the cryptic comment. Yaniff, who had the gift of prophecy as well as "the Sight" was looking beyond—but to what? They knew better than to question this most revered mystic. He would reveal only what he chose to reveal.

Wolthanth spoke, effectively overruling Gelfan: "We agree, Lorgin will remain."

Yaniff nodded an acknowledgment to Wolthanth.

There was silence for a few moments as the assemblage tried to think of another likely candidate. "What about Rejar?" Ernak asked finally.

Alert, Yaniff replied, "What about him?"

"He is now studying to be of the Charl. Though he is new to his training, he is still a son of Krue—"

"Albeit half-Familiar," Gelfan added, insinuatingly.

Yaniff's attention switched to Gelfan for a moment, his piercing gaze speculative. There would be trouble here, he realized . . . but not today. He focused on the discussion at hand.

"Perhaps Rejar is a good choice then." Ernak rubbed his chin, still thinking it over.

"We will choose him," Gelfan stated.

Yaniff viewed them all, his gaze going from one to the other. A flash of annoyance lit his deep eyes. "No we will not."

All eyes focused on Yaniff.

"We will leave Rejar to unfold as he should."

It was then they all knew there was something here; something that Yaniff was not yet ready to expound upon. The group of wizards all sat in deep thought as they watched him, wondering whether to proceed with the topic of sending Rejar.

They were all experienced mentors. One of the problems of dealing with *unfoldment* was the timing. In such matters, timing could be everything. Every mystic present was aware that destiny often rode on the back of timing. And so, as one, they decided to move on to the next candidate.

Only there was no other candidate.

Zysyz, the youngest of the wizards, informed the group of that fact. "We are out of candidates," he baldly stated, making his first contribution.

Though it wasn't exactly an opinion, it *was* true. Several members nodded approvingly at him.

"Bojo," Yaniff grumbled under his breath, "please stop me from banging my head against the wall." Bojo squawked, flapping his wings as though amused. Yaniff glanced at him in mock annoyance.

"There is one other," Yaniff carefully announced.

"Who?"

"Who is it?"

"There is?" They all spoke at once.

Yaniff held up his hands to stop the chatter before he supplied the answer. "Traed."

Dead silence fell over the sacred room like a heavy cloak. Finally Gelfan spoke. *"Traed ta'al Theardar?"* he asked in disbelief.

"Traed ta'al Yaniff," Yaniff corrected him. He had taken Traed to his bloodline, giving him his name after the death of Traed's natural father, Theardar.

Silence reigned at the pointed reminder.

Yaniff's bloodline was one of the most revered in Aviara. Traed now belonged to that line; therefore extreme caution was needed. No one wished to insult Yaniff's bloodline. To do so would be the height of folly.

Finally Ernak mumbled, "We know of his power, of course; he revealed himself to us with his arc when he called upon you to save Rejar. Which was commendable of him," he added as an afterthought. "Are you saying his power is that significant?"

"I am."

"So the son follows the father," Gelfan sneered. "The power in his line drove Theardar mad—it will drive the son mad as well." Traed's father had been a sixth-level mystic who could not control his special gifts. He had turned to darkness and had almost destroyed his son in the process.

"This will not happen to Traed."

"We cannot afford to take such a chance, Yaniff."

Wolthanth agreed. "What if he cannot master his power? He has not been properly trained."

"You need a warrior. Traed is a warrior; an artist of the blade. Trained by Krue himself."

"But mystically! He has not been trained! He could be a danger to us all—a threat to our very existence!" *That* was Gelfan.

"Or our savior." Yaniff mocked the group before him. "Ironic, is it not?"

It was difficult to meet his eye, for each man at the table knew what had been done in the past to Traed; indeed they had all participated in it. Through no fault of his own, they had robbed Traed of his heritage.

Great wizard that he was, Yaniff knew when to press his advantage. "The man will conquer his power. I believe in him. I always have. We owe him a chance to prove himself. *We owe him.*"

An uncomfortable pause followed. "Vote?" Gelfan spoke low.

Thirteen hands rose.

"Very well, Yaniff, we will leave it to you to send him."

Yaniff nodded, turning to leave. Wolthanth came up beside him. "I do not envy you your task in telling the lad, Yaniff. He has always been a most stubborn youth; one who follows the beat of his own tune."

Yaniff smiled ironically. "Yes, he does."

"Obstinate, as I recall." Wolthanth's eyes twinkled.

Yaniff quickly defended Traed's nature. "I have always felt that steadfastness and individuality were very good qualities for a high-level mystic."

"True, true. Not only do they add to his character, but he will never be one to be easily persuaded." Wolthanth grinned wryly. "Again, my condolences on your task."

Yaniff laughed heartily, slapping his old friend on the back as they walked out of the chamber.

Traed ta'al Yaniff sat brooding in the corner of a tavern.

Booted feet hooked over the rungs of a wooden chair, he morosely stared into the depths of his horn of *keeran*.

Yaniff was not overly concerned.

This was the man's normal expression. Traed had ever been like the surface of a lake . . . the dark, quiet exterior hid all kinds of mysteries below the surface.

But not from Yaniff.

Yaniff had glimpsed the real Traed.

The man who kept himself under such firm control was in actuality quite different beneath the exterior shield.

In keeping with his overall demeanor, the waist-length strands of his midnight hair were pulled back tightly from his sculpted features and perfunctorily clasped with a twisted leather thong.

Only the light jade-colored eyes hinted at the roiling emotions below the surface. For all his control, Traed could not completely prevent the sparks of passion kindling in those eyes. They were the sparks of an Aviaran male of considerable power.

For the men of their world, power was an immutable fact of life. It flowed through them like a current and when they were moved by their emotions, this current was always visible in the eyes as tiny bursts of light. The intensity of these sparks was directly related to individual potency. In times of passion, the more power a man contained, the more he sparked.

By their very natures, the Charl were high sparkers.

Yaniff ruminated on Traed's appearance. *One wonders what would happen if he were to truly let that hair come loose. . . . There is untold capacity for emotion within him. Emotion and compassion.*

Compassion was crucial to a man with such power.

Yaniff approached the table and stood before the turbulent man until he finally deigned to acknowledge his presence. Traed's head rose gradually. When he saw who it was who had come to bother him, his nostrils flared in annoyance.

"The answer is *no*."

Chuckling, Yaniff pulled out a chair, seating himself across the table from the green-eyed man. "You do not even know why I have come."

"Yes, I do. You wish me to do something that I do not want to do."

Yaniff's lips twitched. "Now how can you possibly know that?"

"Because . . . you would not seek me out like this if it were otherwise." Traed slammed his horn on the table.

"Hmmm." Yaniff stroked Bojo's feathers. "Perhaps I simply want to converse with you?"

"No."

"Hmm." Yaniff motioned the serving man to bring him a horn of *keeran*. "Perhaps I simply want to share a drink with you?"

"*No*, Yaniff."

The server placed the horn before the old wizard. Picking it up, the ancient wizard sipped it contemplatively. "Come now, Traed, at least give me a chance. A man who does not know what he seeks cannot recognize it when he finds it."

The flat of Traed's palm came down on the tabletop. He leaned forward, pastel eyes glittering. "All you need is a chance! Think you I have forgotten how you maneuvered me the last time, sending me to Ree Gen Cee Ing Land after Rejar? Playing us both so that I would reveal my power to the Guild in order to save him while he would come to acknowledge his place within the Charl? Meddling in our lives?"

The lad had the right of it there. Yaniff shrugged nonchalantly. "I am a wizard—it is what we do."

As if that was an explanation. Traed's eyes sparked briefly. "I will not do it, Yaniff."

"Very well." Yaniff sipped his drink again.

Traed nodded curtly, going back to his own drink.

Whereupon Yaniff tossed a figurative thunderbolt. "I suppose," he mumbled into the horn, "that Gian Ren will be lost to us forever, then."

Traed choked on his drink. Obligingly, the crafty wizard leaned over and slapped his back.

"Are you telling me," he sputtered, "that the Guild had the audacity to ask me to go after him?"

"Well . . . not quite."

The jade eyes narrowed to thin slits.

"They are not exactly asking."

"I see. As usual, they decree and expect others to follow. Well, I might remind them that I was never fully initiated into the Charl. I owe them no allegiance."

"Hmm." Yaniff sipped some more *keeran*. Waiting patiently for the pot to boil.

"How dare they think I would honor such a call!"

"Hmm?"

"Did they think to ensnare me with my 'family honor'? I owe them nothing and will give them the same!"

"Hmmm."

"Perhaps they think I would feel bound to you, Yaniff? Because I wear your Cearix? Then they know me not!"

"Hmmm."

Traed slammed back his chair, his jade eyes sparking. "I care not for such honor I tell you!"

The pot is boiling. As if he had not a care in the world, Yaniff finished his drink. *Time to add the spice.* "One might say Gian is almost a blood relative to you, what with his relation to Rejar and, in a way, Krue."

Traed paused in his tirade.

Ah, the magic word. Yaniff knew that Traed secretly longed for the recognition of Krue, a man he respected and loved as a father. The man who was prevented from raising him as his son-of-the-line.

Bested, Traed closed his eyes. "This is the last time, Yaniff."

The corners of Yaniff's lips lifted ever so slightly. *Not quite.* "You must leave at once, Traed; the situation is most grave."

"Do you know where he was headed when he left M'yan?"

"Not entirely. There is speculation he was headed in the direction of the far rim. There is a planet there that concerns me, called Ganak-ari. I have followed 'sight' of him to that place but lost it. Start there."

Traed nodded resignedly. Yaniff stood to leave.

The green-eyed man forestalled him by placing his hand on his arm. "I am not doing this for the reason you think, Yaniff."

"Of course not. You would never want to be confused with being honorable, Traed."

Traed's hand automatically went to the Cearix on his belt.

Yaniff chuckled. "As I said. In any event, you do not know what *I* think, Traed."

The compelling eyes captured the old man. "That is true. It is what makes you so all-powerful, Yaniff."

Not *all* powerful, the old wizard thought tiredly as he left.

No, not all.

When Yaniff returned to his cottage, his new student, Rejar ta'al Krue, was pacing the floor like a caged beast.

Again, Yaniff was not surprised.

For a man who was Familiar in appearance and abilities, yet held within him a revered Aviaran bloodline, Rejar was a most stubborn apprentice. He resented what he perceived as his loss of autonomy. He was always tugging on the imaginary collar of the Charl that had been placed about him.

Yaniff chuckled. Truly, the bloodline of Krue was a trial to him. Between Lorgin, Rejar, and Traed, he was kept fairly busy. Then again, they were an enjoyable lot. What was more, they were *his* lot. He tickled Bojo under a wing play-fully as he closed the rickety wooden door behind him. Some days it was good to be a cryptic wizard.

Rejar stopped pacing to glare at the old mystic; his blue/gold eyes narrowing.

Here it comes, Yaniff snickered to himself. *Part two.*

Purposely ignoring the Familiar, Yaniff made his way to the table. Tomes of wizardry were scattered about its scarred wooden surface. Bojo rose from his shoulders to settle on his usual perch in the rafters as Yaniff sat down and opened an ancient leather-bound journal.

He began to read a passage out loud to Krue's youngest son.

Rejar began pacing again. Familiars always had to be watched when they paced. It was a sure sign trouble was brewing.

Yaniff ignored the signs, continuing with the particularly boring passage on the obscure nature of elements.

A barely audible groan reached Yaniff.

He tried not to smile as he read aloud. Rejar was a trial, but he had a certain way about him. Yaniff was very fond of Rejar. " 'And so from this we see that the elemental transitions are accomplished when'—Rejar, are you listening to me?" Yaniff did not look up as he perused the passage.

A gust of air left the Familiar's disgusted albeit beautiful lips. Impatient with the endless lessons (which had only just begun), he stormed over to the window and stared moodily outside at the yellow sunshine. It was a perfect day.

Which didn't help matters.

Familiars loved to be out and about looking for mischief on a day such as this. Who knew what delicious adventures awaited the bold? Rejar stared longingly out the window.

Trills sang in the trees, crystal chimes tinkled in a light wind that carried the scent of *tasmin* blossoms. He sighed, wondering what his wife, Lilac, was doing. His lovely "flower" had bloomed on Aviara just as he had predicted. In fact, she was starting to develop some interesting thorns. He shook his head, recalling their past eve together and how it had ended up. He grinned sexily at the heated memory.

Perhaps she was lying under a tree right now taking a midday nap? Yes, with her hair spread out across the grass and her luscious lips slightly parted, waiting for . . .

"Rejar."

"Yes . . . yes . . . I am listening," he murmured distractedly. He would bend over and lightly press—

The corners of Yaniff's lips lifted ever so slightly. As a seventh-level mystic, Yaniff had the ability to read minds. However, he did not have to read Rejar ta'al Krue's mind to know what the frisky Familiar was thinking. Ah, youth.

"That is good . . . that is good," the old wizard replied, not taking his eyes off his book. "Because if you were not, you would be missing a very important lesson."

That was it. Rejar fumed. He was bored beyond belief! Why had he ever agreed to this? These lessons were tedious beyond endurance.

He *had* tried.

It was not as if he hadn't tried!

He could not believe his brother Lorgin had suffered through—No. Knowing Lorgin, he

could believe it. His brother was a paragon.
Nothing ever bothered him! He snorted disgustedly.

Well, he was a Familiar, not a Charl!

Enough was enough.

"Yaniff."

Yaniff went on with the lesson, apparently not
even hearing him.

"Yaniff!" he intoned slightly louder and with
much more authority.

"Hmm?" Yaniff looked up, seemingly perplexed; he seemed oblivious to his student's
boredom.

Rejar's blue/gold eyes flashed in irritation. The
old man had no idea what he was going through!
Hands on lean hips, he emphatically stated,
"These lessons are not to my liking."

"Oh?" Yaniff appeared surprised. "And what
makes you think they should be to your liking?"

Exasperated—and recognizing that the old
mystic was about to ensnare him in a dance of
logic that he would invariably lose—Rejar threw
his hands up in the air, resuming his pacing
back and forth in front of the table. "I cannot
stay caged up in here like this all day!"

The wizard scratched his head. "Why not?"

Rejar all but roared. *"Because it is not my nature!"*

Yaniff's eyes, darker than the darkest night,
gleamed. "Ah."

"Perhaps Lorgin or even Traed could—" Rejar
stopped in mid-stride and pivoted about to stare
at Yaniff. "What mean you, 'ah'?"

Yaniff shrugged. "I never said where the lessons must be."

Rejar scrutinized him through slitted eyes. "Then why have you kept me penned up in here for weeks?"

Yaniff raised an eyebrow. "I have heard that no one can keep a Familiar who does not want to be kept."

It came to Rejar at once. "That was the real lesson, was it not?" He gestured to the books strewn about the table. "Not these other teachings."

"Yes. Always know your true nature, Rejar. When you do, no one, not even me, can pull you from it."

Rejar let the old man's words sink in. He had yet to discover the total scope of his *true* nature, but for now he had learned a valuable thing.

"So we may go outside and walk awhile?" He opened the door, letting the fresh air in. The gentle breeze ruffled the long strands of his jet-black hair.

"Of course." Yaniff got up and joined the Familiar who was also part Aviaran.

"You might have told me sooner," Rejar murmured as they stepped outside into the warm Aviaran sunshine.

"It was not for me to say. It was for you to realize."

"Mmm. I suppose Lorgin realized it much sooner."

"Lorgin never had this particular lesson."

Rejar looked at him, surprised.

"Each student is different inside, Rejar, and so no two are ever trained the same." Yaniff smiled softly. "It is what makes us both student and teacher to each other; it is what makes us always learn."

Rejar seriously considered his master's words. "I see."

"So there is your second lesson for the day, Rejar. Remember that learning is like breathing—once we cease, we are no longer of this plane."

With a flick of his fingers he closed the door behind them.

Chapter Seven

She could not look at him without wanting him.

Jenise walked alongside the Familiar, keeping her head averted, her gaze anywhere but on the sensual feline man. The tips of her ears turned pink with desire as she recalled everything he had done to her during the night. Who would believe a man could have such devastating abilities?

In no time at all he'd had her screaming in ecstasy and yes, begging him for more. Jenise, who had always thought of herself as an extremely independent, reserved person, found it highly embarrassing.

After he had done that—that *thing* to her, she could do naught but moan in his arms like an enflamed *ticna*. Her thoughts strayed back to that incredible moment. Enhancing . . .

It was as if every part of her had become sexually sensitized at the same time. It was as if the Familiar had transferred his own sexual energy to her, making himself pulse throughout her body! The erogenous surge had been too much. It had shattered her, making her scream out the Familiar's name over and over.

She'd lost herself in the alien augmentation. *To him.*

Gian had simply rumbled his approval and taken her to a new peak. Although he was gentle in his movements, that did not stop him from bringing her to incredible heights.

And the more he gave to her, the more lost she became.

Her brow furrowed. She didn't like that part. The surrender.

Afterwards, she had cried in his arms as he held her. Cried for the beautiful yet frightening pleasure he had given her. Gian had comforted her and stroked her, telling her in that husky purr of his that he had shown her only a small portion of what he wished to do for her, what he could do for her.

He had kissed her face tenderly, along her hairline—small scattered kisses—while he hugged her tightly to him. All the while, he whispered things to her in a language she did not understand.

That worried her too.

His deep voice murmured against her, uttering things that sounded forbidden. The soothing, sexy murmurs had a spellbinding effect on her. The Familiar had created a profound need in her, and because of it she was vulnerable to him.

He was overpowering . . . in his mastery, his sensuality, his appearance, his personality, and his command.

Jenise wasn't sure exactly what to do with him!

One steamy glance from those sultry green/gold eyes, which were shadowed over by those thick black lashes, rendered her captive. No wonder women craved these Familiars so!

They were akin to the rarest, finest delicacy. A succulent, delicious, completely unpredictable treat. A delicacy that could deliver untold ecstasy.

These Familiars could become highly addictive!

Which explained why they were hunted after in certain sectors.

Jenise was confused. While she enjoyed the ecstasy part, it seemed to her that such pleasures could prove dangerous. In what way she wasn't sure—but females had to be very cautious, even with ordinary males. With a man like Gian, who knew what trouble would ensue?

Since they had started out across the plains early that morning, she had discovered a new disturbing element in their relationship. It seemed that every time the man caught her in his heated dual-colored stare, she went breathless right to the pit of her stomach.

The other day, when he had helped her out of

the tree and set her down on the ground, his smoldering gaze had perused her length in a slow, deliberate way. She had actually tingled all over. Then the tips of her ears had turned pink.

His mouth had curved in that secret way as he tucked a small reddish purple flower in her hair. She wondered how much he knew.

Perhaps they should part company soon? A pang tugged her at that idea, for she had come to truly like Gian Ren.

Deciding not to think about it any further for the time being, she trudged across the endless plain next to him. The binary suns rose higher in the sky and the temperature became unbearably hot. She started to untie her cloak.

"Leave it." Gian had been constantly scanning the terrain; she was surprised he was so aware of her actions.

She gave him a questioning look.

"Even though it is very hot, the cloak will protect you from the damaging rays of the suns."

"But I just want to remove it for a short time."

"No." His hand stayed hers. "A short time is all it will take. We are close to this planet's equator. The rays of the suns are too potent. Make sure your hood covers you completely, *taja*."

It was then that she noticed how red the skin of his naked back was. Since she had been avoiding looking at him, it hadn't occurred to her that, being shirtless and barefoot, he was almost fully exposed to the lethal rays.

"Gian! You are burned! Here, take my cloak

to protect you." She started to remove it, but he forestalled her.

"No, I will be fine, I assure you." Her attentive gesture touched him. "Later I will transform into my other self. When I change back I will be as I was, free of injury."

"But surely it is painful for you?" A thought struck her. If Gian were in his cat form, his fur would protect him. "Why do you not transform now?"

He did not answer her directly. He pointed to the far horizon. "You see that mountain in the distance? We must head there."

He will not transform because of me, she realized. For some reason the Familiar felt better able to protect her if he remained in his human form. On the one hand, Jenise was touched by the gallant gesture. On the other hand, she did not want the man to bake to a crisp under the blazing suns.

She touched his forearm lightly. "Gian, we have encountered nothing of concern here. Please spare yourself this unnecessary affliction."

Gian looked down at her with hooded eyes. "*Taja*, this landscape is alive with alien life forms just waiting to harm us."

She blanched.

"Do you see the yellowish brush on the rocks as it ripples?"

She nodded warily.

"It is not what it appears. It is a complex symbiotic life form that is extremely dangerous. One of many we have passed."

Jenise swallowed.

"The brush consists of needlelike appendages which are highly toxic. If threatened in any way, they will shoot quills at us as we pass."

Jenise's mouth parted as she scanned the landscape. The entire plain was covered with them! "What is keeping them from attacking?"

"I have been sending them a *flicker-warning*. They seem to understand and respect it—to our benefit. That could change at any moment."

"I—I see."

"It appears we have entered this place at the time of their seasonal migration—when the suns are at their hottest."

"Was that why you took us into the *nanyat* last night?"

"One of the reasons."

Jenise was not sure she wanted to know his other reasons. "But this is a trade route! Between Tunnels!"

"Perhaps that was why that particular Tunnel was so inactive. Apparently it is not peak season for this route." He smiled slightly at his own understatement. The planet was a camouflaged hotbed of danger.

"Would you like me to rub *systale* water on your back? The minerals may help the stinging."

"As much as I would love the feel of your hand upon me, Creamcat, I must decline. We have to conserve the water for now."

Jenise nodded.

"We should make the base of the mountain before nightfall. It should not be too difficult to find a small shelter for the night, on the mountainside."

"Where is the Tunnel point? Are there intelligent beings here, do you think? What kind of trade do you suppose goes on? Will we see a caravan?"

Despite the danger, the creamcat was excited about the adventure. Gian was amused. Yes, she had many traits in common with his people. He reached over and pulled her hood about her face. When he was finished, only her small nose peeked out.

He chuckled, yanking the hood again so it cloaked her entirely. He would not want such an engaging little feature to burn. "The Tunnel point is in the center of the mountain."

Jenise gasped. "How could that be? How will we reach it?"

"We must climb to the top. It will be an exercise, but not too strenuous; I can make out an ascending path carved into the side of the mountain." Familiar eyesight was especially acute.

"Oh." The news of the long climb in the burning heat did not excite her.

Gian smiled. "The mountain is a dormant crater, hollow on the inside. My guess is that a similar carved path will lead us down into its center."

"What an odd place for a people to live," she commented.

"There are no intelligent beings here, Jenise.

This planet is simply a link between your world and a sponsoring world, which sought to broaden its scope by allowing the link. Do you know anything about the sponsoring world at the other side of the next Tunnel?"

"I know only that each of the three Tunnel points on Ganakari leads to a different world. My mother's mate did not wish me to know too much, for fear I would leave when I reached adulthood."

"He loved you like a daughter, did he not?" Gian asked intuitively.

A shield went over her lovely aqua eyes. "He caged us."

Gian watched her carefully. She had much to reveal to him, and perhaps to herself. Again he realized the difficult path he faced with her. "There is a difference between caging and protecting," he said softly.

"I do not wish to discuss this with you."

Gian decided to let the matter rest for now. There would be time enough later for him to explore this with her. *If* they survived. "Very well."

They continued on, neither speaking, each pursuing his own thoughts on the same topic.

By midday the shadow of the mountain stretched over them.

The dome looked higher up close than it had from a distance. Its craggy peaks blocked the suns from view.

Gian knew they would have to make the next Tunnel point as quickly as possible, for there was nothing that could sustain them on this planet.

He was severely burned. Still, he led Jenise along the base of the mountain to the carved-out platforms which trailed up its side. Strange symbols were carved into the edges of the stone platforms, their meaning lost on the two travelers.

Jenise noted that Gian's steps were unsteady.

A few times she had caught him shivering as if he had a chill. There was no doubt in her mind that he had been poisoned by the fierce rays of the suns. She hoped he would be able to end his suffering soon by transforming himself. Never would she forget that he had done this for her, guarded her from the hostile life forms on the planet.

The Familiar had taken responsibility for her. This behavior puzzled Jenise. It was not what she'd expected from one of his kind.

He was a complicated man. And a very ill one. He needed shelter.

"Do you see a place for us to rest the night, Gian? I think I am too weary to go on." She was not that tired; she was thinking of him. The proud Familiar would continue to protect her until he passed out or worse.

"There is an outcropping a little ways up the path. It should lead to shelter." His handsome face was blistered red, his lips cracked and swollen. Despite it all, he was still somehow beautiful.

He stumbled on the path. Jenise winced in

sympathy; she couldn't even imagine the pain he must be in. She quickly went to his aid, lifting his arm over her shoulder.

Without meaning to, her arm brushed against his injured skin. He could not suppress the groan that escaped his lips.

Jenise had had enough of his stubbornness. "Gian, you will transform yourself right now! We have left the floor of the plain and I see none of the spiny creatures anymore."

The authoritative tone she used amused him. If it weren't for the fact that it would hurt too much, he would have grinned. Oh yes, *he*, Guardian of the Mist, would be sure to respond to such a command.

He shook his head, then winced at the pain the movement caused.

"There are other dangers," he replied just as authoritatively. "I will not leave you unprotected."

"I do not understand you! I assure you, I will be most careful, you need not worry about me."

This time he did try to smile, but failed. The woman had no idea of the dangers to watch for here. He could not send a powerful enough *flicker-warning* in his cat form; without his protection she would be overtaken very quickly. "You will forgive me, Creamcat, but it is the way we Familiar men are."

"With everyone?" A line of confusion marred her smooth brow. She hadn't heard that.

"No, not everyone. Now tell me what you see to the right of those steps ahead."

She sucked in her breath. "Why can you not see for yourself?"

"I am having trouble focusing," he reluctantly admitted.

She exhaled heavily. *Males.* "There is an opening in the rock wall; perhaps a small cave."

"Good." He staggered slightly. "We need to get there quickly, Jenise. If I fall here, you will not be able to get me to shelter—I will be too heavy for you."

Jenise nodded. That was definitely true.

They made their way to the small cave. Abruptly, he stopped her before they entered. "Wait!" His eyes were now swollen shut but he seemed to be using his other senses to "see" danger.

"I can detect no life forms within; it appears to be safe, but be on your guard."

"Yes, I will."

They entered the small opening. As soon as they were out of the daylight, Gian sank to the ground, almost taking Jenise with him.

"Please, Gian, change now!" She was beginning to get frightened for him.

"I cannot, Jenise."

"*What?* Why not?" she asked, horrified.

"My energy levels are too low." He shook with a chill.

"Why did you do this?"

His teeth began to chatter. "I have already ex-explained that to you."

Not completely. Jenise gave him a speculative look before she asked, "What will you do?"

155

"I can sense water . . . there is another cavern behind this; if there is a small pool there, I will go into the water to see if it will help the burning. One thing is certain, we must get to the next Tunnel point as soon as possible, for I have seen nothing on this planet that can sustain us."

She wasn't sure he could make it to the next Tunnel point. From what she knew of dual sun exposure, he would become very ill in a very short period of time. "Gian," she whispered, "what if—"

"Get me to the pool, *taja*." His normally beautiful voice was raspy.

Helping him to his feet, she guided him along the rock passage. Soon the corridor widened and a large cavern opened up before them. A small pool lay in the center, its water clear.

"You were right, there is a pool here."

"Good. Unlace my *tracas*."

Unlace his tracas? She looked at him warily. "Why?"

"Because I need to remove them before I enter the water," he explained patiently.

Gingerly, she plucked at the lacings, careful not to brush his burned skin. As a consequence, it took her a very long time to undo them.

When she got to the middle section, she bit her lip as she contemplated the thick bulge in the leather breeches. How could she do this without touching him? She didn't want him to think she was—

"Creamcat, what is taking you so long?"

Her head snapped up. "Um, nothing. Almost

done." She grabbed the bottom end of the lacing and yanked hard. The rawhide flew through the grommets and zipped out; almost flying across the floor.

"By Aiyah!" he roared.

"Sorry," she mumbled.

"Think nothing of it!" he snarled. "I needed a rope burn on my *kani!* To match the sunburn on my back!"

"I said I was sorry." She really felt terrible about what had happened. So she asked the question women universally ask in these situations. "Does it hurt?"

The question universally annoyed males. They never could understand why women asked it. They certainly did not want to answer it and admit to anything. So they usually responded the way Gian did, which was a totally unbelievable "No."

Irritated, he threw his *tracas* to the ground and stormed into the pool.

"At least it gave you some energy," she called after him, helpfully.

Very much the cat, he hissed in response. Then he groaned as his abused body sank into the cool water.

"Look, Gian, someone left some supplies here!"

"What is it?" He cocked his head, listening to her movements. A bag rustled as she excitedly pulled out the contents. He heard her small sigh.

"Not a lot . . . there's a gourd of *systale* . . . a few loaves of dried *pani* . . . some bowls . . . a

fire-starter stick! And some *creote* rocks to ignite
for the fire . . . and . . . a small vial of cleansing
oil."

"Can you bring me some of the *pani?*"

"Of course." *Pani* was a dry, flat loaf of baked
grain. Many travelers carried it as it preserved
well. It tasted awful but was nutritious.

She knelt by the pool's edge and, breaking off
a piece of the *pani*, held it to his lips. He swallowed a few bites and drank the water she
handed him, but it was obvious he was in a lot
of pain.

"I am sorry about the rope burn on your . . . I
am sorry, Gian." She gently smoothed back his
bronzed hair from his forehead.

He caught her hand and squeezed it lightly.
"It is all right." A chill shook him.

"You should rest, perhaps you will feel better."
They both knew that was unlikely.

"I am going to attempt to transform."

"What if you cannot?"

He paused. "If I wait too much longer, I might
become delirious from fever, Jenise, in which
case I will not be able to focus on the transformation. It is best to attempt it now."

It was what he did not say that worried her. If
he waited too long it might be too late. There
was no telling how ill he would become. Her
eyes moistened. He had done this to protect her.
She must do the same for him.

"You must do as you think right, Gian."

Gian wished he could see her at this moment.
He would have liked to remember how the

creamcat looked when she said she trusted him. For whether she knew it or not, that was what she had just admitted. "Jenise—"

She took his hand. "But you must eat some more *pani* first to gather your strength as best you—"

"Jenise."

"Yes?" Even though she tried, she could not hide the shaky timbre of her voice.

"When I transform, I will need to remain in my other form for a while—until my energy level rises. It should not be too long—as long as I can make the initial . . . it should not be too long."

She nodded, then realized he couldn't see her.

He surprised her by returning the nod. Apparently he could sense her movement.

"If you see a flash of light and nothing more, do not be frightened, *taja*. It simply means I am in my third form. If that happens you must continue on to the Tunnel point. I will still be with you, although you will not see me. Will you promise me you will do something for me then, Creamcat?"

"Of course, Gian." After what he had done for her, she would never refuse him.

"You must attempt to get to Aviara. It is very important. Seek out a wizard there named Yaniff. He will see my . . . he will know who you are. You must tell him about the drug they used on me, Jenise. For my people."

"Yes, yes I will."

"Tell him, 'they know of the other.'"

"They know of the other?" She was perplexed. What did this mean?

"Yes. He will know what to do."

"Very well then, Gian. I will do as you ask."

"Trust Yaniff, Jenise. He will help you."

"Help me . . . help me do what?"

Gian hesitated. "Just promise me you will go to him."

"I promise."

"Good," he murmured. "Now, *taja,* if you would help me out of here . . ." He offered her his hand.

She guided him out of the water even though she suspected he was guiding himself and simply wanted to feel her touch.

He stood before her. Virile as always. His hand reached out and stroked her hair. "It seems as though I have done this before," he commented wryly.

"You have." She smiled poignantly. "The time when you jumped out the window."

"Ah, yes. Well, let us not make it a habit after this. The task seems to be getting more difficult." He tried to joke, but she could tell he was concerned.

"No, let this be the last time, Gian."

Blindly, he lifted her chin with his finger. "Remember, if I seem to disperse, I am still with you. I will always be with you."

"Of course." A tear splashed on his hand and he knew then that she didn't believe him. There was no third form; he had been trying to make it easier for her should something go wrong.

Join the Historical Romance Book Club and GET 4 FREE* BOOKS NOW!

A $23.96 Value!

Yes! I want to subscribe to the Historical Romance Book Club.

Please send me my **4 FREE* BOOKS.** I have enclosed $2.00 for shipping/handling. Each month I'll receive the four newest Historical Romance selections to preview for 10 days. If I decide to keep them, I will pay the Special Members Only discounted price of just $4.24 each, a total of $16.96, plus $2.00 shipping/handling ($19.50 US in Canada). This is a **SAVINGS OF AT LEAST $5.00** off the bookstore price. There is no minimum number of books I must buy, and I may cancel the program at any time. In any case, the **4 FREE* BOOKS** are mine to keep.

*In Canada, add $5.00 shipping/handling per order
for the first shipment. For all future shipments to
Canada, the cost of membership is $19.50 US,
which includes shipping and handling.
(All payments must be made in US dollars.)

NAME: _____

ADDRESS: _____

CITY: _____ **STATE:** _____

COUNTRY: _____ **ZIP:** _____

TELEPHONE: _____

E-MAIL: _____

SIGNATURE: _____

"Jenise," he whispered. He inhaled her scent before brushing his swollen lips against hers.

A cry of despair came out of her and she tried to bring him closer to her. What if he could not metamorphose into his other self?

Gian broke away from her abruptly, knowing that if he did not, he would not be able to do what he must. For both of them.

Guardian of the Mist did not hesitate even one instant.

The glowing began and he dissolved right before her eyes. Jenise reached out to the light but it was gone before she could touch it. He was gone. A sob of anguish left her throat. Gian was gone!

Something silky curled around her ankle.

Jenise jumped. Looking down, she saw a cat's tail curled affectionately around her leg. The large black and bronze and gold cat it belonged to was fast asleep at her feet. She smiled through her tears.

His energy had been utterly depleted, but, once again, the man had done it.

Jenise sank to the floor beside the regal looking cat and cried into his soft, thick fur.

Jenise eyed the dozing cat from her vantage point in the center of the pool.

He was still fast asleep, his massive head resting on his powerful front paws. Even in sleep, he appeared master of his universe. Fierce and dominant. Not one to tangle with. This was

Gian, she acknowledged. The traits she saw in one were in the other.

Gathering the vial of cleansing oil, she lathered her long hair, taking her time to wash. The pool was comforting and it felt good simply to relax in its cool depths.

Leaning back in the water, she floated across the gently rippling surface, her hair wafting around her, her eyes closed.

Was the cat watching her? She opened her eyes, glancing his way.

No, the green/gold eyes were closed, his head still resting on his paws. She relaxed, dunking her head under the water to clear the last of the bubbles. She came up sputtering and dripping wet.

Walking out of the pool to the *creote* fire she had lit, she knelt by its edge. Its warmth would help dry her off.

Behind her, the resting cat observed her out of slits of glittering green and gold.

Sitting on her haunches by the warmth of the fire, Jenise closed her eyes and began to doze lightly.

Strong hands threaded through her hair, arranging the waist-length tendrils over her shoulders, bringing them forward to cover her breasts.

"The fire will dry it better this way." The deep voice vibrated against her skin as he nuzzled his chin against her shoulder.

Jenise opened her eyes. Gian had already moved off to the other side of the fire. Picking up another *creote* rock, he tossed it into the fire. Immediately the blaze intensified as flames greedily consumed the stone.

He was whole again and in his human form, she noted.

No red streaking burns marred his smooth, golden-tan skin. His face was as it had been before: devastatingly handsome.

He reached over to the small bag of supplies for a gourd of *systale* and a piece of *pani*.

Covertly, she observed his lithe movements, noting once again the grace with which he moved. She had heard this was a Familiar trait; that they all moved with this sinuous agility. It was captivating to watch.

Naturally, her thoughts went back to what he had done to her the previous evening.

It was a mystery, but he had seemed to retain all his power and command while still losing himself in the sensuality of the experience. He had thrummed inside her, lifting her to new sensations. Sensations that had been far too much for her to deal with.

There was no question that he had taken *her*.

Surreptitiously her glance fell to his capable hands. Those hands had slid down her body, coaxing her, guiding her with every expert caress.

Her focus moved on to his powerful thighs. Muscular, well-shaped, masculine. She remembered the feel of those strong legs sliding against her as he moved. *Oh, how he moved!*

The tips of her ears turned pink as she recalled

the intimate vibration of him. A trickle of desire fluttered through her. *She wanted him.*

Somehow, the Familiar had created this need in her, this craving for that which she had never known before.

She sneaked another peek at him as he slowly chewed the *pani.* Even the simplest act of chewing seemed to be fraught with sensuality. His strong jaw moved slowly; he swallowed the baked grain in a leisurely manner before he sipped some water from the lip of the gourd.

She trembled. She was hungry—for *him.*

She wanted his passion yet she was afraid to experience everything she had last eve. The enhancement . . .

Jenise was frightened of how it overwhelmed her; of the surrender he demanded from her.

She glanced over at the Familiar again. He continued to slowly sip at the water. She wondered if he had any idea what she was thinking.

From beneath lowered lids, he met her look with a smoldering gleam.

He knew.

Leaning back against the rock wall, he casually held his hand out to her.

As if in a trance, Jenise rose, going towards him. She took the proffered hand.

"Not too much pleasure this time, Gian Ren," she instructed him.

"No, not too much, *taja,*" he whispered throatily. *"Just enough."*

Chapter Eight

Traed exited the Tunnel in the royal village on Ganakari.

His cool jade eyes surveyed the scene before him.

Across the way two off-world aliens were arguing with a native about an item for trade; to one side of them a beggar was being thrown from a tavern; and in the foreground a thief was making off with a bolt of fabric.

It was like countless other outlying worlds he had been on.

Barely civilized.

At first glance there seemed nothing out of the ordinary about it. So why had *taj* Gian disappeared here?

Moving off to a relatively quiet corner, he ducked behind a market stall. One of his gifts was the ability to "see." It was an expertise that occured in some but not all high-level mystics. This talent would show him the places where Gian Ren had been. If Gian was here, he should be able to "see" him; if not, he would follow the trail of pictures, "seeing" the places he had been.

Closing his eyes, he concentrated on the image of Gian Ren.

His smooth brow furrowed as the image of a dungeon cell materialized in his mind's eye. Chains hung from the wall. The manacles at their ends were empty. Had Gian been kept prisoner here?

The images continued:

A room with a single window . . .

A stream . . .

A vine-covered valley . . .

A small outlying village by . . . a Tunnel.

Perhaps Gian had escaped and gone through the Tunnel? Traed tried to focus his energy on the image of the Familiar. The picture in his mind wavered suddenly and he saw an ancient sylvan forest. An impression of a small thatched cottage came into view.

Traed delved into the vision, curious as to what it meant. Was the Familiar there?

Now his inner eye focused on the interior of the hut. The furnishings were sparse and old. A bed was by the fireplace. Someone was lying on the bed, a huddled mass writhing in pain.

Traed attempted a closer vision. *Gian?* The strange vision dissolved.

It was not Gian.

Traed did not understand what he had seen, so he passed it off as unimportant. He was here to find Gian Ren and must focus on his task. Obviously the vision had not been accurate.

Had he been mystically trained, he would have known that all visions of the "sight" are significant, if not accurate. A trained Charl would have gone to the hut to investigate.

Once again, fate stepped in and steered the Aviarian away from such a path. He overheard two merchants gossiping about the escape of a prisoner several days before. He listened carefully.

"Took our lady! Stole our princess!"

"They say he forced himself upon her, then made her accompany him."

"What do you expect from one of that kind?" The man spat on the ground. "Aliens!"

Knowing Gian, Traed could only surmise that said princess had begged him to take her along—although he had a difficult time imagining *taj* Gian agreeing to such a thing.

Unless it suited him.

Well, he knew now that Gian had been held prisoner here and that he had already escaped. Discovering the reasons behind his capture would have to wait.

His priority was finding Guardian of the Mist.

From all accounts, he was on the run; undoubtedly he was trying to make his way back to M'yan, his homeworld.

Traed had seen the Tunnel the Familiar had used to flee, but he could not tell which of the other two Tunnel points on this world it was. He approached the two men he had overheard.

"You there!" he said in his usual blunt way. Traed was not one to soften his manner.

The two Ganakari turned, staring at him in astonishment.

It was not often such a rich-looking stranger came to their world. They instantly assessed the clothes he wore. They were of the finest Aviaran weave, enchanted by the Weaver's Guild of Aviara from the look of their perfect appearance. Aviarans rarely visited non-Alliance rim worlds.

One of the men stepped forward, bowing obsequiously. "May I be of service to you?" He eyed Traed's dark maroon cloak, wondering if he could bargain the man out of it.

Traed came right to the point. "What Tunnel point did the prisoner use to escape?"

The man's cheeks flushed. "And why would you be wanting to know that? Are you ally or foe to the Ganakari people?"

"Neither. My business is not your concern. Do you or do you not have this knowledge?"

"I know for a price."

Traed sighed. He detested this kind of work. "What is your price?"

The man eyed Traed's black boots, wondering if he could ask for those as well. Taking in the stranger's steely green gaze, he decided not to press his fortune. "The cloak you wear."

The expression on Traed's face might have been called *deadly* amusement. Anyone who knew Traed knew that this expression meant trouble brewing.

When the handsome Aviaran did not verbally respond, the merchant foolishly added, "And your boots."

A muscle ticked in the firm Aviaran jaw. "I will give you one clarified stone."

The merchant scoffed. "One stone!"

"And . . ."

The merchant's ears picked up. "And what?"

"*This.*" The light saber appeared at his throat so quickly that the merchant did not even see it clear the Aviaran's waistband. He swallowed nervously. Once released from the small black box that served as its hilt, the light blade, or light saber as it is sometimes called, was a lethal weapon.

"Do you accept my terms?" the jade-eyed man murmured in a chillingly low tone.

"Y-yes, I accept!"

"Wise decision." He retracted the blade, returning it to his waist. "Speak."

"He took the second Tunnel point—it is five days' journey on foot from here; although the Familiar made it in two."

"He took a shorter route?"

"There is no shorter route; the deadly *valdt* lies between the valleys and cannot be crossed." The merchant stroked his chin. "It is a mystery to us how he did it."

It was no mystery to Traed; Gian Ren was extremely resourceful. If there was a way, Guardian of the Mist would find it. His acumen was well known in the Alliance. "I need to get there as quickly as possible. How would I go about doing that?"

The other man came forward. "A *safir* beast can shorten the time of your journey somewhat."

Traed raised an eyebrow. "And where would I get such a beast?"

The man bounced forward on the pads of his feet. "I happen to have one for hire, if it suits you."

"How much?"

"Five clarified stones."

Traed tossed him three. The merchant beamed. "Come with me! Perhaps you are hungry? I have many fine supplies fit for a long journey such as yours."

Traed shook his head as he followed the man. It never changed. He only hoped his journey to Gian would be completed quickly.

There was no telling what *tortures* the Familiar was suffering at the moment.

Gian tugged Jenise down next to him so they faced each other, as they knelt on the floor of the cave.

His muscular arm encircled her waist, bringing their upper bodies together. His hand threaded through her long hair, sinking into the mass, entangling it about his fingers.

"I was afraid for you," she admitted shakily, still not over the worry she had felt when she realized he might not be able to make the transformation.

His green/gold eyes captured hers. He stared intently at her. "I know."

A small sound came from her lips, a mixture of desire and wariness. Her experiences with men—all men—had taught her to be cautious.

"What else are you afraid of, Creamcat?"

"Wh-what do you mean?"

He examined her guarded features. "Why do you fear pleasure?"

"I—I do not!" She struggled to break his embrace.

He held her fast. "Do you think it weakens you? Or is it something else?" His fingers splayed against her scalp, forcing her to look at him. To answer him.

"If you take pleasure, then you belong to that which gives it to you. When you belong to something, then you are owned." She lifted her chin, almost daring him to refute her.

Gian easily accepted her challenge. "No, *taja*, if you give pleasure and receive pleasure, then you share the pleasure, and when you come together, the union sets you free."

"You say that because you are a Familiar and Familiars seek only pleasure."

His thumb played with her bottom lip. "Pleasure is our nature, not our goal."

The lovely aqua eyes reflected turmoil. He was reaching her, he knew.

But it would be a slow process.

She said she was afraid for him, which was

true, but she was also afraid *of* him. Of the sensual power he had over her.

She had no idea of the levels of complexity going on here, he acknowledged. It was a new experience for any Familiar, he supposed; for a Familiar woman would be leading the pattern by now.

It mattered not.

He was more than happy to lead both the tone and pace himself.

Guardian of the Mist had discovered he had a partiality for difficult creamcats.

He was also discovering a lot of other things about himself that he had not known before. For one, he was becoming dependent upon her touch. For a man who was a most independent Familiar, it was a new experience indeed.

In any event, he did not ponder the outcome. Such was not his nature. Jenise would come to him gradually but completely. His lips brushed hers; the tip of his tongue giving the satiny surface a soft *lick*.

Lifting his mouth from hers, he stopped a hairsbreadth from the lips he had just moistened to let her feel his breath on her. The hot, light puffs of air blew over her in a tantalizing spice-dream.

She closed her eyes as his scent sensitized her for him.

Then he pressed his mouth to hers. A firm placement which stated who he was and what he was about to do. Gian was a thorough lover whose sexual knowledge was part instinct, part experience, and part Gian Ren. The uniqueness of the Familiar people transcended to the individual; each Familiar brought his own individuality to the experience he delivered. It was another factor that made them prized on so many worlds.

Unaware of the meaning behind his motions, Jenise returned his kiss, craving the feel of him, the taste of him. Smoky *krinang* spice covered her as he delved inside with a wicked thrust of his tongue. His movements, though simple, were surely art just the same.

His fingers splayed on the back of her scalp as he took her mouth. A flood of wanting assailed her along with the evocative taste and touch of the Familiar male.

As his fingers massaged her scalp, his mouth skimmed over her jawline to the edge of her ear. Fiery exhalation feathered the folds. She trembled anew. The hot mouth solidly pressed on the skin of her neck, drawing on the susceptible spot just under her ear.

The peaks of her breasts hardened.

Gian pulled her up tighter to him. He rubbed the firm, pointed tips along the skin of his chest. The sliding abrasion made her shiver.

In response his manhood skimmed her nether curls in a light passing.

Jenise moaned from the exquisite tracing. Unbidden, her hands gripped his wide shoulders, the tips of her fingers making small indentations.

The palm of his hand pressed against a protruding nipple, rotating it around the center. His skilled teasing action heightened the combined feeling of satin lips drawing on her throat and male teeth biting softly.

"Do you know me, Jenise?" he whispered against her moistened skin.

Who could know a cat? Quivering from his expert love-touches, she moaned, "I know you somewhat, Gian."

She was surprised at how true that was—she did know much of him. The life-threatening events they had shared together had formed a certain bond between them. She knew his strength, his steadfastness, his dependability, his pride, his playfulness, and his tendency to take control. But in other ways, the man was a complex puzzle.

She lifted his stunning face between her hands, forcing him to meet her eyes. "Do you know me, Gian?"

His lids lowered as his gaze fixed on her lips. *The lips he had licked.* "What do you think?"

She kissed him fast, taking him by surprise.

There was a new depth to the exchange. Gian held her close, a wild passion building inside him.

They were both becoming hot and damp and they both moaned aloud.

His hands cupped the backs of her thighs, bringing her flush against his desire. Boldly, he moved her onto him while he kneaded her firm buttocks.

Jenise couldn't catch her breath.

White teeth captured the jutting tip of her breast. He suckled vigorously as he observed her watching him; his full regard focused upon her. *It was too much.* Her eyes fluttered shut; a sound of raw need was ripped from her.

The intense utterance of desire reverberated through Gian. In a graceful action, he lowered her to the stone floor of the cavern, immediately coming atop her.

"Let me know if this is too hard for you," he drawled huskily.

Her aqua eyes popped open. *"What?"*

He realized what he had just said. A grin spread across his perfect features. "I meant the stone"—his grin got wider—"floor."

Jenise snorted. He had a teasing sense of humor and it showed at the oddest times. Her arm went around his strong neck, tugging him down to her.

"You will be the first to know if it is too hard," she shot back.

He chuckled against her lips.

And *stroked* into her.

The way he had intended from the very first. A long, penetrating thrust.

She was still narrow from the newness of the experience. Her inner muscles clamped tightly on him.

With fluid agility, he immediately changed her angle by bringing her legs down from around his hips, positioning them straight under him. He gripped her thighs close together as he remained snug within her.

"Lie like this, *taja*." He spoke soothingly into her ear. "It will lessen the discomfort of the deep stroking."

Jenise nodded against his cheek.

He showed her what he meant with a swift, delving thrust. It felt tight, but he was right. He was able to thrust deeper without it bothering her. *Much deeper.*

Both their breathing accelerated wildly. Even so, Jenise would not let him forget his promise to her. "Remember, Gian Ren, not *too* much pleasure."

He smiled against her throat. "Never, *taja*." So he began to pulse inside her with gentle movements. She wrapped him in her embrace, kissing the hollow of his shoulder.

He tossed his hair back. Then he flexed carefully inside her. Jenise jumped at the exquisite sensation.

"Is it too much?" he asked sweetly.

"No," she gasped on a moan.

A small dimple popped into his cheek. "What about this . . . ?" He rotated his hips, pressing more fully inside.

That was when Jenise knew he intended to toy with her. She eyed the felinelike man warily.

"Hmm?" He rested his chin on her chest and smiled like a cat. He flexed again.

It was getting harder for her to catch her breath. Tiny pulses were twitching through her. "N-no."

A completely innocent look crossed his exotic features. The virtuous expression was not an easy accomplishment for one such as Gian.

Jenise knew she was in trouble.

He winked lazily at her.

His long gilded hair swung forward and he murmured throatily into her mouth, "How about this, then, *taja?*"

Withdrawing partway, he captured her earlobe with a sexy little tug and slid into her as far as he could go.

"Gian!"

He pulled her hips up sharply as he bore down a little more. "Mmm?" He *palpitated* from that hidden place inside.

"Ohh!" Jenise came apart, her nails biting into his flesh as the tremors took her.

He liked the scratching. A low growl resonated from his chest. Holding her immobile, he gave her another quick peak by grinding hard against her dampness.

"Please!"

And *again* by waiting for just the right moment in her contractions to rotate and thrust. Reaching an entirely new depth.

The sensation was even too much for him. Jenise was still calling out her satisfaction as he achieved his own peak, a fast, powerful release.

Sitting up dazedly, Jenise placed a hand on her forehead. "I—I think that was just enough."

Guardian of the Mist roared with laughter. His green/gold eyes sparkled. "I am known for the strength of my word."

A Familiar's subtlety could be interpreted in so many ways.

Dara Joy

*   *   *

"We should try to get some rest now." Gian grinned wickedly at her, showcasing white teeth and that sensual lower lip of his.

He had made love to her three times already with nary a pause in between. There was no doubt in Jenise's mind that the Familiar could keep on going. Were all men like this? She was exhausted!

Jenise stared at that masculine lip, remembering its velvety touch. What was happening to her? One moment she had been admiring him, the next, they were . . .

Her brow furrowed. Despite the fact that she enjoyed their loveplay, she was not sure they should be getting this close. Soon they would be forced to go their separate ways. Surely their intimacy would make the parting that much harder.

Gian watched her, highly amused. She was beginning to awaken for him. It was only right that he add to her confusion. He smiled slyly. "However," he tantalized her, "if you prefer to explore—"

"I'll sleep over here! On *this* side of the fire," she stated firmly.

"Think you I would allow that after what we have shared?"

She raised her chin. "It is not your decision, Gian."

"Why would you not want to sleep here where I can keep you warm all night? Where I can hold you and protect you?" He got up and came to-

178

wards her. "Where I can sleep easier knowing you are close and in my embrace?" He picked her up in his arms and carried her back to his side of the fire.

"You will not let me stay on the other side, will you?"

"No." He lay down with her and covered them both with her cloak.

Jenise turned in the circle of his arms until she faced the rock wall, away from him. "You are difficult, Gian."

"Yes."

"Does your name mean Arrogant Beyond Belief in your language?"

He laughed, a rich sound of amusement. "How did you know?" he teased her, rubbing his chin against her shoulder.

She twisted to look up at him. "Really? It does?"

He laughed out loud. "No, *taja*, it does not," He winked roguishly at her. "I am sorry to say . . .."

Jenise made a face. "Then it must mean Infernal Annoyer."

He grinned, liking this. The Familiar adored games of any kind. And, like cats, they were ready to play at an instant's notice. In all ways.

"How about Never Listens? Is that it?"

"Um, what did you say?" He cupped his ear. "I did not hear you."

She poked him in the side with her elbow. "Impossible beast."

"Nooo, that is not it either."

Her lips twitched. "I did not mean . . . never mind. So what does it mean?"

He watched her through lowered lids. "Guardian of the Mist," he said evenly.

"Guardian of the Mist . . . what an odd name. Does it have a certain meaning for you?"

He answered her carefully. "It refers to my abilities."

"In what way?" she asked curiously.

"I am considered a master of the hunt."

That she had already surmised. "But what does—"

"To be an effective hunter, or protector, one must have the ability to seem to hide in mist, to come out of nowhere, to be upon one's prey before the target even realizes it has been marked."

"I see." Jenise knew he referred to much more than a physical situation. He was speaking metaphorically as well. She herself had already noted his acuity, his stealth. He was exactly as she had surmised. *Dangerous.*

"Does it have any other connotations?" she asked shrewdly.

"Yes." The green/gold eyes glittered beneath the black spiky lashes.

Jenise paused a heartbeat. "What?" she asked.

"I will tell you some other time," he drawled. He captured her lips to silence her.

Two small, pretty pebbles were carefully placed on top of her cloak.

Jenise yawned and stretched, trying to wake up. The stones had obviously been chosen with great care for their unusual color and shape. *A gift?* she wondered.

She looked over at Gian curiously.

The Familiar was already gathering their small store of supplies. *First the small flower that he placed in my ear . . . now this. How odd.* Although it was rather sweet in its way.

She decided not to mention it to him. By the covert manner in which he bestowed the little gifts, it seemed as though he might be embarrassed if she did. She tucked the colorful pebbles away in a concealed pocket of her cloak.

Out of the corner of his eye, Gian noted her accepting the gifts of the *t'kan*. It pleased him.

"These supplies were most likely left by some merchants who frequent this route during the trading season." He tied the bag with a *systale* vine, leaving some of the goods behind for the next traveler. "When we get to the next world we must thank them and arrange for payment somehow. I will send something from M'yan for their thoughtfulness."

Jenise felt the concealed compartment of her cloak. There was something she should tell him. "Gian, you do not have to—"

"It is nothing, I assure you." He glanced over at her. "We should leave soon."

She reached for her garment, pulling it on. Before she could pin the clasp he was behind her, taking it from her hands. It never ceased to amaze her how silently he could move.

Or how fast. Clasping her gown for her at her shoulder, he placed a tender kiss on the curve of her arm.

She smiled up at him. "What is that for?"

"Everything." His passionate dual-colored eyes gleamed at her.

Jenise swallowed. It was difficult to get used to his sexual ways. "I am ready."

Amusement lit his face. He raised a brow. "Are you?" he murmured suggestively.

Very difficult. "To leave," she clarified.

"Ahhhh . . ." He smiled slowly. "While you were sleeping I discovered that the path at the far end of this cavern leads directly to the center of the mountain. All we need do is follow it to where it joins the steps down into the center. There we will find the Tunnel entrance."

"I am glad we do not have to go outside again; I do not like this place overly much."

"I agree," he said wryly, rolling the residual stiffness out of his shoulders. Familiars always preferred comfort over bare necessities.

Even if they could make a hard floor seem positively luxurious simply by stretching out on it.

"Although the company has made this cave more than it ever seemed it could be."

Jenise's lips parted at the eloquent and completely unexpected compliment. She lightly touched his arm. "The same for me, Gian."

He inclined his head slightly, acknowledging her words. He took her hand to lead her. "Be careful where you step. Follow my footsteps—

some of the rocks are loose and there are bottomless pits ahead."

She took his advice. After all, when it came to being sure-footed, who better to trust than a Familiar?

"They are no longer on Ganakari, my lord."

Karpon viewed the leader of his elite guard with disdain. "How can that be? You did as I told you? Sent out the extra contingents to stop them?"

"Yes, my lord, of course."

"Then how is it an unarmed man and a woman were able to escape your men?"

"We do not know. All we know for certain is that they somehow reached the second Tunnel ahead of us. Several merchants recalled seeing them enter the portal. I am at a loss to explain it."

"Fool! There has to be an explanation!"

"Not unless he was able to fly like a winged beast across the *valdt*."

Karpon wondered . . . No; that was impossible even for a Familiar! And what about Jenise? From all accounts, she was still with him. His blood boiled at the idea of her in the Familiar's arms.

Unfortunately, at present there was little he could do about it. By this time they could have linked to another portal and their trail would be difficult if not impossible to follow.

So be it.

He had lost Jenise, but he still had his kingdom. Not a bad trade, he supposed. In time, when he had more resources and men, he would go after her to reclaim what was his.

He rolled the vial of amber liquid in his palm. For now he would settle on controlling a world.

And all the Familiar he could capture.

Chapter Nine

"Seeking for Familiar?"

Traed switched his focus from the mouth of the Tunnel to the creaky voice coming from the direction of his elbow.

The being standing before him had a lot of wrinkled skin and a large snout. Two dark brown eyes gleamed out of the folds of skin. "Seeking for Familiar?" It asked again, waving its small, crooked staff.

"And how do you know that?" Traed watched the life form carefully. He was cautious by nature; on a quest especially so.

"Saw Familiar!"

Traed arched a brow. "Really. And where did he go?"

The alien pointed to the Tunnel.

Traed already knew that. "My thanks." He

started walking to the portal. The odd-looking alien rushed up behind him. In an instant Traed pivoted about, light saber drawn and pointed at the protruding snout.

The being stopped short with a small squeak. "No harm!"

Traed wondered if he meant not to harm him or that he would not harm Traed. In either case he did not lower the blade. Krue had trained him always to be on his guard in new situations.

Traed carried the advice one step further; he was always on guard in *every* situation.

"What do you want?" His steely tone caused another squeak to issue forth from the alien.

"Dangerous journey even for warrior. Gruntel guide you!"

"Are you saying you wish to be my guide?"

The snout bobbed up and down.

"I see. And why should I trust you?"

The question seemed to baffle Gruntel. He cocked his head to the side and raised bushy eyebrows. "Not trust?" As if he'd never heard of such a thing.

The expression was so humorous that Traed actually chuckled. The being appeared to be harmless. He lowered his blade. "Are you a . . . what exactly *are* you?"

"Aha-ha-ha!" He did a little dance. "Got warrior fooled, Gruntel does!" He spun around, fat feet pounding the dirt.

Traed watched the show patiently. When the antics had quieted down, he calmly asked, "What are you then?"

One of three leathery fingers pointed to his stubby chest. "Wiggamabob!"

"A *what?*"

"Wiggamabob. Lots Wiggamabob. Go here."

"I see." Although he didn't. "Do you know the terrain beyond the portal?"

Again the snout bobbed up and down. "Gruntel merchant guide. Take many."

In what way? Traed wondered. The creature could be trying to lead him into a trap. Nonetheless, Traed had no idea what existed beyond this Tunnel; it might be wise to engage the alien's services.

"Very well. You may guide me."

Gruntel did another little dance, presumably of glee. He waved his crooked staff in the air as he hobbled in front of Traed, beckoning him to follow.

Traed crossed his arms over his chest and held his ground. He waited patiently, as was his wont, until Gruntel realized he wasn't following him.

The bumpy-headed alien stopped, circling about, a confused look clouding his features. "No follow?"

Traed shook his head slowly from side to side. "No follow. *Lead.* You follow *me* through the portal." He was not about to allow himself to be ambushed by possible accomplices on the other side.

On these outlying worlds, the Tunnel portals were unmanned and to a large extent, ungoverned. Just going through would be a risk. By leading, he felt that if there was a danger of any kind, he would gain a precious instant of reaction time.

Sometimes an instant was all a man with Charl abilities needed.

Traed passed the alien guide and stood before the pulsating maw. The High Guild was not in favor of keeping Tunnels open in stasis for many reasons. For one, certain fluctuations of the space/time continuum could occur at both end sites. For another, the Guild preferred to maintain its control of the Tunnels; such a position strengthened the Alliance as a whole, while curtailing acts of unwarranted aggression.

In spite of this, because of their remoteness, certain areas had to be held in stasis. When Tunnels on remote outposts such as this one were left open, they were routinely phased by the Gatekeepers for maintenance of the temporal continuum.

Traed was thankful the Tunnel was still in its unsealed phase.

"Tell me what to expect on the other side," he commanded.

"Not much. No beings. Place between worlds."

Traed understood; the next world served as a connecting plane. "What is the terrain like?"

"Flat as flat. Must climb to enter next. Listen to Gruntel be fine."

"Hmm." Traed withdrew his Cearix from his waistband as a precaution and stepped through the portal. A lightblade could inadvertently harm someone where it extended while coming through the portal. By using the dagger, there was more risk to him, but Traed would not risk harming an innocent.

He came out onto a flat plain dotted with rocks and brush. A few *nanyats* graced the otherwise barren landscape. Gruntel almost fell into him as he hobbled out of the entrance. Traed threw him a look.

"Most apologetic. Not like Tunnels. Go through fast." He grinned at the tall Aviaran man, showing two pointed teeth.

Traed's returned a stony expression. Which was the normal set of his features. Such obscurity was one of the traits that Yaniff most admired about him. At the moment the Aviaran warrior was conveying patient acceptance of a universe out of his control. Traed was ever the observer on the complexities and incomprehensibility of life.

Seeing no immediate danger, Traed replaced his dagger in its scabbard.

"Way to pass!" Gruntel pointed one of his three leathery fingers towards a distant domed peak. Then he pointed up to the sky at the binary suns. "Most hot now." He covered his bumpy head with a swath of dark gray fabric from his robes. "Protect too, Aviaran."

Traed nodded. He lifted the hood of his cloak over his head. "How did you know I am Aviaran?" He spoke low.

"Knife-dagger. Aviaran."

"Yes, it is."

"Very old. Very powerful."

Traed wondered how Gruntel knew that. Perhaps the strange little alien had gifts of his own. "It is called a Cearix."

"Cearix," he repeated before scurrying past him to begin the long trek across the land.

Traed stepped up beside him, taking one step to the alien's three.

"Cearix," Gruntel repeated again.

"Yes." Traed's thoughts went to the legend of the Cearix, the Aviaran ceremonial dagger.

It was said that the Cearix of each man's line carried with it all of the truths learned by each generation that wielded it. According to Charl mystical belief, one would come whose powers were so great that he would be able to "see" all knowledge passed down from the ages by holding the Cearix within his hand. Such truths were said to be contained within the clarity of a knife's blade.

Although he honored the tradition, Traed did not subscribe to the belief. If it were true, he ruminated as he walked on, then the Cearix he carried—that of the line of Yaniff—would carry with it untold power.

Traed shrugged. Such tales were simply the fables of old Guild members. He preferred the reality of life.

As the day wore on, its unrelenting heat made a misery of the crossing. But finally as the long shadows of the suns inched across the plain, Traed and Gruntel reached the base of the mountain.

*   *   *

"Steps for us to climb!"

The small alien guide placed his curved staff on the first platform, hopping up on it.

Traed gazed up, taking in the distance to the top. Unconcerned with the climb, he started to place his booted foot on the platform.

A sharp pain stung his upper chest above his heart. Tendrils of fiery twinges radiated from the single point, crossing his torso. Clamping on him like a vise.

Stunned, he gazed down at the spot below his shoulder. A thin, pointed quill was stuck in him; its sharp point had cut right through his cloak and shirt.

"Honored Aviaran!" Gruntel had caught sight of the quill. He scrambled down several platforms to aid Traed. Taking the green-eyed man's arm, he tried to yank him onto the platforms, out of reach of the shooting quills.

Despite the acute agony, Traed leapt onto the platform, his opinion of the guide increasing by the moment. "Good, Gruntel."

Gruntel gave him a worried look. A fat, leathery finger pointed at the quill still protruding from Traed's chest.

"It is nothing." Traed grabbed the spine and yanked it out without so much as a flicker of expression. Blood spurted out of the opening, quickly saturating his cloak. The Aviaran warrior ignored the injury.

"You see? Let us continue now." He made two steps before he collapsed.

Gruntel stood over him, clucking his tongue.

"Warrior not as strong as he thinks."

With surprising strength, he picked the man up and flipped him over his knobby shoulder. The warrior's ponytail dragged across the stones as he hefted him up the pathway.

Traed opened his eyes to the sight of a small pool in front of him. He blinked. How had he . . . ?

Then it came to him. *Gruntel . . . the quill . . .*

He sat up fast.

Too fast.

A wave of dizziness assailed him. As was his nature, he ignored it. His hand went to the dull throbbing above his left breastbone. A small bandage covered the spot.

He noted his black shirt and cloak lying on the ground nearby.

"Cleansed wound, Gruntel did. Fix good! Maybe die if not for Gruntel." He knelt beside Traed, offering him some broth.

Traed smiled at him slightly, grateful for his care. He took the broth from him. "I am in your debt, Gruntel."

The odd alien made a rude sound, as if Traed had insulted him. "No debt! Do for right!"

Traed nodded, thinking that all such decisions in life should be so clear cut. Right and wrong. For some strange reason, he thought of his father, Theardar. Light and dark. Life did not follow such narrow guidelines. Edges often blurred. Difficult choices became devastating ones to a man who wielded too much power. . . .

"Called name in your sleep. Many times." Gruntel peered at him curiously, his small, dark eyes penetrating.

Traed lifted the broth to his lips and took a swallow. It was surprisingly tasty. "Did I?" He did not seem overly interested. "What name was it?" He made to take another sip of the liquid.

Gruntel told him.

He paused with the bowl halfway to his lips. Even though no outward emotion showed on his features, it was obvious he was shaken.

"A female?" Gruntel asked with keen interest.

The green eyes became shuttered. "It is of no importance." He drank the broth, ending the topic.

Gruntel was not convinced. He had seen the man's face when he called out for that name. Contrary to what the Aviaran warrior claimed, the name seemed to carry great importance to him.

Traed finished the broth and set the bowl aside. His brow furrowed as he felt the loose strands of his hair. It was full of little twigs and dirt. Frowning at the tangled mess, he looked at Gruntel for an answer.

The Wiggamabob shrugged sheepishly. "Much tall for warrior. Hair regrettably sweep behind." Gruntel snorted playfully. "Clean many steps!" He grinned engagingly at him.

Traed glanced at him out of the corner of his eye. "Hmmm."

Gruntel did a little dance, apparently finding this very humorous.

Traed stood up.

Gruntel stopped his dance with his fat foot poised in the air. "No, no, no, no, no, too soon!"

Traed closed his eyes, willing the slight nausea to pass. With his usual iron determination, he forced the queasiness down and headed for the pool. Pulling off his boots and black *tracas*, he jumped into the cold water, Gruntel clucking disapproval behind him.

He ducked below the surface. When he came up, Gruntel tossed him a vial of cleansing oil. Unconsciously, Traed's arm shot up, his hand catching the tiny vial with perfect precision. Krue had always said he had excellent hands. It was what made him a master of the blade.

With his customary perfunctory movements, he lathered his dark hair, combing the knots out with his fingers. It was not an easy task. A few choice Aviaran epithets followed.

That done, he waded out of the water to don his garments. He searched the ground for the leather thong he used to tie his hair back.

Gruntel sighed loudly. "Gone. Lost on steps."

Traed searched the cave for something else to use.

"Nothing work," Gruntel offered. "Must wear loose." The Wiggamabob grinned.

Traed exhaled, tossing the waist-length strands over his shoulders.

"Look different with hair that way."

"Do I?" Traed answered distractedly. He donned his cloak.

"Most different. Like warrior but . . . not."

"I see." Traed was barely paying attention. He closed his eyes, trying to "see" Gian. Images of this room, the pool, flashed by, followed by a corridor leading to the center of the mountain . . . steps leading down, and lastly, a picture of the next Tunnel.

Gian had already exited this world.

"We must leave now."

"Gruntel say too soon for warrior to travel."

Traed crossed his arms over his chest. "*Warrior* says we leave now."

Gruntel clucked, using his crooked staff to stand. "No want you to fall dead. Got to make sure get payment from you, Charl who is knight."

Traed led the way to the corridor. "I am not a knight of the Charl," he called over his shoulder.

"No?" Gruntel sniffed, his huge snout snuffling the air. "Smell like knight. Look like knight. Maybe taste like knight too?"

Traed narrowed his eyes as he threw him a look.

Gruntel grinned, showing his two pointed teeth.

Gian and Jenise stepped out of the Tunnel onto red sand and blowing red dust.

In the distance, a forest of giant red crystals surrounded the open space.

It had taken them almost a day to reach the Tunnel on the last world. As they walked through the center of the mountain, Gian had led her, carefully monitoring her steps, for the going was treacherous in places.

"Where are we?" She spoke quietly next to him.

Gian's green/gold eyes narrowed as he scanned the area. Several giant egg-shaped boulders dotted the landscape in front of them, forming a semicircular pattern in the red sand.

Jenise was shocked to see someone emerge from the side of one of the boulders through a natural fissure. The being raced to another of the boulders, slipping into a crevice to disappear from view.

Gian exhaled slowly, his eyes scanning the land again. He did not appear happy. "This is a mining world, Jenise. We must be on our guard here; such places are usually lawless and attract a criminal element."

"How many Tunnel points do you sense?"

"Just one other."

"Where does it lead, do you think?"

"That we will find out inside one of those." He pointed to the boulders. His arm came around her shoulders. "Stay near me; there could be danger."

She nodded. The wind began to howl.

Gian lifted his face into the wind. "There is a storm coming."

"How do you know?"

"Familiars have electrical sense; we can predict the coming of a storm. On this world it seems to be a common occurrence. Come, we need to seek shelter." He hurried her through the sand to the nearest boulder. The grit crunched beneath her feet; tiny granules of quartz glinted as the increasing wind sculpted the dunes.

Gian placed himself in front of her as they entered the rock. She realized the protective gesture was simply part of his nature.

Jenise's mouth gaped as she got her first look at the interior. Rose-colored crystal surrounded them, jutting out from the ceiling and walls, projecting towards the center of the space. The flooring was red sand packed down to form a smooth surface. Tiny crystals sparkled across the room.

They appeared to be in a tavern.

Clear crystal glass formed all of the furnishings. Candlelight bounced off the crystal walls and tables and chairs.

Jenise thought it was lovely. "It is beautiful," she marveled.

Several patrons turned to stare at her.

The tavern was full of beings—a jumble of species from various planets. Some had obviously come to test their luck in the mines, seeking their fortunes. Some, like the tavern-keeper, had set up a business, charging a premium for lodging at this end of the world space. Others were there to prey on those they could.

Gian pulled her closer to him. "It is beautiful, *taja*. We are in the center of a giant geode—I have seen them before on other mining worlds. But do not be overcome by the beauty of it; you must be wary of everyone and everything here."

"Are you sure? They seem friendly enough." She glanced over at a Seckla, who was smiling at her and waving one of his tentacles for her to join him.

Gian frowned. "Yes, I am sure." He sent the Seckla a firm *flicker-warning* to stay away. The Seckla wilted in his seat.

Gian led her rapidly through the throng towards the front, where the tavern-keeper was filling horns with *keeran*.

"Do you have lodging for the night?" he asked the woman. She was a Rykan. Her delicately pointed ears twitched with interest as she eyed the comely Familiar.

"For you, my kitty, kitty, I have whatever you need."

Jenise peeked around Gian's broad back with interest. *"Kitty, kitty?"* she mouthed, smothering a laugh.

Gian's hand discreetly motioned her to silence. *{We do not have any clarified stones and we definitely need shelter. Be silent!}*

"And how do you propose to pay for this shelter?" Jenise asked rather loudly. She had no right to feel irritated, but she was.

Gian exhaled noisily. So much for subtlety. He looked over at the tavern-keeper and winked meaningfully.

"Are you thirsty, kitty?" The Rykan leaned forward over the bar, nearly falling out of her shirt.

Gian pretended interest. "Yes, I am." The woman smiled at him, pouring him a huge horn of *keeran*. She ignored Jenise completely.

"Thank you very much," Jenise intoned sarcastically.

[Jenise.] Gian picked up the horn and drank deeply.

Jenise made a face at his back. Gian smiled behind the rim of the brew, knowing exactly what she was doing, for the wall in front of him reflected her infuriated little visage a thousand times in the crystals.

"And what happened to your clothes, kitty?" the Rykan asked suggestively.

Gian flashed her a sultry look. "I lost them."

The Rykan grinned at him. "I like you."

"Good."

"Is she with you?" The tavern-keeper nodded to Jenise, speaking of her as if she were not there.

"Yes, I am delivering her to a friend of mine on the next jump."

"What?" Jenise kicked him in the shin.

"She does not seem happy with the idea." Gian shrugged his broad shoulders as if it were of no concern to him.

"There are no rooms left here—but I also own the tavern across the way. Tell them Jeeva has sent you. They will find a place for you."

Gian smiled seductively at her.

The Rykan looked him over and licked her lips. "And when might I expect *payment?*"

Jenise had heard enough! She started to move forward, but Gian's arm across her chest forestalled her. "I am tired from my journey and need to rest first."

"Of course." She inclined her head. "I want you well-rested, kitty, kitty; the rooms here do not come cheap."

Jenise broke free of Gian's restraining arm. "I choose to pay for my room, if you do not mind, Familiar!" Whereupon she opened her cloak and withdrew a handful of rare clarified stones, slapping them on the glass counter. The tavern-keeper's eyes bulged out.

[Are you mad? Put those away!]

Jenise ignored him. Lifting her chin, she demanded her lodging.

The Rykan scooped the stones off the table-top. "A wealthy patron; how nice." She signaled to a male Rykan, who came forward. "Take them across the way. Tell them I said to give her the red room."

Gian was furious with Jenise. By her actions, she had exposed them to every thief in the vicinity. Word would spread fast that the pale woman was carrying a fortune in stones on her. He gnashed his teeth.

"Is there a place I might replenish my clothing?" he asked the Rykan man.

"Yes, there is a merchant across the way here. His goods are very expensive."

Jenise waved her imperious little hand in the air. "It matters not."

Gian began to simmer.

Outside, the wind was even stronger now than it had been before. The Rykan man sniffed the air. "Be a big storm coming soon." He looked down at Jenise. "You stay here if you know what is good for you. Do not venture out. Storms here are fierce and dangerous. Sometimes they come fast, without warning; sometimes they build slowly like this one. Those are the ones you have to watch for."

He led them into the next boulder.

The first thing Gian noticed was that this tavern seemed to attract an even worse element than the last. Several suspicious-looking beings huddled in poorly lit corners. An opaque red glass partition led to another area in the rear.

Gian realized that several geodes were connected to this one as the man led them up a glass staircase onto a crystal platform. He stopped before a solid red crystal door. Taking out a key, he unlocked the room.

Jenise gasped in delight.

The entire room was made of red crystal points much like the other tavern. In the center, clear crystal lattices formed a bed, which had been covered in sand-stuffed *krilli* cloth. A small bathing pool lay in the far corner.

"It is lovely!" She turned to Gian, beaming.

The smile died on her face at his stern expression.

For an instant she had forgotten the scene in the tavern. Her nostrils flared as she also remembered the shameless way he had tried to barter.

No, it was not right of her to fault him.

Gian could do as he wished. Their pact was at an end; he had more than kept his side. He had delivered her safely out of Ganakari and then some.

A sinking feeling assailed her. Whatever they had shared was now at an end. As a Familiar, he would be wanting to seek his pleasures. It had been wrong of her to interfere.

"You were right. I am sorry to have spoken out of turn."

Her apology took him by surprise. "You understand then?"

"Yes. Of course."

He relaxed. "Good."

"Your obligation to me is finished. I—I thank you for—"

"My obligation?"

"Yes. We are now free of Ganakari. Our pact is over. I understand that you wish to—that is, if you wish to meet that woman . . ."

Gian's eyes narrowed. "Are you saying that it matters not to you one way or the other?"

She fidgeted with her cloak, unsure of how to respond. Of course it mattered to her. She just did not want him to know it.

"I see. For your information, *taja*, I did not know you had any stones. In any case, I had no intention of meeting her; I was simply trying to secure us some lodging."

Jenise waved her hand. "It is your concern."

His eyes narrowed to green/gold slits. A strange light glowed in them.

Jenise was oblivious to the storm brewing inside him. "I have plenty of stones; would you prefer your own room?"

He inhaled and exhaled, reigning in his temper. "I know you have plenty of stones; the entire tavern and probably three quarters of the population here know it!"

"What do you mean?"

"Whatever made you take those stones out, Jenise?"

"I thought—"

"No, you did not. You have made us a target for every cutthroat in the area."

She hadn't realized that. "Oh." She worried her lip. "I have not had much experience with such things."

"So I have seen."

He was referring to more than the stones. Her eyes stung at his comment.

Gian realized at once how she had misinterpreted him. "Jenise, I did not mean—"

"I know what you meant." She turned her back on him. He tried to put his hands on her shoulders but she pulled away from him. "I wish to bathe and rest, Gian."

"Very well. I will go to the merchant that man mentioned and procure some clothing. Afterwards, I will be downstairs in the main room should you need me. Keep this door locked behind me at all times."

He started to leave.

Jenise forestalled him. "You may need some stones to purchase the items you need." She held out a hand brimming with clarified stones.

Gian hesitated, reluctant to take them.

"Unless you have a better way of obtaining

merchandise?" She arched a honey-brown eyebrow. "Perhaps this merchant is female as well."

Her ploy worked. Gian gave her a disgusted look but he took the gems. "They will be returned to you when we reach Aviara."

"You mean when *you* reach Aviara. We need to go our separate ways, Gian." Jenise could not believe the pain it caused her to say those words to him.

Gian hesitated at the door. "I will talk to you later, *taja*." He softly closed the door behind him.

She found him later sitting alone at a table in the tavern.

Apparently no one wanted to test his good fortune by approaching Gian, for his demeanor was quite dark. There was an aura of strength to him that was extemely intimidating.

Seeing him in this new light, from a distance, Jenise was struck by how mysterious Gian could be, how many sides there were to his nature. Throughout these many sides there was a steadfast quality about him, an inner core of strength and *power*.

She had seen him fearless, courageous, mischievous, playful, sexually loving, and concerned. But never like this. . . . Dangerously brooding. Jenise shook off the unsettling intuition.

She noticed that he had purchased and donned a dark green cloak, a white shirt, and

black boots. If possible, he was even more spellbinding dressed in the simple garb.

He looked up in surprise as she approached
the crystal table. "Is something amiss? I understood you were to rest."

Pulling out a crystal seat, she sat opposite
him. "I changed my mind." The truth was that
thoughts of separating from him had plagued
her. After bathing she had tried to rest but could
not.

Jenise thought of what she had gained by leaving Ganakari—her freedom. With that freedom
came the pain of knowing him. Leaving him.

Nothing came without a price, she reasoned
sadly. She was not sorry. She had a brave heart;
she was a Frensi!

Dipping a segment of *paxi* fruit into sweet
sauce, Gian offered her the delicate morsel. She
shook her head. She had no appetite.

He took a bite of the fruit, savoring the tangy
juice. Like everything he did, the action evoked
a certain sensuality.

He watched her through veiled lashes. Like a
cat making plans. Reaching for his horn of
keeran, he took a long swallow of the brew.

Placing the horn down on the table, he began
dipping another segment of fruit as he spoke to
her. "I am headed to Aviara, as you know," he
said in that soft, low voice of his.

"Yes, I know."

"If you will recall, I have told you there is but
one entrance to my homeworld of M'yan and
that is through Aviara."

"Why is that?" she asked, suddenly curious. "Surely the Mystics of the Charl could open as many Tunnels as they chose to your world."

"We have an agreement with them. We explore for them; in return, the entrance to M'yan is watched over by the High Guild and constantly guarded by the Charl knights."

"Sounds pretty one-sided in your favor."

Gian smiled ferally. "Perhaps, but the Guild does not mind. Our allegiance to each other goes back through time. Familiars and wizards are natural allies. You might say we go together like lightning and thunder."

She knew which part was lightning—the Charl. That would make him . . . *thunder*. Before she could fully explore that compelling concept, she wondered why the Familiar would need such an agreement. She asked him.

"To protect us from unwanted and uninvited visitors. We are a private people."

"You are not capable of defending yourselves?"

He arched a brow. "What do you think?"

"I think whoever negotiated such a treaty was brilliant."

"Oh, do you?" He sipped his *keeran* in a measured way.

"It freed your people to pursue other interests without having to expend energy on defense."

"The wizards think we are worth the effort."

Jenise clicked her tongue. "Have them fooled, do you?"

A dimple indented his cheek. He shook his finger at her, sipping his drink again.

"Who negotiated such a treaty? We should send this person to Ganakari."

The Familiar almost choked on his drink. "Why would you even think such a thing? I can assure you Ganakari is the last place he would wish to be."

Jenise shrugged. "Perhaps he could help the Ganakari deal with Karpon?"

Gian looked at her obliquely. "I do not believe he will do that, Jenise. If anything, he will seek retribution on them. You see, it was the King of all Familiar who negotiated that treaty."

That bit of news upset her.

A king would not have a tendency to be lenient in this case.

Jenise worried for the people of Ganakari. From what she had seen of Gian, they would never stand a chance against an entire attack force of Familiar.

She leaned forward in her seat, placing her hand on his arm. "He must not! The people had naught to do with it—it was Karpon!"

He looked down at the table, a muscle ticking in his jaw. Then he looked up, meeting her eyes. "Karpon will pay for what he has done and what he intends to do to my people," he said quietly. "If the Ganakari people stand with him, they will pay as well."

"If this king is as clever as you say, then he will find a way to defeat Karpon without harming the Ganakari!"

A small, secret smile curved his sensuous lips. It was an expression of his she had often noted, and it never failed to captivate her. The enigmatic smile held a wealth of meanings.

"Perhaps you should come to M'yan and tell him yourself."

"I do not think he will listen to me; he would consider me an enemy."

"You helped me escape."

Jenise was not sure she wanted to be pulled into this. When she had left Ganakari, she had left that life behind. "Perhaps he will not see it as you do."

"Who?"

"The king."

He smiled. "Perhaps not."

Jenise decided to change the subject. "Have you found the next Tunnel?"

"Yes." He nodded. "It is a half day's journey from here, in the next mining camp."

"Oh." Jenise folded her hands on the table. "When will you be leaving?"

Gian sat back in the chair and watched her. Did she think he would leave her in a place like this, unprotected and at the mercy of cutthroats? That she would even entertain the idea maddened him.

He tamped down his anger, forcing himself to speak calmly. "What would you do here?"

"I—I do not know. I suppose I will go to the next world to see what awaits me there."

"I thought you might like to accompany me to Aviara."

"What?" Her mouth parted in surprise.

"Of course, it is your choice." He viewed her through his black, spiky lashes. "Since you have no destination in mind, I thought you might consider the journey to Aviara. It will be an interesting journey and once we link to Aviara, you will be in Alliance territory, a much safer place for you to explore."

"Hmmm, I had not thought of that."

"Yes. We could help each other, Jenise."

She was puzzled at that concept. From what she had seen, this Familiar was very self-reliant. "How could I help you?"

His incredible eyes flashed with sudden humor.

Her cheeks colored.

"Other than that," she stated baldly.

Gian grinned. "It is not unusual to see a Familiar in the company of a woman. Together we would not attract as much attention."

He had to be jesting! Alone or in a crowd, as soon as Gian walked into a room, everyone stopped to stare at him. His appearance was that extraordinary. Besides, no Familiar ever spent much time with the same woman.

"I will think on it."

Her evasive answer infuriated him. A rumble of thunder sounded outside.

In addition to having electrical sense, Familiars were sometimes prone to hypersensitivity to atmospheric conditions. Their acute senses were heightened by intense electromagnetic waves. It was another reason the Familiar stayed close to the Mystics of the Charl. They liked the intensification of their senses that occurred around Charl power.

In this case, however, Gian's feelings of possessiveness were combining with his protective instinct. It was a dangerous mix, heightened by the oncoming storm.

When a young miner walked into the tavern a few moments later and Jenise happened to glance his way in a more-than-leisurely manner, Gian's emotions flared up synchronously with the loud crackle of lightning that sounded overhead.

"You would not be satisfied with him," he bluntly stated as he deliberately sipped his *keeran*.

Jenise gasped. She had not been eyeing the youth with anything but idle curiosity! But since Gian had implied otherwise, who was she to disabuse him of the notion! Her own anger flared at his attitude. Who could decipher his shifting moods!

"Oh, why not?" She crossed her arms over her chest.

"He would not be as gentle with you as I have."

"You, *gentle?*" She scoffed at the ridiculous assertion. "The first time we truly . . . You enhanced!"

The next table of patrons looked over at that declaration.

"*Pfft!* It was a simple augmentation." He pointed at her, using the piece of fruit in his hand. "I have not even begun to show you what levels we can attain."

A female miner at the other table dropped her horn of *keeran*.

"And what makes you think I am interested in such levels!" she flung back at him.

He smiled slowly. His cat smile.

"I hate when you do that."

His white teeth bit into the fruit in a leisurely motion. Juice sprayed out. A droplet fell on the corner of his lip. "Do what?" His tongue licked the droplet off in a slow swipe as he watched her through lowered lids. Green and gold gleamed at her.

"Stop it," she gritted out.

He dipped another piece of fruit into the sauce. Instead of biting it, he began delicately licking the sauce off the segment. "Stop what?" He brushed the edge of the fruit along his sensual bottom lip.

The tips of Jenise's ears turned pink with desire.

"He would not satisfy you, Creamcat."

Jenise was tired of his games. Raising a queenly eyebrow, she responded coolly, "As if it is any concern of yours."

At that moment a loud crash of thunder shook the geode. Inside, a few crystals splintered off and fell to the floor. Gian abruptly stood, sending his chair crashing to the floor, where it shattered into pieces. Familiar possessiveness intensified by the violent storm had transformed him into a raging force.

He pulled Jenise up out of her chair in one move.

"Gian!" she squeaked. A few heads turned in interest to view the altercation between the powerful Familiar and his beautiful companion. As casual as Familiars were in their relationships, they became fiercely possessive about those they cared for.

Gian's fingers speared through her hair, pulling her head back so she was forced to lift her face to his. *Who has touched you but me?* he demanded in an arrogant tone. The feline in him was hissing; the cat had been unleashed.

Jenise had never seen him like this. He was wild! "N-no one, Gian."

He knew that, of course; he would sense another touch upon her in an instant.

"Perhaps you need a reminder then of *my* touch." Before she could respond, he tossed her over his shoulder and strode up the glass stairs.

"Gian!" Jenise pounded on his broad, muscular shoulders. "Gian, let me down!"

He ignored her. As far as Gian Ren was concerned, he had been as patient as he was ever going to be. She bounced on his back the entire way.

"What do you think you are doing!" She tried to pinch his buttock but she couldn't get a hold of his firm backside.

"I am going to show you what it is to be truly made love to by a Familiar man. *This* Familiar man!"

It was time for him to pounce.

Chapter Ten

Gian opened the door to their room with a booted kick, slamming it behind him the same way.

His reaction was so powerful that Jenise expected the thick glass to shatter. The door shook ominously but held together.

"Gian, this is madness—put me down and stop this at once!"

If the situation had been different, he might have laughed at her imperious attitude. However, Guardian of the Mist was not in a laughing mood. He was intensely focused and predatory.

All of these feline emotions were gaining strength along with the storm outside.

He quickly brought her forward, standing her in front of him. Whereupon he immediately tossed her cloak to the floor along with her dress. In the brief time it took her to regain her balance, he had already taken one of the *krilli* cloths covering the bed and ripped two long strips of the silken multi-colored fabric.

"What are you doing with—"

He did not answer her. Grabbing her wrist, he turned her from him, and before she realized his intent, tied her securely to the crystal lattice. "Gian! Untie this!"

His response was to fasten her other wrist in the exact same manner.

She tugged at the silk bonds that captured her, keeping her in place, outspread before him. Out of the corner of her eye she saw a dark green cloak float to the floor. It was rapidly followed by a white silken shirt and black leather breeches. Then came the dull thunk of boots.

Jenise sucked in her breath. What did the Familiar plan for her? He was highly aroused, of that she was certain.

Rich *krinang* spice blanketed her, readying her for him. Jenise realized that the intoxicating sexual scent was not simply a Familiars' magnet, it was also his snare. It captured the woman, teased her, made her want him even as he enticed her into the union.

The naked skin of her back felt his warmth behind her, his rapid, scorching breaths on her shoulders. *The room was cool; why is his breath so hot?* She swallowed.

The first heated touch of his satin lips upon her shoulder blade caused her to jump. She gasped. Gian was smoldering! His talented lips and scalding tongue began to trace a determined path from her shoulder blades to the base of her spine.

Jenise wriggled in the restraints trying to escape that devastating mouth.

It did no good.

He had completely trapped her; there was nowhere for her to go. Their situations had been completely reversed; now she was the one who was bound before him.

"Gian." She attempted to break through his intense mood with her no-nonsense tone.

In response, his fingernails rapidly scraped up the front of her thighs. This was followed by the edge of his teeth grazing up the side of her throat. He was not listening to her.

Again he traced the path down her back, his skilled tongue flicking and laving. But not meandering. Gian was focused and all the more dangerous because of it.

He knelt upon the floor behind her. His long hair brushed along the backs of her thighs. Jenise quivered as the dark golden strands lightly passed over her skin.

Capable hands firmly clasped her hips. Suddenly, his mouth press-played with the dimples at the base of her spine, just below her waist. Another tremor ran through her and she tried to suppress the moan which sprang to her lips.

The tip of his tongue ever so lightly traced the centerline of her buttocks. . . .

Jenise was shocked.

Again she twisted in the binding ties. She could not escape his sensual touch! When he rounded the curve of one smooth buttock, he bit her sharply.

Outraged, Jenise hissed at him.

A resonant growl was his response. *Gian apparently liked her reaction!* In fact he was encouraging it. Jenise groaned; how was she to deal with him?

The tips of his thick eyelashes skimmed along her leg until his mouth found the back of her knee. Jenise was very sensitive here and when he swiped the flat of his tongue across the crease she desperately tried to move her leg away from him. His capable palms captured her calf, putting an end to that hope.

Male fingers strummed up and down her inner leg as he continued to torture her with his talent.

He traveled down to her ankle, suddenly catching the tender spot above her heel with a quick grip of his teeth. Tingles flowed up her leg to . . . *right there.* A small sound escaped her parted lips. The Familiar knew every pulse point of sensitivity in the female body; each line that connected the pleasure centers and heightened arousal.

Gian's broad shoulder wedged between her legs from behind, forcing them apart. With a hand on each of her calves, his upper body slipped through the vee of her stance. In a fluid motion, he stretched out on the floor between her legs; his long silken hair spread out under him.

Lazily, he let his burning gaze scorch the length of her inner legs up to the pale curls at her juncture. From his vantage point on the floor he had quite a view.

In the same deliberate yet leisurely manner, he gradually lifted those spiky black lashes to meet her stunned look dead-on.

His green and gold eyes were hazy with dangerous passion.

So intense was his smoky stare that Jenise could feel it igniting her, and could feel herself becoming even more damp for him. It angered her, this sexual power he had over her.

"Stop this! It is not my choice!"

He flinched for a moment as if he had been struck. Then his feline eyes narrowed to slits of burning emerald and amber flames. Adept fingers reached up to lightly stroke back and forth on her dewy curls.

"This is for me, is it not?" he drawled. Boldly, he finger-stroked her overflowing dew. "I see no one else here."

Jenise gasped in outrage. "How dare you! You caused it!"

She had no idea what she had unwittingly said. One side of his sexy mouth lifted in dangerous amusement. "True . . . therefore it appears I *am* your choice; am I not?"

Jenise tried to kick him, failing when his quick reflexes captured her ankle. He had twisted her meaning to suit himself. Despite her obvious desire, she was furious with him.

"Perhaps I feel you, yet think of another," she foolishly goaded him.

It was not a wise thing to do, and if she had

known more about the Familiar nature, she never would have done it. Familiar males responded rather vehemently to such provoking. The expression on his face became lethal, powerful, and merciless. He resembled a fierce cat just before it pounced on its hapless prey.

Her aqua eyes widened. "Gian, do no—"

The commanding hands on the backs of her thighs pulled her forward as he sat up between her legs.

The position brought his mouth and a certain part of her anatomy into perfect alignment. Her mouth parted in disbelief. What she was thinking was . . . Surely he was not going to . . . to . . .

She could feel his hot breath as it ruffled the curls at her juncture. She swallowed nervously. "Release me, Gian, and I will—"

"I have told you that I do not bargain."

The first touch of his silken tongue had her calling out in a combination of shock and ecstasy.

Swiftly, he buried himself in her, then smoothly withdrew with a long, deep lap. He was blatant, masterful; no hinting touches or hesitant movements. He stroked inside her, tasting and teasing, starting a relentless pattern that soon had her begging him to stop the torture.

Jenise began to make a considerable amount of noise.

{You taste even better than I imagined, Creamcat . . . } He mercilessly licked and suckled and grazed her with his teeth.

Jenise stood on tiptoe, trying to get away from

the unbearable, overwhelming sensations. There
was nowhere she could go. She could not even
close her thighs to him, because he had positioned himself between her legs. Firmly, Gian
brought her back down to his mouth. Her entire
body trembled with his exotic touch.

"Ohhh . . . please . . . you must . . ." *Stop.* But
she could not bring herself to say it. The pleasure he was giving her was too intense to walk
away from. Too incredible not to experience.

(Trrrrrr . . .) he purred against her, the tips of
his nails lightly scoring along her lower back.

She did not know that Gian was about to show
her never to tangle with a Familiar man unless
you wished to be *en*tangled. Inserting his tongue
in her, he suckled hard and *growled* low in his
chest.

Jenise screamed. Several times.

Gian leaned back on the palms of his hands,
hair trailing down his back. He looked up at her
through that silky veil of lashes. It was the stare
of a knowing cat.

Breathing raggedly, Jenise gazed down at him
too spent to do anything else. She watched him,
alert for any sign of what he intended to do next;
he was very aroused.

With a fluid agility, he sprang up in front of
her, literally towering over her. Insolently, he
lifted her chin with a flick of his finger. He kissed
her hard and deep. It was a kiss of possession.

Jenise tasted herself on his mouth. And him.
And *krinang* spice.

Abruptly he broke off the exchange and strolled purposely behind her.

She turned her head, following his measured step. The light footfall sounded somehow ominous. "Gian." She tried to speak to him. He would not answer her. It was then she knew that his feral mood had not abated.

In some strange way she wondered if he was purposely ignoring her to heighten the mood; her anticipation and wariness were combining into a heady desire. She did not fear Gian; he would never harm her, of that she was certain. The Familiar had risked his life too many times to save hers.

A strong arm encircled her waist, bringing her back against his hard length. A muscular thigh wedged between her legs.

Jenise's breath came in rapid pants.

He hesitated.

Just enough so that she became aware of her own unsteady breathing. The tantalizing pause of a true predator.

"Gian," she whispered again.

He hitched her into position and slid fast into her. *As far as he could go.*

Jenise cried out at the full, throbbing impact. He was so deep inside!

Behind her Gian snarled softly. His low, sleek voice sent hot puffs of air against her ear. "Do you think he could do this for you?"

"W-who?" She had completely forgotten the young man in the tavern who had so fueled his temper.

Gian bit her shoulder; a sexy, sharp nip designed to chastise and adore at the same time. He rubbed his face in her hair as his other hand reached around to capture a breast in his palm. Squeezing the soft mound, he caught the hardened tip between two outstretched fingers, tugging and rolling.

Jenise shifted her head back, moving with him as he caressed her hair with his face, burying himself in its pale thickness. Much like he had buried himself in her nether curls.

For a moment Gian glanced over her shoulder to watch their shadows flickering across the crystals. His shadow lay over hers, moving synchronously to her moves, entwining around her.

A predatory smile curved his well-shaped lips. It was called *N'taga*. Shadow dance. And it was considered highly provocative. *"N'taga leetan shateer, taja."* He drawled huskily in the Familiar tongue. *I have placed my shadow upon you.*

His hand slipped from around her waist to brush between her cream-colored curls, finding her. There he teased the ultrasensitive spot, rapidly yet lightly flicking the swollen nubbin.

"Do you think he would know when the right moment was to—" He stopped moving his finger.

Jenise cried out in agony, the absence of his touch a torture. She begged him to touch her again.

Instead of obliging her, he flexed inside, where he was still deeply embedded. It was like *thunder* rumbling through her. "By *Aiyah*, Gian! Please."

She did not know what she was asking of him.

But he did.

He began to move inside her, bringing her with him as they rocked in a swaying back-and-forth motion.

"Do you dream he can do this . . ." He barely hinted in a deadly, sultry voice what he was about to do.

Jenise's eyes widened as the full brunt of the enhancement hit her. Unlike last time, this time he moved inside her as he sent wave upon wave of sexual fulmination skipping through her. Jenise was devastated. *"No, Gian, no!"*

It was too late for both of them.

Gian became wild, pagan, animalistic. For the first time in her embrace, he released his true Familiar passion and his feral cries rose with hers.

The mingled sounds of their lovemaking almost took down the crystal room around them. With each and every untamed thrust he took them higher and higher. Deeper and deeper.

His beautiful, spirited Jenise matched him move for move. She followed his lead; she led him when she could. *She shattered him.*

And Gian Ren, Guardian of the Mist, loved her so much he thought he would die of it.

Afterwards, she sagged limply against the *krilli* bonds.

Gian quickly untied her and carried her to the lattice bed. Placing her on top of the silken coverlet, he got in beside her, taking her in his arms. His special hunt was over.

She was his.

He covered her with himself and promptly fell asleep.

She was going to leave him.

Jenise peeked over the broad male shoulder covering her. If she was very careful, she could possibly slip out from under him without waking him. It was a very tricky thing to do. She wondered how he could be such a deep sleeper yet wake in the blink of an eye.

As usual he had wrapped himself around her in the oddest position. This time luck was with her. Just as she was about to make an attempt, he rolled off her onto his side. She jumped up before he rolled back.

Experience told her he would not sleep long without wrapping himself about her again. It was as if he needed to be assured of her safety even in repose. Often, he actually shielded her with his body as he slept! She wondered if it was a Familiar trait or simply Gian's own. The man had a very large streak of protector in him. She supposed that was one of the reasons he was called Guardian.

Jenise shrugged. It was no concern of hers. Not anymore.

For the man also had a great deal of feline sensuality in him that could apparently be fueled by the oddest occurrences. The terrible storm had since abated; it would be safe to leave now.

Or as safe as it was likely to get on a world full of itinerant miners.

She sighed.

She would have preferred to wait until the next world to part company. A small lump formed in her throat. That was not quite true, either.

Nonetheless, Jenise was a realist. They were going to have to part company sooner or later. The man was a Familiar, wild and free. As far as she knew, Familiars were never serious in their sexual relationships. Even if he was—though she assured herself he wasn't—she had waited her entire life to escape Ganakari so that she might develop her own true nature. The Frensi nature.

He had overwhelmed her this eve. His actions, his lovemaking, his passion, his boldness.

Gian Ren, she discovered, was like the Hlix River on Ganakari: ever-changing, completely unfathomable. A mysterious adventure that would never be solved. It was good she was leaving.

She kept repeating that to herself as she started to get dressed.

Pulling her gown on, she bent to pick up the clasp *and bumped into something very solid*. She jumped and whirled around.

Gian was standing directly behind her. The gown she had just put on but had not clasped slithered to the floor.

Like a true feline, Guardian of the Mist watched her silently, going over his options. As he saw it, he had three choices. He could be aggressive. He could be enraged, as was his right. Or he could show her his kindness and understanding.

Another Familiar, in the same circumstances, would have chosen one of the first two options; Guardian of the Mist chose the latter.

"You are leaving me without saying good-bye, Jenise?" He *was* genuinely hurt.

Her gaze dropped. She could not look him in the eye. The way he had phrased his question combined with the disappointed tone in his voice made her feel terrible. She swallowed the lump in her throat. "I—Yes, I must."

He examined her features. Her jaw had a set, determined appearance but the slight tremble of her lips told the whole story. He needed to be very careful. Much stealth was called for and he planned to tread cautiously.

"I would worry for you if you left now," he said softly, beguilingly. "It is the middle of the night. Come back to bed. You can leave on the morrow, when it is safer."

She chewed her lower lip. "You will let me leave?"

"Of course. It is your choice. Come back to bed now." He held out his hand to her, coaxing her to take it.

He was right—it was too dangerous to leave now. And he did say she could leave on the morrow. She swallowed again as moisture filled her eyes.

Gingerly she took the proffered hand. He led

her back to bed. When they were lying down again, he hugged her to him. "I should not have . . . I have shocked you." He kissed her forehead tenderly. "I keep forgetting that you have not—no, that is not true. I do not forget that for a moment, you are such a rarity, Jenise. It is simply that I . . ." He stopped, not sure how to continue.

Familiars did not generally apologize for their sexual activities. On the contrary, sensuality was always encouraged. Gian knew that it would not be the last time he experienced something new with her. She was different—not Familiar.

Gian was an experienced man in all ways of life. He knew he would have to bend in some areas for her, and he was prepared to do just that. He wanted her that much.

He tried again. "I am . . ."

"What?" she whispered.

He stroked her hair. "I am sorry. Truly sorry. I never meant to upset you like this. Not to the point that you felt you had to leave in the middle of the night."

When she burst into tears and hugged him to her, he was more sorry than he could say. Above all, Familiars had kind hearts. Predatory but kind. They played the game to win, but for fun. They never intentionally hurt women, for they loved them too well.

"Gian, oh, Gian, I do not want to leave; it is just that—"

"Shh, shh. I know. I know." He began kissing

her face, her nose, her forehead, her eyelids and lashes. A litany of small kisses.

Jenise was hardly aware of returning his tiny kisses. She, too, pressed her lips to his chin, his nose, his lashes.

He slipped inside her naturally, as he gently loved her. Showing her that he could.

She pressed her tear-streaked face to his, kissing him sweetly. Her middle finger glided down the centerline of his chest.

Gian shivered and purred appreciatively. She had found one of those special spots on him.

He paused to gaze down at her in a most innocent way.

She reached up, cupping his incredibly handsome face. "You can be so sweet, Gian."

He had beguiled her back into his bed. Where she would remain.

He smiled at her.

And took her.

There is an old Familiar saying: Just because the cat is not in sight—it does not mean he is not there.

Jenise stretched out against a warm body.

The Familiar was lying on top of her, wrapped around her in one of his usual tangled positions.

It was time they got up. She nudged the sleeping man with a roll of her hip.

He was too cozy to move. Gian gave her shoulder a little bite in his sleep and burrowed his face deeper into her neck.

Jenise grabbed a hank of his hair, trying to lift his face. "We have to leave."

Without opening his eyes, he sleepily sought out her lips. Gian started to kiss her but fell back asleep before he could finish. He slid off her mouth and back into the nice warm nook in the curve of her neck.

They had been up long into the night making love. Between outrunning the *valdt*, getting burned to a crisp, and everything else he had gone through on Ganakari, Gian was happy to be in a nice soft bed with a nice soft woman. A sheer lassitude of feline comfort overtook him and he just wanted to stay where he was, in total bliss.

Jenise kicked him. "Get up!"

He snarled softly but got up. Sitting on the edge of the bed, he yawned, stretching sinuously. Then he mussed up his already tousled hair by rubbing at his scalp with splayed fingers.

Jenise's lips twitched. He looked adorable. She had never seen him look adorable before. Breathtakingly handsome, yes. Sizzlingly sensual, definitely. But not adorable.

Putting her hand to her mouth, she attempted to hide her smile.

He glanced at her out of the corner of his eye. "What?"

"Oh, nothing." She grinned at him. Adorable.

"Mmm . . ." He stood up slowly, stretched again, and lumbered in the direction of the pool.

Full of energy, Jenise mischievously jumped

out of bed. Passing him, she reached the small bathing area first. He frowned.

Waving her fingers at him, she got into the tiny pool and started to wash.

Crossing his arms, Gian leaned against the smooth part of the crystal wall. Jenise cupped some water in her hands and, lifting them, let the warm water trickle down her arms and chest.

"Ahhh—that feels good."

He arched his brow.

She did it again. "So relaxing!"

No response.

A third time. "Completely . . . *EEEE!*" Gian had bent over and scooped two large handfuls of water at her.

Leaning on the edge of the pool, she flipped a sodden strand of hair out of her eyes. She gazed up his impressive length. "It still feels wonderful." Her grin dimpled her face.

Gian roared with laughter, shaking his finger at her. She laughed.

He got down on his haunches beside the pool, leaning close to her face. "And why are you in such a good mood this day?" he whispered.

Coyly, her lashes shielded her aqua eyes. A becoming blush bloomed on her cheeks.

"I see."

She raised her lashes for an instant, sending him a smoldering glance, then quickly lowered them. She crooked her finger, beckoning him closer.

Gian leaned in further, entranced by the se-

229

ductive look she had given him. He had never seen such a look on her before; he was not even aware she was capable of such a look. His blood thickened.

"Gian?"

"Mmmm," he purred near her lips.

"How long does it take to get to the next Tunnel?"

He paused, green/gold eyes flashing with amusement. Clever as a kitten. *"Whhhhy?"* he mouthed, letting his lips barely touch the corner of her mouth.

"Because I wish to reach it before dark."

"Ummmm—It will take *us* about half a day." The tip of his tongue touched the tiny indentation in the curve of her upper lip.

She tested him. "You did say that—"

"So I did. But *my* choice is to accompany you." He licked her lips.

She shivered at the delicious contact. "I suppose you are entitled to your choice."

"Yes."

She smiled, nipping his mouth.

"Come with me to Aviara, Jenise. I know you will be safe there."

"Very well. I will start my journeys from there. I believe you are right about staying in Alliance space. From what I have seen thus far, it is probably better for the single traveler."

Not much better in some quarters. She was naive to think so. And even more naive to think he would ever let her travel unescorted anywhere but on M'yan. "Good choice," he purred.

Once on Aviara, it would be an easy thing to bring her to his homeworld.

And he felt not the slightest twinge of remorse at his scheme.

Gian Ren never denied his nature. He was Guardian of the Mist; a full-blooded male Familiar who played with her in all seriousness.

Chapter Eleven

The dust had died down with the wind.

Jenise and Gian made their way along a crude red dirt path which they were told led to the next encampment and Tunnel.

The winding path led them through numerous crystalline structures, their odd, twisted shapes starkly beautiful. When the wind blew, a whirring sound ensued, humming to the very ground. Jenise thought it wonderfully alien. Gian smiled at her delight. He enjoyed the experience with her, sensing the joy of her first impressions.

The journey was pleasant until they reached a flat plain. In front of them, not too far in the distance, stood a towering crystalline structure.

Jenise began relating to him an incident from her childhood. She had found a small, clear crystal. Thinking the pretty sliver was magical, she had lovingly treasured it. Somehow, Karpon had found out. He had asked her why she would like a piece of rock and not him. Jenise had answered that the face of the crystal told no lies. He took the stone from her and crushed it under his boot heel. From that day on she had hated him.

Gian listened to her story thoughtfully. Suddenly, he stopped her forward step. He scanned the structure in front of them, a concerned look on his face.

"What is it?" she asked worriedly.

"There are beings concealing themselves within the large crystal structure ahead."

"Is it a danger?"

"I believe it is, *taja.*"

He had no sooner finished saying that than a voice called out to them. "*We want the stones the woman has in her cloak. Give them to us and we will let you live!*"

The being was lying, of course. Gian could tell that.

Jenise began untying her cloak.

"What are you doing?"

"Giving them the stones, naturally. You were right, it was foolish of me to show them."

"Do not take off the cloak, Jenise."

"Do not be foolish! A few stones are not worth dying over."

"They have no intention of letting us go. Once they have the stones, they will kill us."

She blanched. "But they will kill us—"

233

"Regardless," he finished, letting her know the truth. Checking their position, he saw at once that they had no defense to speak of—they were out in the open with nowhere to hide.

Something whizzed through the air. Gian's hand snapped out and caught a long crystal shard in midair, not a hand's length from Jenise's face. She sucked in her breath.

A voice called out, *"That was a warning. Give up the stones."*

"If what you say is true, why do they not simply kill us? Why pretend?"

A muscle flexed in his cheek. "You are a beautiful woman. . . ." He let her draw the only conclusion.

She gazed out towards the crystal formation. A veil of fear crossed her features.

"I will not let that happen," he said.

Her head whipped to him. "What do you mean?"

"Stand behind me," was all he would say.

She did as he bade. The man called out once more, "What is your answer?"

"I will give you an answer," Gian yelled back. He hurled the shard in a powerful arc towards the structure. Unerringly, it found its way into a narrow space in the wall. A scream issued forth, followed by silence.

Four shards were hurled at them at once.

Gian caught the shards one after another, immediately sending them back the way they came. Every one hit its mark cleanly, ending its deadly trajectory with the final cry of its victim.

"*We are done playing, Familiar! It is over for you both!*"

Gian pulled Jenise up against him. Even with his incredible reflexes, there was no way he could fend off fifteen or twenty shards at once. The situation was grave, to say the least. He would try his best to fight off the attack, but he doubted he could. Ultimately, he would protect Jenise. Rather than let her fall into their clutches, he would disintegrate them both by dispersion. Such a thing could occur during a metamorphosis, if he did not take form.

{Put your hands upon my back, Creamcat, so I may feel them.} She would have to be in contact with him at the exact moment.

"Yes," she whispered shakily; doing as he bade. She did not understand his request fully, but she trusted him.

A barrage of shards came hissing through the air at them. Gian stood tall, making himself a broader target. He circled one arm back around Jenise.

His senses told him thirteen spears were coming directly at him. Too many, he acknowledged resignedly. *{Jenise, I—}*

A flash of light singed the air in front of his chest. Instantly thirteen shards exploded, pulverized in a crackling explosion. The Aviaran light blade arced through the air in a blur of movement.

"*Taj* Gian." Traed inclined his head in greeting as he stepped protectively in front of the couple. His incredibly adept blade continued to connect with the deadly missiles being hurled at them.

"Traed," Gian responded wryly. "Good to see you again." Gian feinted left, taking Jenise with him as he dodged several shards. "And I mean that most sincerely."

Traed's enigmatic lips curved. "How many are there behind the barricade?" The warrior knew Gian's Familiar senses would tell him how many he faced.

"I have taken down five already, so seventeen." He threw another shard he had caught. A scream followed. "Sixteen."

Traed nodded in acknowledgment, never taking his eyes from the lethal weapons being thrown at them.

"You do realize we have a problem here." Gian spoke matter-of-factly as he deflected yet another spear.

"Yes, I do." Traed answered just as blandly. Jenise marveled that the two men could speak so calmly. As if they weren't fighting for their lives!

Both men did their best to fend off the attack. However, there were too many marauders; Gian and Traed could not keep this up indefinitely.

Traed pulverized seven shards in a lightning-fast display of swordsmanship. The explosion of the crystal for some reason made him think of the crystal point Yaniff always wore in his ear. The symbol of the ever-changing facets of Charl power . . .

Crystal can transmute energy, a voice whispered in his head. Traed raised his brows at the sudden idea. "Stand back from me, *taj* Gian."

Gathering Jenise to his side, Gian carefully moved a few paces back from the Aviaran warrior. While Traed's left arm plied his blade in lightning-fast maneuvers, he stretched out his other hand—five fingers splayed—in the direction of the crystal formations to his right.

He called forth his latent power.

It rose up in him as it always did, greedily.

Arcs of light traveled up his body, circling around him, growing in strength and number. The sky above them, which had been clear just an instant before, now darkened ominously. A rumble of thunder sounded overhead.

Jenise stared in wonder at the chiseled features of the Aviaran warrior who had saved their lives. His green eyes were sparking with his power! She had heard of this, but had never seen it. It was often said that the Charl carried a light within them and therefore could endure any darkness that surrounded them. Looking at this tall, contained man, she could well believe it.

Five jagged bolts crackled from his widespread fingers, aimed precisely at the crystalline structure to his right. The bolts hit their mark, illuminating the facets of the crystal. It almost seemed as if they were absorbed into it.

At first nothing happened.

Suddenly star bursts began to appear in random patterns throughout the crystal, gaining in strength and number. Traed's power bolts were changing the internal structure of the crystal, causing it to generate a strong piezoelectric field.

Five deadly arcs came back, aimed directly at them.

"We will be scorched to cinders!" Terrified, Jenise hugged Gian tightly to her.

Just as the bolts were almost upon them, Traed lifted his light blade straight out, capturing the killer bolts on it. The arcs hissed and snapped as they circled hungrily around the blade.

In a smooth action, Traed pivoted the pulsing blade, aiming it directly at the outcropping in front of him.

The augmented power bolts zinged from the blade, pulverizing a section of the outcropping in a shower of red dust.

The bandits began to yell as they attempted to run for shelter, *"He is a Charl warrior!"*

In a calm manner, Traed sent out another five bolts to the crystal, repeating the procedure. The bandits scurried about like insects. The second blast took off half of the front facade of the barricade they hid behind.

"You do not waste time, I see." Gian spoke approvingly as he watched the beings who would have destroyed him and Jenise meet their own fate.

The corners of Traed's lips curled. "It was becoming tedious."

A final BOOOM! rent the air, decimating what was left of the barricade. He lowered his weapon as the last of the bandits scurried off.

Someone was running up on them from behind. . . .

Gian whipped Jenise behind him and crouched low, preparing to attack.

An odd-looking alien was huffing and puffing to reach them.

Traed's arm on Gian's shoulder forestalled him. "It is my guide, Gruntel—he is harmless, if a bit slow."

"Wait for Gruntel to fight!" the guide called out. As if the bandits would have the courtesy to begin fighting on his arrival.

"It is already finished, Gruntel." Traed folded his arms across his chest, shaking his head as the Wiggamabob lumbered toward them. Traed rolled his eyes. Well, at least his heart was in the right place.

When the Wiggamabob finally reached them, Gian stared at the alien in a piercing way. The guide looked familiar to him. Then he recalled that he had seen him just as Jenise and he had entered the first Tunnel on Ganakari. The Familiar attempted to use his special senses to ascertain what he could about the strange alien.

Gruntel, not understanding the Familiar's action, responded by sniffing the proud Familiar in a meddlesome way.

"Stop that at once!" Gian brushed the snuffling snout away.

Jenise giggled behind her hand.

Traed glanced aside, eyes twinkling with mirth. An unusual occurrence for him.

"So Traed, how did you find me?" Gian ignored the guide, who was still sniffing at him from a distance.

"Yaniff sent me."

Gian grinned. "Yaniff, my old friend. I will have to thank him for coming to my aid, and you as well, Traed. You saved our lives. I will not forget it."

Uncomfortable with praise, Traed shrugged off the valiant deed he had performed as if it were a mundane thing.

"One who smells tasty is correct," Gruntel chimed in.

Gian frowned at the odd guide, but Gruntel was oblivious. He leaned on his crooked little staff, catching his breath.

Jenise stepped forward. "I am Jenise." She held out her hand to the Aviaran. "I, too, thank you."

"Forgive me, *taja;* in all the excitement, I have not introduced you. This is Traed ta'al Yaniff. He is a member of my extended family."

Traed's eyes flicked to Gian. He had heard him call the woman *taja.* And she was not a Familiar woman. Was this the princess the Ganakari claimed he had stolen?

{She does not know.} Gian sent the thought only to Traed.

Traed raised an eyebrow, looking questioningly at Gian over Jenise's head. *{It is complicated. Leave it for now.}*

Traed inclined his head at Gian, taking Jenise's proffered hand. "There is no need to thank me."

"Of course there is." She smiled prettily at him. Traed could tell at once why Gian would abscond with such a woman. She was captivatingly beautiful in a unique way. While they had been fighting, she had stood her ground bravely. She was exactly the kind of woman Traed admired. Unusual and bold.

His admiration must have been apparent. Gian sent him a *flicker-warning*. Traed smiled ever so slightly. Familiars were extremely possessive of what they considered theirs. He acknowledged Gian's right with a respectful nod.

In fact, Gian was one of the few men that Traed did respect. Guardian of the Mist was universally admired throughout the Alliance and especially on Aviara. He had the reputation of a man who was cunning yet fair. A courageous and honorable Familiar, whose word in all things was his bond. Among his own people, he was well loved.

"Jenise is accompanying me to Aviara." Gian met Traed's eyes. A wealth of subtlety lay in that statement.

"Then our journey will be all the more—"

Gian raised his brow.

"Enchanting," Traed finished diplomatically.

Jenise smiled. "What a love¹· thing to say. If you are an example of all Aviarans, then I must confess I look forward to visiting your homeworld."

Gian immediately bristled with feline jealousy. "I am afraid, Creamcat, that you will find that Traed is *unlike* most Aviarans."

241

"Really?" She examined the strong, controlled warrior speculatively—from his waist-length dark hair to his sparking jade eyes. "In what way?" she asked curiously.

Hands on hips, Gian turned to Traed, daring him to answer *that* question. Traed actually smiled.

It wasn't until much later that Traed wondered if the voice he heard in his head reminding him that crystals transmute power was actually his own.

The rest of the journey to the mining camp was uneventful except for Gruntel constantly snuffling at Gian and Gian shooing the Wigga-mabob away in irritation.

They reached the Tunnel point before nightfall, grateful to leave this world behind.

This mining camp was completely deserted. Gian told the group that he had heard this was not unusual when a strike had been found. Though they were glad not to have to come in contact with any more of the disreputable inhabitants of this place, they would have liked the opportunity to question the locals about the next world.

Jenise took a deep breath. "I wonder what we will find on the other side." So far they had not had much luck with the planets connecting through this line of Tunnels.

Gian squeezed her hand, offering her his support. "I will be right by you, *taja*."

"No worry!" Gruntel piped up. "All nice. Good place. Good people. You like."

Traed turned to the guide. "Are you sure, Gruntel?"

The guide bobbed his bumpy head up and down. "Much good place. Very comfortable."

Traed turned to Gian and Jenise. "We can hope it is so." He sidestepped in front of Gian, saying in an aside to him, "In case he is wrong, I will go first, *taj* Gian." He removed his Cearix from his waistband.

Gian nodded, grateful for the additional protection for Jenise.

Traed set one foot inside the Tunnel. He pivoted halfway, saying to Gruntel, "Much nice, hmmm?"

"Much nice," Gruntel affirmed.

Traed stepped through the corridor that joined worlds.

Gian waited a few moments in case Traed sent them a warning, but none came. Which might mean nothing or everything.

"Come, Creamcat." Gian led Jenise into the maw. Gruntel was close at their heels, sniffing.

If anyone had been in the mining camp, he would have heard the Familiar man hissing at the Wiggamabob.

Followed by the imperative, "*Stop it!*"

Followed by feminine amused laughter.

The land before them was starkly beautiful. Until the cold hit them.

"Did you not say much nice?" Traed pulled his

cloak about him, giving Gruntel a skeptical look.

The guide beamed, taking a deep breath in the icy air. He exhaled with great satisfaction, grinning broadly. "Much nice!"

Jenise smiled even as she shivered. "It seems he likes the cold."

"It would seem so." Traed replaced his Cearix.

"I wonder which way we go?" Jenise pointed to the three icy paths in front of them. They were standing on a hillock in a forest covered with ice and moonlight. The air, though cold, was crisp and clean and invigorating. It was night on this world.

"Follow path to center!" Gruntel chirped. He bounced to the front of the group and happily led the way.

Gian looked at Traed, questioning if they should follow. Traed shrugged. "It is as good a way as any."

"True."

They fell in behind the self-proclaimed guide. Gian brought Jenise under the warmth of his cloak.

"Is this better?" he whispered to her.

"A little." She nodded, feeling his sultry heat through the double layer of cloaks. "You are always nice and warm, Gian."

A smile tugged at his lips. "I was thinking the same of you." His hand under the cloak tickled her side.

She laughed, enjoying the moment with him. A thin layer of snow coated the ice on the path. Their footfalls made crunching sounds in the night and everything around them was bathed in silver light. "Silver and ice," she spoke softly. "It is almost magical here."

Gian gazed down at her. "Yes."

Her breath caught in her throat. The silvery moonlight made him even more stunning, if that was possible. "I am so glad to share this moment with you, Guardian of the Mist."

Jenise believed in moments. The Frensi taught that ultimately one perceives the reality of one's life by the moments he chooses to commit to memory. When these chosen moments are strung together throughout a lifetime, their patterns form a mystical helix that the inner spirit climbs. The Familiar belief was much the same.

Her simple words touched him greatly. "I as well, Creamcat." He brushed her lips with his own.

Gian reached inside the waistband of his *tracas*. "For you." He handed her a small faceted sliver of red crystal. "To replace the one Karpon took from you."

Tears came to her eyes at the Familiar's kind gesture.

She held the treasure in her palm protectively, closing her hand over the tiny gift. For the rest of her life she knew that every time she gazed upon Gian's gift she would remember the incredible night they had shared in the crystal room.

He had given her yet another moment to vibrate along her lifeline. "I will treasure it always."

"As I treasure you." He kissed her mouth, purring against her sweet lips.

Gruntel tugged Traed's sleeve. "Look! See what they do!" He pointed to the embracing couple.

Traed shook his head at the nosy guide. "Do not look upon that!" he hissed.

Gruntel scratched his bumpy head. "No?"

"No." Traed turned the wayward guide about to face front as they marched along.

"Hmf! She think he tasty too!" Gruntel complained.

"Not in the same manner." Traed rolled his eyes, continuing on the path. *Quests!*

Towards dawn, they came upon a stone abode next to an icy, flowing stream. They had not seen any beings during their journey through the night and Jenise was starting to wonder if Gruntel had been correct.

"Go there!" Gruntel said excitedly. "Friend. Rest for day."

"Is he saying we are to find shelter ahead?" Gian asked Traed.

"It would seem so."

"Are you tired, Jenise?" He hugged her to him. "Or do you wish to go on?"

"No go on!" Gruntel jumped up and down. "Too far to Tunnel. Too dangerous. Must have help!"

"Dangerous? What do you mean by dangerous?" Gian demanded, concerned for Jenise.

"Way too steep. Need help."

"I believe he is saying that the route becomes difficult to navigate."

Gruntel bobbed his head at Traed.

"Perhaps we should take his advice, *taj* Gian. He has proven correct thus far."

Gian glanced down at Jenise. He knew she would not admit it, but he could tell she was wearying. "We will stop."

Traed and Gruntel went ahead.

"Why does he ask you what to do, Gian? Traed seems like a man who would not ordinarily do such a thing." Jenise gazed up at him, an inquiring expression gracing her soft features.

Gian paused. "It is his way."

"It does not seem to be his way," she responded shrewdly.

Gian shrugged, pretending no interest in the topic. In reality he was astounded by her astute observation. He would have to warn Traed to be more circumspect.

Gruntel pounded on the wooden door with his crooked staff.

High-pitched yipping came from inside, followed by raspy grumbling. The door opened a few moments later to reveal a fur-covered being who stood almost as tall as the two men. He had round brown eyes, a round black nose, and two small, pointy ears sitting at an angle on the top of his head. He tapped the side of his forehead to indicate he had no translator device.

Gruntel took over the conversation for them, speaking to the being in snorts and guttural sounds. They obviously knew each other.

Gruntel turned to them, grinning his two-toothed smile. "Ogga let you stay for rest."

Traed nodded. "Tell him we thank him for his kindness."

Gruntel translated. Ogga's tongue hung out of his open mouth in what everyone assumed was his version of a grin. He ushered them inside into the warmth.

Jenise looked around the main room of the small abode, happy they had decided to stay here. The room was lit by a huge fireplace. Heavy woven rugs covered the floors and there were low cushions scattered about for resting upon. A kettle of soup was heating over the fire, its fragrant herbs filling the room.

She sighed. Shedding her cloak, she sank wearily down upon the nearest cushion. Gian sat next to her. Jenise marveled anew at his feline ways. The Familiar sat very close to her, touching her at various points of her body with his. It was as if he were silently letting her know of his presence and protection while at the same time telling anyone watching that he considered this person one of his own.

Traed recognized the pose immediately, for he had seen it countless times in the past with other Familiars, both male and female. It was another Familiar enigma—they were fiercely independent and yet they positioned themselves as guardians to those they cared for.

Ogga was a gracious host. He offered them all bowls of the steaming soup, handing the first bowl to Gian. Somehow he knew the Familiar was the one whose approval he had to gain.

Guardian of the Mist cocked his head to one side and examined the brew. Using his special senses, he ascertained that the concoction would not be harmful to them. "It is safe," he said in a low tone. Even though Ogga could not understand him, he did not wish to insult the generous alien in his home. He handed the bowl to Jenise so that she might refresh herself first.

She gratefully took the brew, for she was quite hungry. She swallowed several times before stopping to inform them that it was delicious.

They all eagerly drank theirs.

After they had finished eating, Gruntel and Ogga carried on a conversation by the fire—much like old friends do. After a time, Gruntel turned to Traed. "Ogga say he take you on to Tunnel with his Wee-chukchuk."

"Wee-chukchuk . . . what is that?" Traed was stretched out across several cushions, his hands folded behind his head. Despite the relaxed pose, the Aviaran was, as always, fully alert.

"He say very fierce, very brave. Can go over ice. Wee-chukchuk respected by all. Only take if they like."

"Hmmm." A strand of his hair caught under his cloak as he turned on his side. He yanked it out, irritated. "Ask him if he has a leather thong to tie back my hair."

Gruntel snorted something to Ogga. Ogga's tongue lolled out in a grin. "He say no. Too bad for warrior who think he not Charl."

Traed narrowed his eyes. Ignoring Gruntel's

obvious pleasure over the situation, he watched Gian place a sleeping Jenise carefully down on one of the cushions. He idly wondered what it was like to care for a woman that much. To feel that kind of . . .

The path of thought disturbed him on many levels, so as was his wont, he squelched it.

"She was exhausted." Gian covered her with his cloak.

"Is she your *tajan*, Gian?" Traed asked bluntly.

"I have said so, have I not?"

"I know you were captured on Ganakari—I saw your physical path."

Gian was impressed with Traed's ability. "I did not know you possessed the Sight, Traed."

A small, ironic smile curved the dark-haired man's chiseled lips. "No, not many do. I revealed myself to the Guild to save Rejar."

Gian sat up. "Rejar has been found?"

"Yes." Traed filled him in on the story. "And he brought back a non-Familiar mate, Gian."

Gian had to hold back his laughter so as not to waken Jenise. "Rejar always did have to be first when it came to blazing new paths."

"True," Traed agreed as he thought of his capricious brother-of-the-line. He was sure the half-Familiar was not having an easy time of Yaniff's lessons. The few he had taken as a youth were enough to tell him that someone like Rejar must be tugging at the harness. Traed's eyes gleamed as he pictured how Lorgin must be mercilessly teasing him.

"So you have saved Rejar as well. I owe you much, Traed."

The Aviaran bristled. "You owe me nothing." Traed did not like to owe or be owed. Such was his nature.

"Nonetheless . . ." Gian stated firmly.

A dull bronze colored Traed's high cheekbones. "How did you get free on Ganakari?"

"Jenise helped me to escape."

"It had to be more complicated than that."

"It always is. She is not Ganakari; she is Frensi."

"Frensi?" Traed looked over at her speculatively.

"What is it?"

"Do you know anything about the Frensi?"

"Not much. Just that they are a nomadic people."

"There were some Frensi on Zarrain where I lived. They are a passionate people."

A very male smile crossed Gian's face but he said nothing.

"Ah." Traed could just imagine. "Has she danced for you?"

"What do you mean?"

"You would not have to ask if she had. They say a Frensi female has one special dance in her and she performs it only once in her life for one person. It is rumored to be a mystical, beauteous thing. She uses no words, just movements, to resonate with the soul of the watcher. The dance depicts the image of pure love. Once seen, the one who has witnessed it is forever moved."

Gian was stunned. He gazed at her as she lay sleeping. "I did not know," he murmured.

Traed switched the subject away from love and devotion, wondering what had ever made him bring *that* up. It was unlike him. "The Guild is most anxious to see you."

"And I them. We have much to discuss. The Familiar are in grave danger, Traed. I will call in every favor owed us by the Charl."

Traed raised his eyebrows. For Gian to say such a thing, it was serious indeed. "I will get you and your *tajan* safely to Aviara, Gian."

"Of that I have no doubt. Yaniff has sent only the best to me, for which I am grateful."

Traed inclined his head at the words of praise coming from a man he respected.

"Let us get some rest. I have the feeling our journey will not be a peaceful one."

"True. We must deal with these fierce Wee-chukchuks." Traed paused, saying in his usual bland way, "Perhaps they will like your tasty smell, Gian."

Gian arched his brow. "Why should they be an exception? It appears everyone else does."

Traed snorted.

Both men lay down on the cushions to get a brief rest.

The following night when the moon rose, Ogga led the group around the back of the cottage.

A low, raftlike platform rested there on rails. In the center of the platform were two waist-high poles with crossbars. Ogga motioned for Gian and Traed to stand at the poles while Jenise and Gruntel sat at their feet, facing forward.

"He get Wee-chukchuk now," Gruntel informed them. "Hope they like. Very fierce."

Gian and Traed nodded seriously.

Loud barking sounds came from behind the shed. By the sound of it, Ogga had his hands full. The two men prepared for the battle of wills that was sure to ensue.

Ogga rounded the corner.

Leading him were eight tube-shaped animals with fluffy heads, lolling tongues, wide paws, and wagging double tails. They stood only one-and-a-half hands high. Gian's and Traed's eyes both widened incredulously but neither man said anything. Out loud. Both, however, were thinking the same thought: *This is the fierce beast?*

Ogga hitched up the Wee-chukchuks and climbed onto the platform. He waited anxiously.

At first the Wee-chukchuks did nothing but fuss around, checking everything out. Ogga seemed nervous.

Then as one they lifted their round noses in the air and tested the scent. At the same time, they all turned their heads and stared at Gian.

The Familiar narrowed his eyes at them.

Eight Wee-chukchuks broke into actual little grins, their smiling mouths showing their little white teeth. Then they faced forward and began to pull the platform.

"We go now!" Gruntel shouted happily.

They went. *At a* zorph's *pace*.

Sometime later they still hadn't cleared the front yard.

Gian's mouth twitched. The absurdity of the situation got to him. He was trying desperately not to laugh. Jenise began giggling into her cloak. Traed blinked and stared off to the right. A suspicious snort came from his direction.

Gian pinched the bridge of his nose. *[What are we doing?]* he asked anyone who would listen. The platform barely crawled onto the main pathway.

Traed turned to him and said quite seriously, "We are Wee-chukchuking."

Both Jenise and Gian roared with laughter. The corners of Traed's lips twitched.

"Good thing they liked your scent, Gian," Jenise added facetiously. "Who knows how long it would have taken us otherwise?"

This time even Traed laughed as the strange cart crept along the path.

The Wee-chukchuk proved themselves useful when the land started to dip down into gullies. Their wide, sharp paws dug into the ice and they were able to pass through areas that would have been difficult for the travelers to navigate on foot.

Jenise thought the starlit journey through the icy forest was particularly lovely. The cool, crisp air, the silvery branches against the dark sky, created a magical scene before her that she knew she would never forget.

Gian stood behind her, his muscular, leather-clad legs bracing her back. His presence added to the mood of this night, for even though she still would have enjoyed the scenery had he not been with her, it would not have been the same. There was a sense of excitement around the Familiar. He was like an adventure unto himself.

What was more, he made her feel so incredibly alive! Not simply because of his sensual expertise; it was everything about him. She suspected her impression was not due only to this journey they were on. It would always be that way around him. Gian was a unique, vital presence.

Once again she grew sad at the thought of leaving him.

As if he sensed the momentary change in her mood, he reached down and stroked the side of her neck with two fingers as he spoke to Traed. The unconscious, tender gesture affected her deeply. She affectionately rubbed her cheek against the back of his hand.

Near daybreak, they reached the Tunnel entrance.

It stood alone in the middle of the woods, a silent, pulsating maw of light. Jenise guessed that its location was significant in that it was hidden. She was proven correct when Gruntel informed them in his stilted speech that this Tunnel led to an Alliance world. Once they exited this Tunnel, there would be another close by that would lead directly to Aviara.

Both men cheered at the news.

Though Jenise was also happy that the most dangerous part of their journey was apparently over, she was also somewhat downhearted, for she knew her time with Gian would soon be over. Back in the beginning, when she had gone to him as he lay chained to the wall, she had never imagined the relationship that would develop between them.

But then, she hadn't anticipated someone like Guardian of the Mist. *How could she have?* Surely there was no one like him.

Gruntel surprised everyone by saying his good-byes.

"You are not coming with us?" Traed asked the guide as he took him aside.

"No come. Gruntel finished here. Take you as promised. Need go home now."

"I see." For some strange reason, Traed felt somewhat sad to see him go. He had actually come to like the Wiggamabob. And the guide had helped him when he had been struck with the poisonous quill. "Would you like to come to Aviara with us?" he surprised himself by asking. "I am sure we can find a place for you."

Gruntel shook his head, his small eyes bright. "Need go home," he repeated sadly.

Traed nodded acceptingly. Taking from his cloak a uniquely designed black and silver pouch heavy with stones, he held it out to Gruntel as payment for his services.

Gruntel grinned, eagerly scooping up the pouch. "Much good pay, Charl knight!" He did his little dance, turning around on his fat feet.

Traed smiled slightly. "Gruntel, I am not a Charl knight."

Gruntel secured the stones inside his gray robes, ignoring Traed's claim as he had from the beginning. "Accomplish great deed—save us all. Maybe get special reward from Charl!"

Traed's features instantly turned to stone. "There is nothing I want from the Charl."

Gruntel cocked his bumpy head to the side. "Want something. In heart. Deep. Gruntel know."

A dull bronze highlighted the Aviaran's high cheekbones. He turned away.

"Ask for heart's need. Never hurt." He patted the warrior's back with his fat, leathery hand.

The Aviaran paused before saying softly, "Farewell, Gruntel. I wish you well." He began walking toward the Tunnel entrance.

"Remember Gruntel's words, Charl knight!" Gruntel called after him as he entered the portal.

Traed hesitated briefly but continued on.

Gruntel leaned on his crooked little staff, making sure they all entered the Tunnel safely. Satisfied, he continued on his way.

A Wiggamabob always took his job as guide very seriously.

Chapter Twelve

By their own reckoning of time passage, they arrived in the Hall of Tunnels on Aviara later that same day.

Jenise marveled at the beauty of the planet. The wide streets in the village were of paved stone and led to a center plaza flanked by shops. There were blooming trees and flowers everywhere, their exotic scent sweetening the air.

It was daytime here on Aviara and Jenise looked up, noting the clear, light blue sky. Just a hint of breeze wafted her hair. Trills sang in the trees and bushes and she saw that crystal chimes were hung in numerous places; their soft, tinkling sounds lent a harmonious atmosphere to the lovely scene.

Aviara was even more beautiful than she had

heard. Inhaling deeply of the flower-scented air, she sighed.

"It is beautiful, is it not?" Gian smiled as he took in the welcome sight.

"Yes, even more lovely than I imagined." She beamed up at him. "I am so glad I came here with you! It was one of the places I had always longed to see."

His gaze shifted to her. "Your joy pleases me." He lifted his hand to remove a stray lock of hair from her face. "It is your choice, but perhaps you would like to see M'yan as well," he offered.

Overhearing the Familiar, Traed raised an eyebrow. Gian was a wise and deadly hunter. Such tactics as these were not unknown to Aviaran warriors. He watched the scene play out before him, fascinated.

Jenise's eyes widened in surprise. "The Familiar homeworld?" No one was ever allowed on M'yan except by personal invitation. The Familiar guarded their privacy zealously. All kinds of rumors circulated about the place. Some said it was a mysterious world, harsh and unforgiving. Others claimed it was a place of untold ecstasy.

Whatever its nature, Jenise was sure such an opportunity would never come her way again. She would be foolish not to take the chance to see it for herself.

"That is very generous of you, Gian."

Traed folded his arms across his chest. *Generous.* Gian had her completely ensnared. He patiently watched Guardian of the Mist appear to act humble. It was a sight not to be missed.

"Then you will come?" Gian beseeched in a sincere tone. He knew very well what such an invitation to explore would mean to her.

"If you do not think it would be any trouble . . ." She no idea that the Familiar had purposely waited for just the right moment to issue such an invitation.

Gian smiled much like the cat he was . . . the one in control of the intricate game he played. "No trouble at all, *taja*."

"Then I should like that." She smiled gratefully up at him.

"Good." He took her hand. "You shall be ours, of course."

"Ours?" she looked at him, puzzled.

"A figure of speech."

It was more than that, Traed knew. When a Familiar took you into his home and said those words, he was claiming you to his family. His home was open to you as if it were your own.

Before she could question him about what the saying meant, he firmly led her in the direction of the home of Krue and Suleila.

It was a lovely day; they had survived to reach Aviara; she was going to have the rare opportunity to view M'yan; and she would not be leaving Gian for some time to come. All in all, she suddenly felt happy.

Traed noted Jenise's light step and shining eyes and had to hand the victory to Guardian of the Mist.

Not that there had ever been any doubt of the

outcome. Still, he wondered what her reaction was going to be when *taj* Gian got her safely ensconced on his homeworld.

Traed's chiseled lips curled. From what he had seen of Jenise, he did not think she was going to take the situation lightly.

He almost envied Gian his battle to come. Speaking for himself, he had always had a liking for danger.

Of *any* kind.

Before they could reach Krue's home, the ancient wizard Yaniff met them on the road.

"Gian!" He heartily slapped the Familiar on the back.

"Yaniff, my old friend." He hugged the wizard in greeting. "I have much to thank you for, it appears."

"*Pssht!* You have nothing to thank me for. I am only glad to see you are well and unharmed."

"Yes, but you must thank Traed for that. If it were not for him we would not be here."

Yaniff looked at Traed approvingly. "I never doubted you would do less, my son."

Bronze highlighted Traed's cheeks. Uncomfortable with praise of any kind, he muttered, "*Taj* Gian makes more of it than it was."

"Are you saying that *taj* Gian exaggerates, Traed?" Yaniff shrewdly rejoined.

Either way he answered, Traed was caught. Annoyed at the wizard's ability to trap him in such a way, he stared stonily ahead, refusing to say anything.

Yaniff chuckled. "You have done a valiant thing for the Guild and for the Familiar, Traed. Do not be shy to say so." Yaniff turned to Gian. "I can glean what has transpired from your mind." He looked pointedly at Jenise. "I will apprise the others of the situation. Do you wish to speak to the High Guild now?"

Gian thought for a moment. "Yes, I will. Jenise, Traed will take you to Krue's home, where you may rest until I come. Suleila, his wife, is a member of my family."

Jenise bit her lip, hesitant about going to a stranger's home expecting shelter. Gian cupped her cheek. "It is all right, Creamcat. She will be happy to have you. You will like her very much, I am sure."

"Perhaps I should go to an inn?"

"No. Traed, take her to Krue's."

Immediately Traed came forward to do so.

"Gian!" Jenise protested his high-handed attitude.

"I know you will be cared for there in the home of my family. I will see you soon." He bent down and imperiously kissed her lips. *[Tell Suleila to keep silent.]* He sent the thought to Traed, who inclined his head in acknowledgment.

It wasn't until she was being led away that Jenise wondered how the Familiar had managed to get her to do exactly as he wanted. She had never heard that tone of command from him before! It was rather . . . forceful. A niggling worry crossed her mind.

Mine to Take

* * *

Gian entered Krue's home some time later, finding Traed in the great room. The warrior's hair was once more pulled tightly back in a ponytail. He was sipping a cup of warm *mir* as he idly thumbed through a book.

Obviously he was waiting for Gian to return so that he might leave. Despite the fact that three other warriors resided in this household, *taj* Gian had entrusted Jenise to him. Traed would not leave until the trust was returned to Gian. Such was the Aviaran way.

"Where is Jenise?"

Traed looked up as the Familiar entered the room. "She is resting upstairs."

"Where is everyone else?"

"Krue and Suleila went to see Melody."

"Ah, Lorgin's babe. Yaniff has told me Krue is besotted."

Traed smiled slightly. "Yes, it is something to see. The babe has him at her bidding. He claims she looks just like him."

Gian laughed at the picture of a legendary warrior such as Krue being brought to heel by a mere babe. "Does she?"

Traed shrugged. "I am not one to ask of such things."

Gian had observed that although Traed was a part of the family of Krue, he was apart. It was unfortunate for all concerned. "Where is Rejar?"

Traed steepled his fingers, resting his chin on the tips. His mood was indecipherable. "Rejar is at Yaniff's."

"Yaniff's? What does he there?"

"Ah . . . you would not have heard. Rejar has joined the Charl."

Gian's brow raised. *"Willingly?"* he asked disbelievingly. He could not imagine Rejar subjecting himself to the discipline needed to become a Charl warrior. Rejar had ever been of a capricious nature. Loving life and women. And not always in that order. In all ways that Gian could see, he was a true Familiar.

Traed smirked. "Willingly . . . that is a matter of some debate."

Both men chuckled. Although half Familiar and half Aviaran, Rejar seemed to have inherited the most independent qualities from both sides. Rejar's father Krue and Yaniff had both railed at him for years to join the Charl, but to no avail. The men of Krue's bloodline followed the path of the Charl warrior. Gian could only speculate on what machinations Yaniff had employed to get the frisky Rejar to comply. He would find that out later, but right now, he had more pressing matters on his mind.

Gian became serious. "I have apprised the guild of the situation on Ganakari."

Traed put down his drink. "And?"

"Karpon must be stopped, of course. And the nature of the drug they administered to me must be ascertained. It is my belief that certain steps should be taken in the meantime to ensure the safety of the Familiar. I have done what I thought best." He did not elaborate on what that was, but Traed sensed there was much on Gian's mind.

"I am sure you have done the right thing, Gian."

"The Sages wish to see you, Traed," Gian said in a quiet voice.

Traed was not happy with this. He had no desire to be embroiled further with the mystics' unending schemes. "Why do they wish to see me?"

"I have told them what you did to save us."

Traed's nostrils flared. "I wish you had not, Gian."

"They would have seen it, regardless . . . in my mind."

"No. You could have shielded your thoughts from them."

Gian sighed. So, Traed knew that Familiars could shield themselves from high-level Charls. "It would not have been right. You deserve recognition for such a deed. They wish to speak to you."

Traed stood resignedly. When the House of Sages requested an audience, there was little choice in the matter. "No, they want something from me."

"It was not the impression I received."

"You know them not. Believe me, in the end, they will want something. If not this day, then the next." He quietly closed the door behind him.

"Then I am sorry, Traed," Gian said to the empty room. A warrior with such power as

Traed's, who refused to be Charl, was walking a very dangerous path.

Perhaps it would be good for Traed to come to M'yan for a while as well. The more Gian considered it, the more he realized what an excellent idea it was. For both of them.

In fact, he would insist.

Traed stood tall before the House of Sages in the High Guild. Insolently, he threw his shoulders back, meeting each and every eye that faced him.

It was his first time to be called before them as a group, even though separately, he had met them all.

Although they had never made any decrees regarding him personally, their actions against his natural father had punished him as well. It was an unjust chastisement of an innocent boy that had affected his entire life.

And he had suffered greatly because of it.

He would not welcome a summons to this chamber on any day.

Gelfan was first to speak. "We would compensate you, son of . . . Yaniff."

Traed's pale green gaze narrowed. The man could not even bring himself to say his name. "It is not necessary. I seek no compensation from *you*."

Ernak cleared his throat, clearly embarrassed by Gelfan's rudeness. "You misunderstand, Traed. We, the Sages of the High Guild seek to make up for . . . for the way we have dealt with you."

"The way you have dealt with me." Traed's dry tone caused several to avoid his piercing look.

Ernak was one of them. He looked away uneasily. "The way we ignored your position in all of this. Surely you see that was not our intention. In light of your abilities, we seek to mend this error. A power such as yours cannot be overlooked or ignored. Whether you desire it or not."

Traed snorted, crossing his arms contemptuously over his chest.

Gelfan's palm slapped down on the table. "He needs guidance; that is obvious! That power cannot be allowed to run amok!"

Traed raised a scornful eyebrow. "Really. And which one of you will designate to not *allow* me to go about my way?" The challenge was there. He impaled each member save Yaniff with a chilling glare.

As expected, no one spoke. Who in his right mind would challenge such a power?

Yaniff stepped forward. "This is not necessary, Traed." He used the voice of a Charl master to his student. *"Think well ere you speak your next words."*

Traed hesitated despite himself. He had been about to challenge Gelfan. Yaniff's warning resonated through him. Besides protecting him, Yaniff was letting him know that Gelfan might welcome such a challenge for his own ends. Traed would not go against Yaniff. "As you wish,

Yaniff. Out of respect to you and you alone, I hold my tongue."

Wolthanth was impressed. "What can we do for you, Traed? Surely there is something. I, for one, do not feel right about what has transpired in the past. In any event, even if the incidents of the past had not affected us all, we still would wish to compensate you for this valiant service you have performed. You have saved Guardian of the Mist, something both our peoples applaud. Under the circumstances, there was not another who could have brought him out alive. It was your level of power and ingenuity that delivered him back to us. You have rewarded our trust in you and now we wish to reward you in kind."

It was an eloquent speech. Wolthanth had neatly turned aside his past grievances and focused instead on the present. By his words he had made it very difficult for Traed to refuse a reward. Nonetheless, there was nothing he wanted from them.

Suddenly he heard Gruntel's words again. *". . . ask heart's desire . . ."*

Why not? What did he have to lose? "Very well, Wolthanth. The Guild may begin to make amends by granting me my rightful name, which has been denied me these many years."

Silence reigned in the cavernous room.

Finally Zysyz spoke. "What name is that, Traed ta'al Yaniff?"

Only the slight flickering of an eyelash betrayed Traed's hurt. "There is a name that be-

longs to me—indeed is part of my bloodline—
which you in your wisdom have denied me." He
bit the bitter words out.

Traed turned to Yaniff, genuine sorrow etched
on his face. "Forgive me, Yaniff, and know that
I do this not to dishonor your name, which I
hold above all others. There is another whose
name I should bear, however. One whose bloodline is directly tied to mine. Does he not stand
for my mother's line?"

"He does!"

All eyes turned towards the sound of the powerful voice which spoke from the doorway to the
chamber. Krue.

He strode forward, his commanding presence
a force in the hall. He came to a halt abreast of
Traed.

"The lad is right." Krue placed his hand on
Traed's shoulder. "Reverse your ruling; it is past
time to put away old hurts. The Tan-Shi will
have to understand and if they do not, it will be
their misfortune. For I *will* claim this Traed as
my son. I should have done so when he was but
a child and would have if not for the constraints
you placed upon me. Constraints, I would add,
that doubled my sorrow—to lose my sister and
my son-of-the-line as well."

Wolthanth spoke. "Krue, there was more to
that decision than you realize. As retribution for
Theardar's insult to the Lodarres line, you would
have sought to face Theardar for the rights to
his son. This we could not allow."

"Yes, Krue," Gelfan added. "Theardar was a

sixth-level mystic even then. At the time, you were but a four. Against such power, you would have been helpless."

Krue's lavender eyes captured the Sages in their steely glow. "Think you so?" he uttered in a chilling tone, causing a few members to look away. Krue's reputation as a legendary warrior was well known.

Gelfan narrowed his eyes, not liking the way the conversation was going. Sages were not to be questioned. "Perhaps not," he admitted. "But we could not take such a risk."

"You should have allowed *me* to make that decision! It involved the honor of my family."

Yaniff spoke to Krue. "We could not. It was my say the Guild followed."

Krue turned a shocked face to Yaniff. "Your say? But why? You were on my side of it—you told me so yourself! Why would you do such a thing?"

"Rejar."

Both Traed and Krue appeared stunned.

Finally Krue spoke. "But Rejar was not an issue then. Why, I had not—that is, Suleila and I . . . I had not yet performed the Transference with Suleila."

"Exactly." Yaniff pierced Krue with a steady look. "As I say, we could not risk your going against Theardar."

Everyone was silent for many moments. What had Yaniff seen? Somehow it involved Rejar and was of vital importance. But what? The Sages pondered.

"I do not understand these things, Yaniff. I confess they disturb me more oft than not. For I wonder where the line between vision and manipulation lies. Lately these lines blur for me and I begin to resent much."

"It grieves me to hear you speak thus, Krue."

"And me."

"I have known you all your days; I beseech you to listen when I ask you to honor my words. It is Rejar and it has always been Rejar."

"I cannot credit this!" Krue spat.

"What do you speak of?" Traed was completely left out of this exchange of mystical significance.

The Sages turned horrified eyes to Yaniff. "We cannot credit this either. Surely you have misread the signs, Yaniff?" Gelfan was clearly shaken. "He is of the Familiar; he is not—"

"It *is* as I say."

Strangely enough, it was Krue who recovered first. "I am not here to argue my son's place in your visions, Yaniff. I am here to claim another son to me. This son."

He faced Traed, placing his hand upon his shoulder. "I claim this Traed as my right by bloodline, by Charl mystical belief, by Aviaran law, by my heart as well, as Traed ta'al Krue, acknowledged brother to the sons of my loins Lorgin and Rejar. It is done. Embrace your father, Traed. Though it grieves me that this moment comes so late, better than never."

Moved, Traed embraced Krue. Jade eyes damp, he went down on one knee before him. "I

271

acknowledge you as father of my bloodline and of my heart as well. I hereby know myself. *I am Traed ta'al Krue!*"

Not one voice called out to dispute the fact.

Yaniff watched, more pleased than he had been in many a year as Traed rose to his feet, bringing with him his rightful heritage and the name of his mother's bloodline. On Aviara, when a father disgraced his lineage, he forever lost the right to claim his sons. Such sons by law then belonged to he who would stand for the mother's line. In this case, Krue had the right to claim Traed.

Krue and Traed left the hall together, and Yaniff thought it was just.

"Are you sure the babe is getting enough rest?" Krue glowered down the table at his eldest son, Lorgin.

"Yes, father, I am sure," Lorgin answered him dully. He casually turned away from his father towards his brother Rejar and crossed his eyes. Krue was driving him mad! Yes, it was his first child but, by *Aiyah*, he was not an idiot!

Rejar smirked at his brother, glad for once not to be the one under scrutiny.

Lorgin's wife, Adeeann, beamed at Krue as if he were the wisest and most caring of olde-fathers. In truth, she was enjoying this. For which he would make her pay later.

"I do not think it safe for her in that tree you live in," Krue grumbled.

Lorgin knew what was coming next. His father was once again going to "suggest" his son move back to the family home.

Temporarily.

For the next twenty years.

He wondered if his father was still suffering from the shock of his errant son, Rejar, bringing home a wife. Yes, that must be it. Had to be.

Lorgin fumed. Why did he always have to suffer because of his brother? He glowered at him across the table, brows lowered. Rejar blinked innocently at him.

"Oh, but the tree is so pretty." Lilac winked at her husband, Rejar. They had found a nice, secluded spot on one of the branches a few nights ago. She shivered as she remembered what he had done to her that night.

Rejar glanced at her out of the corner of his eye. He discreetly ran the tip of his tongue across his sultry lower lip. Lilac shivered anew. Her husband had not been named "Gifted" in the Familiar tongue for nothing.

"The tree is perfectly safe, Father," Lorgin reiterated for the hundredth time.

"I fail to see how it is safe when she can crawl off a limb and—"

Lorgin rubbed the side of his forehead, where the throbbing was starting. Krue had been going on like this for weeks and he was getting worse. "She cannot crawl yet, Father." He groaned as he imagined what Krue would be like by that time.

"Nonetheless, who can say what—"

A loud shriek of disgust came from the direction of Krue's Familiar wife, Suleila. Everyone stopped eating to stare at her, stupefied. Including Krue.

Suleila had had enough. "I vow, Krue, if you do not stop with this ridiculousness, I will scratch your eyes out!"

Krue's mouth parted in shock.

Suleila threw her hands up in the air. "The babe is perfectly fine! She eats well, she sleeps well, her digestion is perfect, and yes, she looks like you! Now will you let us have some peace!"

All eyes shifted to Krue to see what his response was going to be to this most unusual but highly applauded set-down by his wife.

"Hmf." He resumed his meal.

The rest of the diners gratefully followed suit.

"Scratch my eyes out?" he murmured to Suleila in a low tone.

Suleila's lips twitched. "At the very least."

He flashed her a look she knew well. "I look forward to it," he drawled in a low tone, so no one could hear. He could still make her blush.

"My boy, would you pass me that purple woodcock over there?" Aunt Agatha peered at the plate through her lorgnette as she nudged Traed.

No one had a clue what woodcock was, but Traed passed the old woman the dish of Aviaran *calan* stew just the same. Aunt Agatha had come back from Ree Gen Cee Ing Land with Rejar and his wife, Lilac. Aviara had not been the same since.

A single knock sounded on the door.

Malkin, their servant, opened the door and was so unnerved by the person who stood there that he lost his ability to speak. So the visitor simply let herself in and entered the room where they sat.

All conversation came to a dead stop as each person looked up.

"Who is it?" Jenise whispered to Gian when no one would speak.

{It is the revered Tan-Shi Mother. She is the mystical leader of the feminine sect. They say she is the knowledge-bearer of all female wisdom on Aviara. It is unheard of for her to leave the monastery.}

"Why has she come do you suppose?" Jenise murmured.

{She has heard that Krue has acknowledged Traed to his line. In doing so he has violated an oath between the Charl and the Tan-Shi.}

Both Lorgin and Rejar had already been told about Traed and both were relieved. Although the brothers themselves had long acknowledged Traed, they knew of the strain placed upon their father by the Tan-Shi.

Jenise eyed the elderly woman closely. Her hair was silver and hung down her back. Her robes were black and unadorned yet somehow they did not look plain with her proud carriage. Like Yaniff, she carried a long staff with a crystal at the end. Her eyes were clear silver, fathomless. Even though she never glanced Jenise's way, Jenise had the distinct impression that the woman knew she was studying her.

Krue found his voice first. "Revered Mother, we are honored by your presence here. Come and sit at my table." He stood, offering her his own seat at the head.

The Tan-Shi Mother declined. "I am not here to sit at your table, Krue, although I thank you for your gesture."

He frowned. "If you have come about Traed, then you waste your time. I have claimed him, as is my right."

Traed, who was obviously uncomfortable at being the center of all this attention, stared down at his plate, a muscle ticking in his jaw. His anger at the Guild and the Tan-Shi was deep-seated.

"I am not here to discuss your right either," she informed the Aviaran warrior. The Tan-Shi Mother never minced her words. She was direct and to the point.

Krue responded with like boldness, seeing no reason to temper himself despite his immense respect for her. "I will fight for him," he said in a soft but deadly voice.

Traed looked at Krue, surprised.

"He is my son—you will not take him from me again."

The corners of the Tan-Shi Mother's lips twitched. "You will not have to fight for him, Warrior. It is time we set aside the past. The debt has been paid. The destruction that was caused by one Charl was made right by another." She looked pointedly at Yaniff, who remained silent at his end of the table. Then she nodded at Traed, acknowledging him and his right to sit beside Krue in his home.

Traed pointedly ignored her.

Krue, in his first act as father, kicked Traed under the table with his boot. Grudgingly, Traed inclined his head. Slightly.

The woman's silver eyes twinkled as if she found some amusement in his reluctance. "Stubbornness can be a good trait for a Charl warrior, Son of Krue."

Yaniff snorted. "So I have been telling him since he has been a youth."

Traed narrowed his eyes. "I am not a Charl warrior. Nor will I ever be."

"We will speak of that later, Traed." Krue returned to his seat.

"No, Krue, we will not."

Rejar and Lorgin both winced, knowing what was coming. Gian, watching the scene play out before him, waited for Traed to find out what it truly meant to be a son.

Krue did not disappoint. He set his goblet on the table with a clink and pierced the younger man with a steely look. "*I* said we will discuss it later."

The muscle played in Traed's jaw but he remained silent.

Excellent, Gian thought, *already he takes the role of a son*. Gian wagered that many a battle of wills would take place in the future between the two strong-willed men. *Yes, I think I will ask*

Traed to come to M'yan for a while. He will need the time to adjust to what taking the name of Krue truly means.

But Gian was in for his own surprise when the Tan-Shi Mother suddenly said, "I will speak with the *tajan* of Ren."

Gian raised his steady gaze to hers. *{On what matter?}*

"It is a private matter."

Gian knew he could not refuse such a request, even if it was stated as a demand. *{Very well,}* he assented. *{But she does not know.}*

The Tan-Shi Mother's voice came back to him in his mind and he realized she too had the ability to send her thoughts. *{Your secret is safe,* taj *Gian. I wish to speak to her of . . . other things.}*

Gian inclined his head, although he was wondering what those other matters could be. "Jenise, the Tan-Shi Mother wishes to speak with you."

Jenise, who was in the process of tasting a colorful leafy thing on her plate, squeaked, "Me?"

Gian almost grinned at the comical expression of apprehension on her sweet face. "Yes. In private."

She looked from the Mother to Gian, then back to the Mother. "Why does she want to speak with me?" she whispered nervously.

Gian was amused. "I do not know," he whispered back teasingly. "Why do you not ask her?"

"Come, child. We will go sit in the garden for a few moments. There are matters I must speak to you about."

Jenise rose and, throwing Gian one last beseeching look, followed the robed woman outside. Gian chuckled as he watched her hesitant steps.

Yaniff also watched them leave as he calmly fed Bojo a strip of meat.

"What do you wish to speak to me of?" Jenise sat down next to the elderly woman on a stone bench.

"I would speak to you about your perceptions of power, my child."

Jenise fidgeted in her seat, somewhat surprised that this old woman had been able to see into her in such a way. Power had ever been a touchstone to Jenise.

"What of it?" she asked quietly.

"You tell me," the Tan-Shi Mother wisely instructed.

Jenise sighed. "I like not the way men wield it, the trappings of it, how they use it to control . . . I want no part of it."

"Explain."

"Karpon . . . he is—"

"I know about Karpon. Continue."

"He twists and turns his power; he thinks he uses it, but it uses him."

"Excellent." The Mother nodded. "Go on."

"Traed appears to have incredible abilities and yet he is not in harmony with his power. . . ."

The Mother's silver eyes gleamed. "Most astute."

"And Gian . . . Gian has incredible *sexual*

power. He uses it to his advantage in whatever way he can."

"Gian has more power than you think."

Jenise snorted, not understanding what the Mother was implying. "I am well aware of his gifts; he has fairly beguiled me."

The old woman smiled. "Of course he has; I would have expected no less from him."

Blushing, Jenise returned her smile.

"Tell me, Jenise, does he overwhelm you?"

"Yes," she admitted.

"And this bothers you because you fear you lose yourself to his passion."

"Yes. It is the way with men and power—no matter what power they wield. I do not wish to be part of their play of power."

"You already are and always have been. You cannot deny the path your destiny takes."

"Perhaps not." Jenise shrugged. "But I can seek to alter the route of it, can I not?"

The Mother's expression was enigmatic. "In matters of reasoning, you would have made an excellent Tan-Shi."

Jenise's aqua eyes flashed at the compliment. "Perhaps I should join you?" She hadn't thought of it before, but maybe she would like such a life.

A dry, crackling laugh rumbled through the old woman's chest. "Child, you are not of the temperament."

"Why not?"

The Mother's lips twitched. "In order to be a Tan-Shi, you must divest yourself of . . . let us simply say that you enjoy your Gian too much."

"Oh." She colored.

The Mother patted her arm in a kind way. "Which is a good thing as well—simply a different pathway. Besides, I think Gian Ren would have something to say if you suddenly declared your wish to join us." She winked at her.

Jenise was surprised at the Mother's misconception. She immediately corrected her. "He has nothing to say! It is my choice."

The Mother chuckled. "He was always clever," she murmured to herself.

"What?"

"I said you are clever and will make the right choice."

Jenise nodded, her hand playing with the folds of her garment. "I understand your need to be apart though. I have seen the power the men here wield. In a way, you have done as I have. Removed yourself from their ceaseless strategies and quests."

"You are wrong, Jenise. We are nothing alike in that regard, for what motivates the Tan-Shi is the opposite of what drives you."

"What do you mean?"

"You are running away because you distrust power. We of the Tan-Shi choose not to be warriors; instead we seek to explore our true female power."

"Female power? What is this female power you speak of?"

"I can only tell you what it is not. It is not male power. It does not come with the flash of a blade or the strength of a fist. It is not born of physical strength but intuitive recognition. That is where our true power lies. In the knowing and in the wisdom."

"Against male power, what is that? You would do better to become warriors."

"No. Though it is true we could become as strong as warriors, that is not the way to become our most powerful."

"How can you say that?" Jenise knew well the power that men brandished. She had been subjected to it her entire life.

"Our Tan-Shi power is likened unto water; it is a gentle and soothing ripple. It is fluid and ever-changing; it flows with life and when it meets an immutable obstacle, it knows to flow around it. Yet it is water that will wear away the mighty rock."

Jenise thought about what the Tan-Shi Mother was saying. "Why are you telling me this?"

"Because you are who you are, Jenise," she replied ambiguously. "In the future you will need to think of these things in your life. When you hold a babe in your arms, you have much influence on the perceptions of that child."

"*Babe?* What are you speaking of? I will have no babe! I will not mate."

The Mother's eyes gleamed. "There will come a time soon when you will be faced with a vital decision. Remember that male energy is likened to fire; it roars and crackles and consumes, for such is its nature. Then think of the water which flows with life. Fire cannot consume water but water can consume fire. Which do you think is ultimately the stronger?"

Jenise stared at her, staggered by this insight.

"Fire commands all to be his and so becomes enslaved by his rule; water yields to change direction and so flows with freedom."

Jenise had never viewed it in such a way before. Nonetheless, it had naught to do with her. Her course was set.

The Tan-Shi Mother stood. "Water can continually change its course; remember that too. It is what makes the female so very powerful."

With that she left.

Jenise sat there for a long time wondering exactly what the mysterious epigrams meant.

And why the Revered Tan-Shi Mother had chosen her to tell it to.

Chapter Thirteen

When Jenise returned to the others, Gian told her they must leave immediately for M'yan.

"So soon?" She had hoped to stay and explore Aviara.

"Yes; the situation with Karpon is very grave, Jenise."

She flushed at her own insensitivity. Here she had been worried about seeing the sights of Aviara, while Gian's people were faced with a serious threat from Ganakari. "I am sorry, Gian. Perhaps it would be best if I visit another time? After . . . when things are . . ." She was not sure how to finish.

Gian rose from the table to approach her. "I will not hear of it," he intoned softly. Ambiguously.

"If you are sure." Jenise did not want to be an imposition.

"I am sure." He turned to Krue and Suleila. "I will keep you both informed."

"Please, Gian." Suleila was also concerned for her people. "You will come soon to visit us again?" she asked Jenise.

"I would like that. I am grateful for your hospitality and kindness."

Suleila smiled, liking her very much. *{You have found yourself a treasure, Gian.}*

His lips curled. *{One might say so.}* He sent Krue a glance as he said out loud, "Traed, I would like you to come to M'yan on the morrow."

Traed paused in the process of taking a bite of food. "For what purpose, Gian?"

Krue met Gian's eyes and understood. The Familiar was going to give his new son some breathing room. He recognized the wisdom of Gian's plan. He silently thanked Gian with his eyes, before saying, "It matters not the purpose, Traed. When *taj* Gian invites a member of the Lodarres line to his home, we accept unconditionally. Is that not so, Gian?"

"That is so, Krue."

Traed's nostrils flared. There was naught he could do—except go to M'yan on the morrow. "Very well," he bit out, annoyed at being so maneuvered. "I will be there."

Rejar, who had been watching the whole exchange, exhaled ruefully. His brother Traed had a slight reprieve, but it would not last long. Krue expected his sons—all his sons—to be Charl warriors. Rejar had a hard time picturing his dour brother, Traed, on the happy, frolicsome world of the Familiar, where the senses ruled all. It would almost be worth going there just to see such a thing. Rejar reflected on the possibility of fascinating entertainment.

{Do not even think it.} Gian leveled a nononsense look at him.

Rejar flashed his relative a mischievous grin.

Before they left, Gian asked Yaniff to clear Jenise's translating device so that she could understand the Familiar tongue while on M'yan. Yaniff briefly touched her forehead, saying to the Familiar that it was done.

For a reason she could not name, Jenise had a very peculiar feeling. The Tan-Shi Mother would have told her it was the power of her woman's intuition.

Gian and Jenise stepped onto the Familiar world of M'yan just as the sun was beginning to set.

It was a world of tropical splendor.

A profusion of heavy red and purple flowers greeted her eye. The humid air was scented with the foliage surrounding them. There were so many species of animals! It was a world of sounds and color and scents. A place where the senses were heightened and stimulated.

She took a deep breath of the sultry air and as

it tingled through her, she realized she had never felt so alive!

"What causes it?" she asked Gian in wonder.

"We know not, but M'yan has this effect on all who come here. It is why we guard our home the way we do. There are those like Karpon who would seek to take it from us were they to learn of its nature."

Jenise watched Gian; watched him here in his own world where he belonged so completely. It came to her that M'yan and the Familiar people were strangely connected. The elusive beauty of both touched upon those they met to echo forever. No wonder rumors abounded about this place. Would it call to her in the recesses of her mind now that she had glimpsed its tantalizing essence?

As the Familiar undoubtedly would?

They encountered no one en route to his home. Gian explained that it was the time of day most Familiars liked to take a brief rest. They would be rising soon with the setting sun. Secretly, he had planned their arrival exactly at this time to avoid meeting anyone.

Gian observed Jenise's delight with everything around her. She was smiling now, but she would not be soon. A pang of sorrow hit him; he wished he did not have to do what he was about to do. He sighed.

There was no other way.

It was the nature of moons and stars and Familiars.

He took her hand in his large one and resolutely led her to the home of he who was known as Guardian of the Mist.

It was a rather imposing jumble of a residence, Jenise concluded as she glanced up at the enormous structure, topped by crenellated turrets and open-air verandas.

As soon as they entered the enormous abode, they were surrounded by servants and others—all exclaiming over his return. One authoritative man finally shooed everyone way.

"What can I get you, Your Majesty?"

Jenise gasped, her incredulous gaze flying to Gian. She knew he had heard her shocked exclamation. Apparently he was choosing to ignore it.

"Nothing, Nirim, we will retire to my chambers immediately." If the servant was curious—and Gian was positive he was—he admirably held his tongue.

The servant Nirim bowed.

"What do—" Jenise began.

Not answering, Gian simply tugged her after him as Nirim escorted them down several halls, up a level, then down more halls until he stopped before a wide, heavy door.

"Your *utal* will wish to speak with you."

No doubt he would. His mother's brother was his first advisor. He was definitely going to have something to say. "Not now. Tell him I will speak with him on the morrow."

Nirim nodded. "Should I send someone to Her Majesty?" he asked solicitously.

"No."

Jenise's brow furrowed. Gian opened the door, yanked her inside and slammed it shut.

They stared at each other in silence.

Finally Jenise spoke. "You are Ruler here?"

He pierced her with a steady look. "Yes."

She lifted her chin a notch, a terrible feeling sinking into her bones. "Of this principality?" she asked in a shaky voice.

"Of *every* principality. I am King of all Familiar, Jenise."

His words were like a blow to her. "I see."

"Do you? My eye color determined my destiny the moment I was born, for there is but one child born per generation who has three golden flecks on green. Such a male is said to be 'king' Familiar; that none can compete with his abilities and so he rules."

"I see."

"Although not customary, this trait has been passed down through my family for many generations; so it was that my father ruled before me. The trait does have a tendency to stay in royal houses."

"I see."

"We are a clan people. Each clan has its own ruler. I rule them all."

"I see."

He crossed his arms over his chest. "Can you say naught but 'I see'?"

She inhaled a short breath and exhaled it as her temper flared. With an iron will, she tamped it down. "I did not know that Familiar eye color was significant."

"No, we keep that knowledge amongst ourselves. You can imagine what would have occurred if Karpon knew who I was."

That much was true. *But he could have told me.* Her temper rose another notch. "Rejar's eyes—blue and gold . . ."

"Blue denotes that the house he comes from is also royal. There are many variations and subtleties amongst the clans."

"I see."

Gian watched her carefully. Like a hunter patiently waiting for his prey to spring. "The Mist is another, secret name for my people. *Taj* Gian—literally, King Guardian; Gian Ren—Guardian of the Mist."

Jenise looked at the wall behind him, too furious to meet his calm gaze. *Taja* . . . The word echoed in her mind. A word she foolishly had assumed was a simple endearment! Her hands shook with anger. "When did you mate with me?"

"The very first time."

She felt her eyes moisten but she staunchly refused to give in to *that* emotion. "How did Nirim know?"

"Our senses are different from yours. I placed my mark upon you."

She glanced down at herself. "I do not see anything."

He smiled without humor. "I assure you, it is there for all to see."

She sucked in her breath and finally raised her eyes to his. "You cannot mean this!"

"It was your choice," he intoned evenly.

That did it. Jenise's controlled facade cracked just as Gian had intended. "My choice?! My choice!" she ranted, throwing her arms up in the air. Like a *true* Familiar, she began to pace before him. Gian's eyes flashed with sudden heat as he watched her.

She stopped before him, her head snapping up to capture him in her outraged look. "You took the choice from me just as Karpon did! Wherein lies the difference?"

Gian visibly flinched. "You dare say that to me?" he rasped. "Compare me to such a man?"

She regretted the words the moment they left her mouth, for in truth there was no similarity between the two. Karpon had tried to force her to bend to his will for the sake of his power. Gian had protected her and pleasured her and showed her what it meant to—

It mattered not!

"You lured me and tricked me, setting the parameters to suit you!"

"You did not mind when you wished to use me in a similar fashion and you believed yourself to have power over me. Think on that." His low voice was a rumbling purr.

Jenise blanched. "It was not the same!"

"Really. I will remind you that you bargained with me for the use of my body. What right did you think you had to do that?"

She looked away.

"Tell me," he said softly, with a thread of menace, "would you have left me there to rot if I had refused you?"

She swallowed. "You are twisting things. It was not my doing that you were captured."

"True. But it was your *responsibility* once you knew the situation."

He staggered her.

"This is why you have such a reputation, Guardian of the Mist! You can twist reality with words to muddle your opponent! You should be proud of such an ability."

He viewed her obliquely. "Are you my opponent, Jenise?"

"If not, then what?" she flung back at him.

He exhaled heavily. "I warned you back on Ganakari that appearances can be deceiving. You *chose* not to heed that warning. Now you are mine—how did you put it? Ah, yes—*to take.*"

Her breath hitched in her throat. "What are you saying?"

"I am a male Familiar."

"So? What point are you trying to make?"

"That *is* my point." He began pacing toward her with deliberate steps. "Did you expect me to behave in a way foreign to my nature? We sense our mates; I knew who you were the instant you entered that cell. I am who I am. You are who you are . . . to *me*. Therefore, I am—"

"A *predator*," she sneered.

"When it suits me." He stalked closer to her.

"A hunter!" she threw at him, incensed.

"Depends on what you deem the hunt," he murmured, coming closer.

"A king! You are a king!" She yelled what she considered the worst offense.

"Very much so." He caught her face between his strong palms, forcing her to look up at him. Then he lowered his silken mouth close to hers.

"And you, Creamcat, are my queen." He covered her lips and took her breath. A sharp, quick inhalation.

Jenise panicked, pounding on his broad chest. The warm, dry lips cleaved to hers, a firm, unyielding siege.

And when she began to grow faint, he casually blew into her mouth.

Letting her know it was his breath alone.

His.

She ignored him after he released her.

She disrobed silently and got into the enormous, low bed, which was covered in silken jade and gold *krilli* cloth and cushions. The same color as his eyes . . . In fact, many of the fabrics and furnishings seemed to reflect his eye color, as if the tones represented a symbol of—

She did not want to think of those mesmerizing eyes or anything else about Guardian of the Mist.

When Gian disrobed and joined her, she turned her back on him.

He slid in next to her and took her in his arms.

"Leave me be." Her voice was cold.

"You are my mate."

"Then that is unfortunate for you." His eyes sparked with anger but he released her. Familiar

293

men did not take well to being denied their mates. And Gian was very much a Familiar male.

Tired from the events of the past days, Jenise quickly fell asleep.

In the middle of the night she awoke with an intense desire that bordered on pain. Her breasts throbbed, her nipples tingled, her skin hummed with arousal. The curls between her legs were wet.

Gian came over her, the moon surrounding him with a halo of muted light. His incredibly handsome features were starkly sensual and starkly resolved.

She wanted him so much she ached with it. "What did you do to me?" she moaned.

He did not speak to her. His fingers delved into her hair to capture her in his possessive, feral hold. He did not take his eyes from her as he slid fast into her, hot and determined.

Jenise threw her head back and cried out at the sensual torture that was at once pleasure and pain. Pleasure from his touch and pain from needing it.

"What do you do to me, Gian?" she gasped as he silently answered her with ecstasy from his body.

His bold thrusts told her.

His lapping tongue told her.

His grazing teeth told her.

His stroking palms told her.

He was Guardian of the Mist. King of all Familiar. And she was his to take.

* * *

When Gian entered his official chambers the following morning, he was not surprised to see that H'riar, his *utal*, was already waiting for him. His first advisor had the reputation of being relentless; no matter how small the matter at hand, he never rested until it was resolved.

The man's dark hair was slightly graying at the temples; he was past his incarnations. Gian respected H'riar immensely and often sought his wise council.

He wondered which topic H'riar would bring up first . . . Jenise or Karpon. Whichever one it was would indicate to Gian which of the two his advisor considered the more urgent.

Gian hoped it was the latter. He was in no mood for an altercation with his *utal*.

Especially not after the turbulent night he had spent with Jenise. When he left, she had still been sleeping.

During the night, he had made her give herself to him . . . in every way. He had mastered her with his sensual skills, but he had no illusion as to what her reaction was going to be to him in the light of day.

His hopes were not to be answered by H'riar. The advisor wasted no time in confronting him. "She is not Familiar," he stated bluntly.

Gian exhaled deeply. "So have I noticed."

H'riar raised a brow. "I am serious, Gian."

Gian sighed. "What would you have me say?"

"The people are concerned . . . about many things."

"They need not be concerned about Jenise—she had naught to do with the situation on Gan-akari. If it were not for her, I might not be here right now—she aided my escape."

H'riar was impressed. "I will let it be known. Although a *tajan* who is not Familiar will take some getting used to."

"They will come to love her." He faced H'riar. "You will see."

H'riar accepted his king's assessment. "Traed has arrived. I have placed him in the third spoke. Already word has spread of what he has done for our Guardian." He snickered. "I vow he is very uncomfortable with all the praise he is receiving."

Gian grinned. "No, he would not like it."

"The people wish to have a mating celebration for you tonight. I have approved the festivities. The heads of the clans, their advisors and families are already journeying here. I am sure the people will wish to honor Traed for his heroic deed as well."

A muscle worked in Gian's jaw. Jenise was not going to be amenable to any marriage celebration. H'riar would not know that, of course. "You should have consulted with me first."

The advisor was surprised. "I truly did not think it necessary. There is always a celebration when the *taj* takes a mate."

Gian wiped a hand over his face. What could he say? He did not want anyone, including H'riar, privy to his personal problems. He would just have to think of a way to get Jenise to go along with it. "You are right, of course. My apologies."

H'riar smiled softly. "I understand—it is the situation on Ganakari that has you worried. What of Dariq, Gian?"

Gian shook his head sadly.

H'riar's eyes moistened with tears. "This news saddens me greatly. He was a sweet, kind youth and on his first adventure too."

"I know. He would not have had much of a chance against them, H'riar." Gian was pained by the young Familiar's terrible fate.

"I will let his family know."

Gian nodded in sorrow.

"Tell me what has transpired on Aviara with the Guild."

"I have told them that Karpon is not alone—he has an accomplice. They seemed very interested in that and asked me to recollect what I had gleaned. As they usually do, they looked into my mind to see if they could learn more than I from the glimpses I had—a black fingernail and part of an orange ring."

"Could they?"

"No. They were all as baffled as I had ever seen them, including Yaniff. They are still debating what to do about this situation. Yaniff seemed most concerned. He later told me that he wondered if the real danger was not Karpon but this unseen threat."

H'riar rubbed the back of his neck. "If Yaniff was concerned, then I am truly worried."

"Yes, I as well."

"What of the poison? Can they neutralize the drug?"

"No, not unless they obtain a sample of it. None of the High Mystics could get a sense of its essence from me."

H'riar was concerned. "What will we do, Gian? Our people will be powerless against such a threat."

Gian took a deep breath. "I have told the Sages to seal the Tunnel."

H'riar gasped. "But Gian! That will curtail the freedom of the Familiar people! Are all of our activities to be monitored by Aviara now? The second Tunnel was our secret door!"

"Think you I do not know that? I assure you, I have thought on this well, *utal*, there is no other alternative—not if we want to ensure the safety of our children. There is nothing to prevent Karpon from stealing them from us; there is nothing to stop him!"

"Could we not guard the Tunnel against such an attack?"

"There are too many of them and they are well armed. In addition, we know not what friends they have. The potential losses are too great." His fist slammed down on a tabletop. "I will not lose another Familiar to Ganakari. Dariq was the last! It is bad enough that for years Oberion slavers have hunted us in certain sectors, but now this! I vow I am heartily sick of it! If Karpon should gain entrance to M'yan our very world will be in jeopardy. I know his kind; he will not stop until he can call M'yan his."

"We could fight him." H'riar said seriously. "No Ganakari could stand up to a Familiar."

"True; I took down many, but what of the drug, *utal*? It renders us helpless at their feet. We must bide our time and find out the source of this drug. Until we do, I will protect the Mist."

"There will be a great sadness amongst the people. To lose one's freedom—is there a worse thing for a Familiar?" H'riar asked sadly.

Gian looked at him evenly. Never would he forget the effect the insidious drug had had on him. The horror of it. "Yes, *utal*, there is."

H'riar knew then what Gian had gone through. He wisely acquiesced to his decision. "When will the Sages do it?"

"Tonight."

"I will inform the people."

Gian inclined his head. Walking over to a window, he stared out at the incomparable view of the Placid Lagoon. M'yan, his home. So beautiful. So untamed. Like his people. The sealing of the secret Tunnel had been the most difficult decision he had ever been forced to make. Somehow, he suspected it was only the first in a long line to come.

A sudden tremor shook him. A bead of sweat formed on his brow. Closing his eyes, he rested his forehead against the window frame.

"Your Incarnation approaches." H'riar spoke quietly. Even from across the room, he had noted the signs. The man had been through enough of them himself to recognize the symptoms.

"Yes." Gian tried to regulate his breathing, which suddenly fluctuated erratically before becoming even again.

"Does she know?" H'riar walked over to stand behind him.

"No." Another body tremor seized him.

H'riar placed a kind hand on his shoulder. "What will you do, my sister's son?"

"I will tell her soon. It will be her choice."

"She may not survive it," H'riar felt compelled to point out. "There never has been a non-Familiar woman who—"

"*She* will survive it." Gian pierced him with a meaningful look.

H'riar sucked in his breath. "You mean to sacrifice yourself?"

"If need be."

H'riar squeezed his shoulder. "Who will rule us then?" he asked devotedly.

Gian smiled faintly. "There is no reason to think she cannot go through an Incarnation." Whether she wanted to or not was the essential question, but that doubt he kept to himself.

"That is true. We have nothing to go by— yours will be the first between a male Familiar and a non-Familiar mate. A fitting place to start . . . with the ruler of us all!" He slapped Gian's back affectionately, trying to lighten the seriousness of the situation.

Gian appreciated his *utal*'s gesture.

"You will have no Familiar child, though, Gian. Whatever chance existed that a son of yours would be *taj* is forever gone." It had been a great source of pride to Gian's family that for many generations the *taj* had come from their direct blood descendants. Such an unusual occurrence denoted the exceptional strain within their house and clan.

Familiar offspring from mixed unions were rare. Only one child had ever been born Familiar from such a union, and that was Rejar.

Gian glanced at his advisor from under veiled eyes as he flexed his shoulders. "She will birth a Familiar babe."

H'riar grinned. "Oh, what are you now—a Charl mystic? Think you to possess their gift of prophecy?"

Gian threw back his head in a leonine pose. "Of course not! I possess something much better, *utal*."

"And what is that, son of my sister?"

"Familiar arrogance!"

H'riar's deep laughter echoed through the halls.

Jenise rose from the bed and walked over to the wide window.

The scene before her was one of utter beauty. A lagoon of aqua water surrounded by tropical plants and fronds.

A soft breeze laden with the scent of *krinang* spice ruffled her hair. *Gian*. He was this world. Mysterious and beautiful to look upon. Dangerous and unpredictable to know.

She was furious with him!

He had left her while she slept and she was

glad of it. Last night he had ravaged her. Over and over. He had brought her to peak so many times she lost count. And throughout it all he remained steadfastly silent.

He let his body speak for him.

In no uncertain terms, he showed her this other side to his nature. Dominant and conquering.

He had tricked her as to who he was.

Tricked her in the worst way possible! Although the clues had been there. . . .

The way he had saved them from the *valdt*, the steadfast endurance of the man, his extraordinary abilities, his refusal to give up even in the face of the overwhelming odds against them. All of those attributes pointed to a superior individual.

To a man who was King of all Familiar.

Her mind went back to that first time, in the cell on Ganakari when he had "accepted" her terms. She remembered he had told her then that appearances could be deceiving. How right he was!

At the time, she had not known what he meant. In her conceit, she had thought herself in control of the situation and the chained captive. Now she knew better. Who could ever control a Familiar?

He had been right about one thing yesterday— she had had no right to propose such a bargain to him.

But desperate situations called for desperate measures. And she had been so very desperate.

He knew that. They both had been desperate. The memory of his breath teasing at her ear weakened her in a way she could not name. He had been so very passionate as he stood behind her, ready to take her. *Ready to snag his unsuspecting prey.*

His heated, soulful murmurs came back to her. Hot, sensual phrases, which at the time she believed to be words of passion. How wrong she had been.

With her new knowledge of the Familiar tongue, she recalled a few of the arcane phrases he had uttered . . .

Ei mahana ne Tuan, I discard all others. . . .

A jhan vri re Tuan, For me there is no other. . . .

Jenise bit her lip as tears welled in her eyes. *Why had he done such a thing?* He had told her that Familiars could sense their mates. If that was so—and from everything she had seen of the Familiar, she had no reason to doubt it— why had he not let her make her own choice?

Why had he not waited?

His purring voice came back to her anew. His powerful hand had been wrapped securely around her hair and his silken lips were at her throat. *"I ask you to wait . . . tell me to stop . . ."*

She had told him he must not stop. And so he'd done as she had demanded of him.

But she had not known!

If you had, a voice inside her said, *would it have made a difference?* She had been desperate to escape Karpon and had been ready to do, indeed *had done,* anything to accomplish it.

It was a complicated, tangled mess. And it all centered, as everything had in her life, on power.

Perhaps Gian had no choice initially. Perhaps since he realized what she could be to him, he was bound to do what he did. But after? All those days they had traveled together—he could have told her.

But then he was a predator. His purpose was to ensnare her.

Her nostrils flared. It would not do. He must release her now.

A tear found its way down her face. She staunchly wiped it away.

As far as she was concerned it must be over between them.

If in the future she had a longing for *krinang* spice and ached for the feel of smooth, dark golden hair with singular black strands, she would just have to remember what price is demanded of those who embrace the source of power.

Resolved, she waited patiently for his return.

Chapter Fourteen

Despite her morose mood, Jenise gazed up in amazement at the twisting trunk of the gnarled tree that grew through a hole in the flooring and on through the roof above. It was mid-morn and she was still waiting for Gian to appear.

Small trills sang happily in the leafy branches. *Inside the room.*

She had never seen a tree growing inside an abode before but decided she liked the effect of it. It was a rather peaceful addition which conveyed a nice feeling to the room.

There was a rock-lined pool in the chamber as well, its source continually refreshed by a small fountain which trickled forth streams of warmed water. The gentle, bubbling sound of the fountain soothed her frayed nerves somewhat as she relaxed in the scented water.

Dara Joy

Someone had placed flower blossoms in the pool. The exotic white blooms had pale pink centers and were really lovely. Jenise picked one up in her cupped palms to sniff at it. The sultry fragrance teased her, evoking images of warm tropical nights and even warmer passion. *Sparkling green and gold eyes dilated with lambent hunger. . . .* She shivered at the memory.

A rich, purring voice brought her out of her reverie.

"The *tasmin* flower is believed by some to be a sexual stimulant." Gian stood in the doorway intently watching her.

Jenise looked away from him, blushing as she recalled the things the Familiar had done to her in the middle of the night. With his lips and tongue and teeth. He had licked her from head to foot and back again.

He bit her the same way too. Gian liked to bite.

She shivered anew.

As angry as she was at him for his subterfuge, she could not deny the way she had responded to him physically. Towards dawn, she had actually turned it about and taken *him*. Something she had enjoyed tremendously. As had he.

She almost moaned aloud as she recalled the way Gian had looked as he lay, sprawled beneath her, watching her with a slumberous expression as he urged her to continue by whispering a multitude of naughty things he expected her to do to him.

Her initial shock had abated somewhat with

her understanding of his nature, but her resolve
concerning their future would not.

Her initial shock and hurt had abated somewhat with her understanding; but her resolve
had not.

Since the early morn, Jenise had given a lot of
thought to her present situation. Gian was reasonable. She would just have to make him understand that as far as she was concerned, this
mating of his was impossible.

It was not as if she did not *want* him. That she
would never be foolish enough to deny.

In truth, she was quite taken with him. But
this had nothing to do with her desires. She simply had a need to be free of any entanglements.

Once the Familiar listened to her—really
listened to her—she knew he would see her side
of it.

"Is it?" she asked. "A sexual stimulant, I
mean."

He strolled over to the pool, kneeling at its
edge. "I will tell you a secret about such things,
taja."

My queen.

From what she had learned of him, there
wasn't a doubt in her mind that he purposely
called her by that particular endearment. The
implication irked her.

She glared up at him, crystal droplets of water
sparkling on her gold-tipped lashes. "And what
is that secret, Gian?"

Before answering, he snapped off a petal of
the flower she was holding and brushed its vel-

vety surface tantalizingly across the surface of her lips. "Almost anything can be a sexual stimulant in the proper hands."

By way of demonstration, the tip of his talented tongue lapped languorously over the same petal. The handsome Familiar viewed her from beneath lowered lids as he did so. The effect was highly provocative to say the least.

Jenise drew in a quivery breath. Last eve, he had done much the same to her. With his tongue. *Back and forth . . .*

"I can taste your essence. It is combined with the essence of the *tasmin* flower. As rich as the *tasmin* flower is, Creamcat, your taste is still richer."

The tips of her ears turned pink.

"Sometimes," he continued in a husky voice, "our senses let us 'see' taste as colors."

The idea fascinated her. "Do you see color now?"

"Yes." He purred low.

"What—what color do you see?"

He smiled slowly. "Red with a hint of purple beneath a cool wash of white."

Jenise fumed. She was sure he was provoking her. "And what does that mean?"

"It means," he drawled sexily, "that you are both very angry at me and very aroused *for* me beneath that cool exterior you are showing."

Jenise crossed her arms over her pointed breasts and immediately showed him her back.

He chuckled, low. "Also an enticing view."

Her shoulders hunched; she ducked lower in

the water. She did not want Gian enticed! She wanted him to listen to her!

"I can also sense many variations in your flavor that I cannot describe to you in words."

"And do you like this flavor?" she asked quietly.

"I crave it." His sexy voice rolled in his throat.

A shiver washed down her back. She glanced at him over her shoulder and spoke the truth. "As I crave your flavor."

"Jenise," he breathed on a purr. He was deeply moved by her admission. Another strong tremor raced through him.

She turned away from him again. "But Gian, you must see that this notion you have of us being mated is not realistic."

He was silent for a few moments. Completely silent. She wondered what he was thinking. Unable to take the suspense any longer, she peeked over her shoulder at him once more.

He had folded his arms across his chest and his brow was arched. Apparently he did not agree with her assessment.

"I mean it, Gian. We are not suited. And I have no desire—"

He snorted.

She ignored him. "No desire to be mated. Please do not take this personally."

A dimple popped into his cheek. "Of course not. Why would I?"

"I wish to explore, as I have explained to you. Like the Frensi. I need to be free, Gian. If it were not for that . . . perhaps . . . that is, you . . ."

Green and gold eyes flashed with amusement. He wasn't supposed to be enjoying this! He was supposed to be agreeing with her! She cupped some water in her palms and splashed him with it.

He laughed as he stepped back out of harm's way. It was that rich, rolling laugh of his that always tingled down her spine.

"I am serious!"

Grinning, he held out his hand to her. "I would like to show you our home."

He was definitely not listening to her. "It is your home, not mine."

"Come." Smiling, he motioned with his outstretched hand, compelling her to take it.

Gingerly, she did.

She would convince him . . . it would just take a little time. After all, he was a Familiar, used to ensnaring what he desired. This tour would be an excellent opportunity to enlighten him. She couldn't expect the man to have her elevated sense of reason—he lived by instinct. It was up to her to point that out to him. Loudly.

Gian lifted her easily out of the water. Her wet body, glistening with water droplets, brushed against him.

Once again she noticed that a tremor shook him.

"Here, use this." He handed her a large, soft cloth to dry herself. She was surprised that he did not do the drying himself, taking advantage of the opportunity to caress her curves.

Instead, he was looking at the wall, away from

her. This was unlike him. Curiously, she observed him. A slight sheen of sweat dotted his upper lip.

"On my instructions, several *krilli* caftans, imported from the *sacri* on Aviara, have been delivered for your pleasure. They are in the next room awaiting your choice. *I* will await you at the bottom of the stairs."

Jenise gave him an odd look. It was also unlike him to leave like this . . . especially if he thought he could watch her as she dressed. In the past, she had noted that the small task seemed to give him immense enjoyment.

But then Familiars were so unpredictable; who could fathom what they would do next?

"During our jaunt, you may *try* to convince me of your need to wander unguarded through dangerous worlds filled with all manner of unscrupulous beings." He gave her a very male look that said, "not in this millennium" just before he slipped through the door.

He knew what she was about! The entire time, he had simply been playing with her! The boot she threw at his arrogant head bounced off the door frame.

"I *am* leaving, Gian!" she yelled through the closed partition.

"Of course. I will see you downstairs, Creamcat." His voice trailed off as he left.

Jenise muttered to herself as she grabbed the first caftan she found, putting it on without looking at it. Familiars could be so infuriating!

As soon as she was dressed she stormed after

him. She had no intention on letting up on him. Gian was waiting for her exactly where he'd said—at the bottom of the stairs.

Gian watched her stomp towards him, amusement highlighting his features as he took in the caftan she had donned. Jenise glanced down at herself, shocked to discover that the beautiful, rare *krilli* cloth was in tones of red and purple shot through with strands of white. According to him, the exact colors of her present taste!

"It was an accident," she gritted out.

"*Mmmm-hmmm,*" he drawled.

"You are impossible!"

He smiled in an altogether feline way.

"I do not understand how you can even think a woman could possibly tame you!"

"What makes you even think I would wish such a thing?" he whispered back in challenge.

"Well, you speak of mating and such!" she sputtered.

"Mating has naught to do with taming. Or other things you have confused it with." His spellbinding eyes glittered with secrets. "Familiars cannot be tamed, Jenise."

"What does mating have to do with, then?" she flung back at him, exasperated with his feline ways. "According to you?"

"I will let you discover that. Now come."

M'yan was a world of delights.

Everywhere she looked there was something new and fascinating to see.

The royal abode, she quickly learned, was a

structure of impossible angles, levels, convoluted halls, and hidden nooks. It appeared to her as if a tradesman-builder had gone mad.

Gian explained to her that to a Familiar it was a place of great interest, for there were endless intricacies to explore.

"But it is so . . . so odd."

His well-shaped lips twitched. "We enjoy such oddities. This being the royal ruling house, you might say it is by far the oddest." He smiled boyishly at her.

She gave him a suspicious look.

"Our people always long to come here; invitations are coveted." He blinked playfully. "Truly."

She could see why. Despite its unpredictable layout and decor, it was a beautiful place. Familiars had an eye for detail and it was evident in the silken fabrics and furnishings, which were rich in both color and design.

There were all kinds of pleasing places to lose oneself. Hidden alcoves. Secret stairways. Winding stairways and mysterious stairwells.

As Gian continued the tour of the house, Jenise also noted that the chambers were sumptuously appointed without being overbearing or stately. The focus seemed to be on comfort. Beds and furnishings were low and sprawling, with an overabundance of cushions.

Familiars appeared to be enamored of textures as well; in one chamber she counted twenty-five different fabrics! All of them exquisitely blended. On Ganakari, even the ruling house did not have such wealth, for these fabrics were highly costly, not to mention extremely rare. She had never seen such vibrant colors! They flooded her senses, instantly elevating her mood.

"It is so unusual, Gian!" An exclamation of delight escaped her lips upon discovering a window garden complete with thick, soft cushions and fragrant spice plants.

"I will come back to this spot"—she grinned— "If I can find it!" The house, designed for Familiars, who never got lost, relied on their innate tracking ability rather than any logical layout. After the numerous twists and turns they had taken, she truly doubted she could find the spot again.

Gian chuckled. "We adore such complexity, as I said; but you will eventually learn your way about. And if you should become lost, you need not worry; I will always find you."

That was what worried her.

"What if I do not wish to be found?" she murmured pointedly.

He raised his eyebrow. "Tell me, in what way do you believe that will affect my actions?"

Her face flushed in irritation. "Gian, we need to talk about—"

He interrupted her by pointing out the window to a small child who had fallen asleep in the garden below. Surrounding her in slumber were eight little kittens. He chuckled. "It appears they got tired from their play."

Jenise could not help smiling as she gazed on

the endearing scene. During their tour, Jenise's mouth had fallen open as scores of cats scampered about everywhere. She had never seen so many cats. They walked and played among the people, doing as they pleased, some causing great mischief.

She had observed that they all had two different-colored eyes. They were Familiars, of course.

"Do the children get into much trouble?" She glanced at two of the kittens, who had woken up and were now hissing at each other in playful sport. One suddenly pounced on the other and the two balls of fur rolled down an incline tangled up together.

"Yes." He laughed as he watched them. "They get into much trouble."

"But surely you discipline them?"

He shrugged. "Not too much. We like them to get into trouble. Such mischief-making is part of our attractive nature, is it not, Jenise?" He gave her a beguiling look.

She scoffed.

He took her hand and led her to yet another wing of delights. Here she caught the smell of food cooking nearby. Her stomach growled.

He chuckled. "I thought you might be getting hungry. You will find our food is as varied as everything else here and just as tempting." He led her out onto a balcony, motioning for her to sit at a small, low table. A trellis of flowering vines secluded the choice spot. A light breeze ruffled her hair.

"I will be right back."

He quickly returned, bearing a plate of delicacies for her. The small appetizers were intricately shaped and of many colors. Her features lit up as she recognized a tiny face painted on one of the round pieces. Until she noticed it was *her* face.

"Why—how did they do this?"

"During our walk, you passed by one of the cooks. She has made these to honor and welcome you."

"What a dear thing to do." She picked up the tiny confection, laughing as she noted the set of the features. The cook had drawn her with her eyes rolling upward. She must have seen her this morning, when she was having her discussion with Gian at the bottom of the stairs. Placing a hand to her mouth, she giggled.

Gian took the confection from her and, grinning, popped it into his own mouth.

"Gian! I was to eat that!"

"You will have your chance, for she is making hundreds of them for the feast tonight."

"What feast tonight?" She picked up another confection, which looked suspiciously like Traed, and bit into it. She could not wait to see the dour Aviaran's face when he realized his miniature head was painted on these tiny treats. Just the thought of it made her giggle again.

Two dimples curved Gian's cheek. "You see how it is here, Creamcat? There is always something whimsical to delight you."

"Mmm . . . What feast, Gian?" She noted that he had not answered her question.

"Ah, that." He stretched out beside her across several cushions.

"Yes, that." She picked up another treat. "Who is this?" She indicated the unknown face.

Gian looked over her shoulder. "That is my *utal*, H'riar. He is my first advisor. You will meet him tonight."

"At the feast."

"Yes."

"Gian. What—is—this—feast—for?"

He smoothed back a strand of her pale, waist-length hair. "It is to honor Traed as a hero of M'yan. . . ."

"Oh. Well in that—"

"And to celebrate our mating."

"No."

"Taja"—he took a deep breath—"it is customary for—"

"No. I will not." She placed the treat back on the tray.

Gian bent over her, lifted it off tray, and swallowed it. Jenise frowned at him.

"The people are expecting this, Creamcat. There is naught I can do. Already the clan heads are on their way here for the celebration. H'riar approved it without my knowledge." He did not add that he would have approved it regardless.

"Is that true?" She peered at him intently.

"Yes, we always speak the truth." He looked at her through half-veiled eyes.

Dara Joy

"Then I am sorry for you, Gian, but you must cancel it."

"I cannot."

Jenise sighed. "Gian, I do not—"

"I ask you for this, Jenise. Come this eve and enjoy yourself. Be my *tajan*. If you will do this for me, then you may discuss what you wish with me on the morrow."

She stopped. It was a concession. A big concession. And one she was not expecting from Guardian of the Mist. He was saying that he would consider what she had to say if she did this for him. Once again, the Familiar had surprised her. "Do you mean it, Gian?"

"Of course."

Jenise took a deep breath. She owed the favor to him. He had saved her life countless times; without him she never would have left Ganakari. "Very well. As long as we understand each other. What do I have to do?"

His green/gold eyes shimmered triumphantly. "Something terrible," he drawled in a teasing manner.

Her mouth formed an O.

He snickered. "Simply be yourself and have a wonderful time . . . *as my* tajan."

She looked at him suspiciously. "That is all?"

"Yes."

"What will happen when they realize there is no mating?"

He snagged the same strand of hair that he had earlier smoothed and drew it between his

318

lips as if it were a blade of grass. "Allow me to worry over these matters, hmmm?"

"Very well. Since you are king, you can worry over everything," she said, teasing him back.

"I do, Jenise. I do." His pulled her over his hip and covered her lips firmly with his own.

Yaniff and Rejar walked through the forest, following an ancient trail.

It was late in the day and Rejar was thinking of returning home soon to Lilac. He missed her when he was not near her.

He smiled faintly. She often teased him about his "kitten" ways. He could not deny that it was a new experience for him. An experience he treasured.

Foliage carpeted the forest floor and it was cool and green and silent where they walked. Rejar noted the pleasurable crinkling sounds their boots made as they traversed the needle-strewn ground.

Somehow, it was a good sound.

The revelation struck him that he *liked* walking with Yaniff; especially when they were relaxed, simply speaking of this matter or that. Not that he would ever admit it to the old man.

Unnoticed by Rejar, Yaniff cast the Familiar a small, pleased smile.

"Yaniff, do you think all will be well with the Familiar people? I vow, I am concerned."

"We all are, Rejar. My confidence is in Gian. He will safeguard the Familiar. My real concern lies in what he has told us about this mysterious accomplice of Karpon's."

"You had no warning of this in your sight?" Yaniff often had premonitions. In the past, many of his premonitions had warded off disaster for both Aviara and the Alliance.

"No, I saw nothing. And that worries me." Yaniff absently stroked Bojo's feathers.

"Perhaps there was nothing to see and we make too much of this accomplice." Rejar scanned the treetops, noting their rich color against the sky.

Yaniff's dark eyes pierced the younger man. Of all the things that Rejar needed to learn, one of the most important was to focus. "Do *you* believe this to be so?"

Rejar looked at the old mystic, surprised. Yaniff was asking him if *he* had sensed anything. What was he thinking? "Yaniff, you know I have naught of those abilities."

"Mmmm." They walked on.

Rejar knew the wizard was implying something. "What *mmmm?*"

Yaniff gestured with his staff. When the old wizard did that, he usually was up to something.

Rejar gnashed his teeth together, positive another esoteric lesson was coming! What had he been thinking about—a nice, relaxed walk? For once he would like to take a simple stroll without having to think so deeply!

Yaniff chuckled. "Why waste the opportunity? Surely you can move and think together, my young friend. I, myself, have witnessed you doing thus on many an occasion when you were in the company of females."

Rejar flushed, realizing too late he had not been shielding his thoughts from Yaniff. "As I have been telling you all of my life, Yaniff, I do not have this Charl power you speak of."

The old wizard waved his staff about, confirming Rejar's suspicions about the lesson with his next words. "The nature of power comes from within. If you believe you do not have it inside, then you are truly powerless. Conversely, if you think you have it within you, then there it resides."

Rejar blinked as the meaning of his master's words sank in. "You are saying I do not show my Charl power because I believe it is not there?"

"You have never acknowledged it to yourself, Rejar, and so it sleeps within you."

Rejar snorted in disbelief. "I cannot credit this! Am I to just say yes, you are here inside"— he thumped his chest—"and there it will be?"

"It is more complicated than that and yet in some ways it is that simple."

Rejar arched a black eyebrow as he teased the wizard. "You speak in riddles again, Yaniff."

Yaniff snickered. Rejar and his ways . . . "You cannot simply think these things into being, Rejar." At least not at this stage.

"I am not sure I understand you, Yaniff."

"Let us look at Guardian of the Mist."

"Very well." They rounded a curve in the path and headed deeper into the forest.

"Gian never wonders about his power because

it is not in him to do so. That is why he is so very much in control. His strength comes from his instinct and this he knows. He never questions himself." Yaniff glanced at Rejar shrewdly. "But then *he* is a Familiar."

"As am I."

"Not entirely."

Rejar shot him a look. True; not entirely. "So you are saying if I reflect upon my inner strength then I am powerless?"

"Not so."

The wizard confounded him. Rejar threw up his hands in disgust. He did not have the patience for these lessons that led him in circles!

Yaniff's eyes twinkled as he watched him. "It is the nature of a Charl to reflect. You, Rejar, are also Charl."

"So you say," he flippantly responded.

"So it is."

Rejar's mouth firmed in annoyance. "Then how am I to balance these sides of myself? The Charl reflects; the Familiar reacts!"

They both bent under a low-lying branch. The forest suddenly gave way to a hidden lake. The men stopped by its edge to gaze across the calm water.

"You must learn to take those qualities from each side that will be most beneficial at any particular moment. Not an easy thing to master, but an important one."

Rejar let the intriguing notion sink in as he stared out across the water. Water, Yaniff had told him, was always mystical. Sometimes it had the ability to bring forth revelations. He idly wondered if Yaniff had deliberately brought him on this path to this place for just such a purpose.

"If you think to ask that then you already know the answer." Yaniff stared straight ahead.

Rejar exhaled heavily. "And how am I to do as you say," he asked quietly, "balance my inner self?"

Yaniff's lips curved mysteriously. "You must rely on your Familiar *instinct* to lead you. Mystical growth comes from an opening within, not by a show of outward force. Might must never be mistaken for true strength. Our abilities can be the catalyst to our deeper power if we but heed this lesson. That is the real strength of a Charl."

Rejar concentrated on Yaniff's words, his blue and gold eyes reflective as he gazed upon the water before him. The Familiar in him would bring out the—

Power.

Instinct and Charl power . . .

His blue/gold Familiar eyes gleamed as comprehension sank in. Willingly, he unveiled his special senses, letting everything flow through him at once; letting his instincts guide him home.

Something seemed to stir within him . . . a deep, nestled consciousness that began to unwind. It uncoiled from the pit of his belly, tingling up his back to travel down his arms. It grew and grew, building and building, this feeling, this something that was coming from inside him!

He felt the vibrations clear to his toes before they seemed to resound, reverberating through him.

Blue and gold Familiar eyes began to flame with incandescent glowing sparks. Brighter and brighter they blazed. His captivating eyes ignited, gathering strength and luminescence. His entire body began to hum with this strange vibration.

The forest around them literally quaked! The wind whipped through the trees and the sky itself suddenly roiled with turbulent masses of dark, gathering clouds. *It was then that the very ground shook beneath his feet.*

Before he knew what was happening, twin beams of crystal-white light shot from his Familiar eyes. They were aimed directly at the lake he had been viewing.

A deafening crack resounded.

In a flash, a great ball of steam rose high into the sky, evaporating immediately into threads of mist. Whereupon everything became still once more.

Silent, yet not the same for the lake that had been there an instant before was no more. Its water had been instantly vaporized by the tremendous flux of energy.

Shocked, Rejar turned a stunned look upon his master. The twin beams of light had come from his own eyes! *What kind of power was this?* He had never seen anything like it.

Yaniff chuckled dryly at his student's awe-stricken expression. A student should have more faith in his Charl master. "Thus you see a small measure of your abilities, Rejar."

"What kind of thing is it, Yaniff?" Rejar was visibly shaken. He could still feel the power crackling through his veins. An undertone of concern laced his voice. "What does this mean?"

A satisfied look crossed the old wizard's face. "It means, my student, that your *true* nature has shown itself at last!"

And in that same instant of being, all the mystics in the realm of Aviara and beyond, in this plane of existence and beyond, in the Tunnels and beyond, stopped to recognize, to acknowledge, and to pay homage to the staggering power that had just been revealed to them.

Power unbound.

Power foretold.

Power that could see truth.

It came from he who was named Gifted.

Chapter Fifteen

A white caftan laced with gold had been laid out for her.

Jenise assumed it was for the festivities that evening. She picked up an edge of the garment, fingering its smooth, soft texture. It was an extraordinary fabric. The material would glide against her skin and shift with the movements of her body as she danced.

As I dance . . .

She sat down on the edge of the bed. As far as she knew, Gian did not know of the Frensi custom of the Dance. Not that it would be an issue between them.

From what she knew of him, Gian was not a man to expect anything that was not freely given. He might use feline strategy to obtain his desired results, but in the end, he would never take that which was not offered to him. Still . . . her mother's consort was ever bitter that her mother would not perform the Dance for him. She could not, for she had performed the Dance for Jenise's father.

Frensi women loved best only once. Their perfect love. Sometimes, for various reasons, this love was given to someone they would never mate with. Rarely they were fortunate enough to find that perfect love and mate with him as well.

Her hand glided down the satiny fabric. The garment she was to wear to celebrate their mating. Her mind registered its feel upon her palm, but her thoughts were on Gian. . . .

"You look lovely, *taja*." Gian picked up her hand to warmly kiss the center of her palm.

The tip of his tongue delivered a quick, steamy message before he released her. "Our men will be desirous of your beauty tonight." The look on his face was one of pride.

Jenise blushed at the compliment; although after viewing him, she could see why the Familiar had such reputations for perfection of form. He was, as he always had been, breathtaking.

He was dressed all in white, much like her. His white boots, white breeches, and white flowing shirt were all laced with gold strands. The stark white color against his golden-tan skin and long, bronze-gold hair created a vivid contrast. And there was always that mysterious curve to those lips of his.

"It is you who are beautiful, Gian." The only time she had ever seen him more handsome was when he wore nothing at all.

Her lips twitched at the indecent thought. *Jenise, what has happened to you?* she asked herself. She wondered at the changes that had recently taken place inside her that she could view a man so . . . so . . . *sexually*.

His fingertip brushed her pliant lips. "And what are you thinking, hmmm?"

She grinned wickedly. "Nothing."

He raised an eyebrow in plain doubt. "I see. Are you ready to go?"

"Yes." Taking her arm, he led her to the massive chamber that had been designated for the mating celebration.

The massive double doors were thrown wide as they entered the chamber. Jenise was amazed by the sheer size of the room as well as the number of Familiar who were there to attend.

Everyone stopped speaking when they entered.

A sea of Familiar faces, male and female, all strikingly beautiful, greeted her. She could see that some of the Familiar were grouped together, presumably by the clans Gian had mentioned before.

Not a sound was heard in the chamber as everyone stared at her in shock. Clearly, they had been expecting a Familiar woman. Jenise stiffened by Gian's side, again questioning the wisdom of appearing together this way.

{Relax and give them a moment to adjust.} Gian squeezed her hand.

A distinguished man stepped forward. His hair was slightly silvered at the temples and there was an air of reserved wisdom about him. He stood directly by Gian's side. Jenise recognized him from the face on the treat she had taken earlier as Gian's *utal,* H'riar.

The advisor's gesture was definitely a message of strong support for the *taj* and his choice of bride.

Unconcerned by his people's silent reaction, Gian smiled warmly at her. Taking their joined hands, H'riar raised them high into the air. "The *tajan* of Ren!" he yelled out, his rich voice booming throughout the hall.

There was a pause, then fifty men came forward—all the heads of Familiar clans. They joined their fists as one, raising them together to the ceiling. "*The* tajan *of Ren!*" they all shouted together.

Gian's eyes lit up in an altogether feline way. He smiled broadly.

Without warning, he whipped Jenise around in front of him and lifted her high in the air, twirling her about. A deafening roar reverberated through the room as all the Familiar shouted at once with a joyous sound.

After that, things got amazingly boisterous.

Jenise was soon to learn that the Familiar were a fun-loving people who adored celebration. Several clan musicians picked up their *obats.* The unique, concordant sounds they produced were sensual, exotic, and at present, lively.

Many Familiar broke into unrestrained dance, swinging their partners through the air in provocative movements which revealed their wild, free nature. They didn't seem to care whom they danced with—as long as they danced. Men danced with men, women with women; they wove about, switching off until, in a seamless pattern, men were dancing with women, then back again. The intricate steps were flawlessly executed.

Jenise watched, wide-eyed. "Are they always like this?" she asked, amazed by the dexterity and passion she was witnessing.

"No. Usually they are wilder. Wait until the night progresses, Jenise. Then you will see how the Familiar can celebrate happiness." He winked at her, his face alight with pleasure.

Jenise's breath stopped. She would remember Gian like this, she thought. Always. His captivating features glowed with the pure happiness of the moment.

"Look, Gian, there is Traed." Sure enough, the Aviaran warrior stood at one side of the chamber, apart from everyone else, as was his wont.

Jenise watched as he glanced over at the table, which was overflowing with all manner of delicacies. She could tell the exact moment the warrior spotted the treats with his likeness painted on them, for his eyes glanced over them, then immediately shifted back.

His handsome brow furrowed as he inspected

the tiny treats with a puzzled expression.

While he was peering at them in mystification, a pretty Familiar woman strolled over and picked up the Traed treat. She placed it in her mouth, letting it dissolve slowly.

Traed arched his brow.

Jenise giggled.

Gian chuckled. "He will find his experience here a new one, to be sure. Let us greet him, Jenise."

She nodded, happy to see the Aviaran again. His quiet, controlled manner had impressed her greatly during their journey. No matter how he tried to conceal himself, there was a caring side of his nature that always drew others to him.

"I am glad you have found your way here, Traed." Gian clasped his shoulder.

"*Taj* Gian." He inclined his head at Jenise. "*Tajan.*"

"Traed, I am happy you have come."

"Tonight, in addition to welcoming the *tajan*, we honor Traed ta'al Krue!" H'riar came forward, his sure voice quieting down the chamber. "For his valiant service to our Guardian of the Mist, we gift him with entrance to M'yan whenever he so desires. From this day forward he will be considered as one of us!" A great cheer rose as all saluted the Aviaran warrior who had saved their king and queen.

Traed was speechless. He faced Gian. "This is not necessary. It was nothing—"

"Do not speak further lest you insult me.

Surely you do not mean to indicate our lives are nothing."

Bronze highlighted his cheeks. "Of course not. However, I—"

"Good!" Gian slapped him heartily on the back.

Traed was clearly irritated by the turn of events. The Aviaran warrior glowered.

Gian grinned. "You will have to endure it, I am afraid, my friend." He gestured in the direction of the pretty woman Traed had noticed earlier. *{Have you ever been with a Familiar woman?}* He sent his thought only to Traed.

Traed shook his head, his jade eyes sparking briefly as he watched the sensual dark-haired Familiar woman move to the music.

{You will find it unlike any of your other experiences. They claim they are not satisfied until they scream and scratch and beg for more.}

Traed cocked his brow.

{Although, I admit, I prefer creamcats.} Gian glanced down at Jenise, then winked at Traed.

Jenise looked back and forth between the two of them. "What are you saying to him?"

"What makes you think I am speaking with him?" He gave her his most innocent look.

"Now I know for sure."

Both men smiled.

"I must introduce Jenise to the clans." Gian took her hand. "I will speak with you later, Traed." Gian glanced meaningfully at the young woman who had caught Traed's eye.

Traed started to nod, then froze. His chiseled

face paled as he looked straight ahead into nothing as if he had been physically staggered by a sharp blow.

Concerned, Gian rushed to his side. "What is it, Traed?" He looked down and noticed that the Aviaran's Cearix was glowing. The dagger at his waistband lit to a bright flash before fading back to its usual appearance.

"*Something miraculous has happened. . . .*" Traed was still shaken by whatever it was he had felt.

"What? What is it, Traed?" Gian put a hand out to steady him.

"It is . . . Rejar? . . . *It is Rejar.*" He seemed stunned.

"What about Rejar? Is he all right?" Gian was concerned for his blood relative.

Traed blinked, coming back to himself. "Nothing. I am fine now."

He did not look fine. The man was still white around the mouth. Whatever had occurred had shaken the normally controlled warrior.

Gian scrutinized him closely. "If you are sure you are all right, then I will see you shortly."

"Yes."

He led Jenise away, still wondering what could have so moved the stolid Aviaran. Whatever it was, it involved his kinsman Rejar. Gian made a note to ask Yaniff about it. The mystic would arrive later this eve along with the Sages, who were to seal the Tunnel.

So far the people were putting on brave faces, but Gian knew their happiness would be short-lived. Joy would be shadowed by sorrow on this occasion.

Gian brought Jenise forward, introducing her individually to the heads of all the clans. The process took a long time, lasting well into the evening as each in turn introduced her to his family and advisors. Gian laughed to himself, knowing that Jenise would never remember all of these people's names.

But Jenise was making her own observations.

The males, she curiously noted, were almost all in their prime. All striking. All supremely virile. All sensual. All *different*. No wonder these men were so sought after!

Jenise wondered what Gian was going to tell these people when she left. She shrugged. He had told her he would deal with it, and she was more than content to let him. Tonight was to be her gift to him. She knew Gian was not a man who would ask for much, but he had asked her for this.

The request alone had convinced her to do it for him. Karpon's brother had never asked her mother for anything. Over the course of their tumultuous relationship, Jenise had developed an immense fondness for Guardian of the Mist. There was little, she realized, she would not do for him.

Except stay here as his wife.

A pang struck her chest.

No. Frensi women needed to be free. . . . She could not allow herself to become a pawn of power again.

So she smiled at his subjects and took their best wishes and praise with the best of grace. And Jenise ached inside.

She ached for what she possessed yet could not have.

Gian glanced at her as she met his people. He engraved upon his memory her lovely face and delicate profile, whose subtleties he had mapped with the touch of his lips on more than one occasion. She was his, and yet . . .

He ached for what he had, yet did not possess.

A buzzing of voices started up near the tall windows. Like a wave, the voices gained in volume. A litany of sorrow. Gian's features instantly sobered. The Sages had arrived.

Putting an arm around Jenise's shoulders, he led her to the nearest window; a path opened before them between the Familiar. He gazed down at the center courtyard below, where the secret Tunnel of the Familiar lay, surrounded on all sides by the protection of the royal abode.

Jenise gasped. "I did not know there was another Tunnel!"

"None but the Familiar do," Gian explained. "At least not until recently."

"What do you mean?" She turned to him, bafflement marring her smooth features.

"Karpon somehow learned of it. His threat to my people is on many levels, Jenise."

Jenise felt terrible. "But you—" she swallowed—"you never told me."

"No."

"Why, Gian? Did you not trust me?"

His finger stroked the downy softness of her cheek; his thumb grazed her lower lip. His green and gold gaze captured hers as his mouth touched hers lightly.

He had not wanted her to leave.

If she had known of the second Tunnel in the courtyard, she might have been able to—

A hurt expression crossed her features. "I would not have, Gian. Not without saying good-bye."

"You almost did once before." He spoke low.

"That was different." She doubted she would have been able to do it then, either. But he did not need to know that. "You cannot keep something that does not want to be kept, Gian. You, a Familiar, should know this."

"I do know it. You misunderstand. I was protecting you from Karpon. Since he knows of this Tunnel, he could easily overtake you along the connecting portal routes. Already I have sent out word to call all Familiar home. Some will not make it."

Her eyes filled with tears. He had been protecting her once again. Protecting them all. "I had not thought of that."

"No."

She turned to the window. "What are they doing?" She pointed to a group of men below.

"They are from the House of Sages. They come here under my direction to seal the Tunnel."

She was shocked. "They can do that?"

"Under extreme circumstances, yes. It is

rarely done, though. There can be mystical repercussions." Just what those repercussions were, he would not say.

They both watched the group of thirteen—ancient and powerful wizards all—as they formed a triangle before the portal.

Yaniff was alone at the front, his power being the greatest. Behind him stood Wolthanth and Gelfan. And behind them four other mystics. And six behind that, forming the Triangle of Sages. The formation was a highly specific placement designed to augment their individual powers into a unified flow.

There was no greater power in their universe than the Formation of Thirteen.

At least there hadn't been until a short time ago.

The chamber became utterly silent as the Familiar sadly watched an avenue of their freedom being closed off to them forever.

Yaniff lifted his staff high, beginning the ritual by calling forth his power. It flowed around him, gathering strength, its bright, lightninglike arcs curling over his legs and arms and torso. Yaniff directed the current of his power up the staff to the faceted crystal at the end, where it glowed brightly. Tipping the staff in his hand, he released the guided current into the maw of the portal.

The clans' *obats* began to play a mournful dirge as Wolthanth called forth his power in much the same manner. He tipped his staff and his arc joined Yaniff's as it flowed into the Tunnel.

Jenise would never forget the awesome, sobering sight of the ritual or the sound of the dirge that played around them. She felt the spirit of the people, felt their sorrow and tears. They had been persecuted—and in some cases enslaved—simply for the beauty of their being. Now they would be forced to stay close to their home planet as well. How would they adjust to such restriction?

Gelfan joined the first two wizards, his power leaping into the combined beam. And so it went; one by one the mystics' individual powers joined side by side, connecting forces to seal the opening.

{You have reminded me of what is important, Creamcat.}

"I have?" She looked at him, perplexed.

"Yes." Gian suddenly turned away from the scene below. He faced the crowd. "A Familiar cannot be contained!" he called out, loud and clear.

The stricken crowd heard his words. The call began to ring through the hall as more and more joined in his chant, each avowing the same. *"A Familiar cannot be contained! A Familiar cannot be contained!"*

Gian motioned to the *obat* players. "I prefer to dance in joy than watch in sorrow!" He caught Jenise, pulling her to the center of the floor. "For our freedom is in here!" He pounded his chest with his fist. "In *here!*"

A boisterous clamor rose in the air as all cheered their flamboyant king's response to the situation.

In that moment Jenise could see why he was so loved by his people.

The music changed. Now it was spirited, sensual, its beat contagious. Gian tossed back his hair in a proud stance. He encircled Jenise slowly, his slumberous gaze capturing her. Then he placed his palm firmly on her waist.

"What do I do?" Jenise whispered frantically, having no notion how to perform this Familiar dance and not wanting to disappoint them all at such an important moment.

{Encircle my waist with your right arm. Throw your left arm in the air like this.} He demonstrated. She followed his lead as he swung her about gradually.

He started slowly but soon went faster and faster, turning her round and round.

Jenise began laughing gaily. Gian smiled at her, the music infusing him with spirit.

He released her suddenly as his boot heels rapped on the floor, a series of intricate masculine steps pulsing to the beat. The onlookers began clapping to the rhythm of his staccato steps. Jenise watched, spellbound by his masculine grace of movement, his style, his beauty. He entranced her with his striking steps, making love to her with expressive movements that were at once highly sensual and commanding.

He leapt into the air and landed on one knee. With a sweep of his arm, the dance spoke of his claim to her and his joy in it.

He slid across the floor on his knees, coming to a stop exactly in front of her. He tossd his hair back and became the untamed male. Powerful hands clasped her waist. In an unorthodox manner, his face pressed lovingly into her stomach. Feeling passion's beat, he *swayed* with her to the music in a sensual undulation she would never forget.

Without warning, he sprung into the air again, taking her with him as he whirled her about in his arms.

His wild spirit infected the crowd. Soon others joined them; to dance; to celebrate. To be free.

Gian gathered her to him, tight in his embrace, still twirling with her. With his strength, he easily picked her up in his arms, kissing her hard and fast on the mouth before releasing her once more.

They both laughed.

The dance picked up speed. Jenise became breathless, unrestrained with the movements as the enchanting music flowed through her too.

She walked around him slowly, just as he had done to her, and spun him about. She moved up to him and back, swaying seductively with the music. She showed him a small portion of a Frensi woman's talent for the dance.

Gian's dual-colored eyes flashed with admiration and more.

{I will always find my freedom in you, Jenise.}

Jenise's mouth parted in astonishment. Before she had a chance to consider his revealing words, he lifted her again high in the air and twirled around with her.

The celebration continued long into the night as the strange glow from the sealing of the Tunnel lit the room with odd flashes of light. The Familiar people danced with their king and queen.

To freedom of the spirit.

Traed walked through the night jungle.

The slithers and sounds of nocturnal creatures shadowed his steps. The dark tangle was full of deadly menace. He did not care. On the contrary, the silent Aviaran welcomed it.

He embraced the danger, the shadows.

Coarse vegetation surrounded him like a thick shield. He liked that too. To be hidden yet not hidden. Breathing deeply of the humid air, he could discern the scent of earth, vegetation, and elemental life.

A *santark* suddenly growled to his left.

He spun about on his boot heel, light blade already drawn. The immense beast stopped in its tracks, its lethal fangs bared. The two stared at each other.

The *santark*'s pink eyes reflected the Aviaran in their depths—a fierce warrior on the verge of battle.

Traed willed the wild beast to attack him.

The *santark* watched him, frozen in its place. For the span of three heartbeats, Traed did not take a breath. His entire being was alert, ready to fight. To battle for his survival. To *feel* alive.

The beast snarled a deadly warning.

Traed's pale green eyes sparked with the light of challenge, a flash of satisfaction glowing there. In a puzzling move, the Aviaran lifted his chin arrogantly, standing straight before his adversary. Then he slowly *lowered* his blade, making himself a perfect target.

The beast crouched low, preparing to strike.

Traed actually smiled, his hand motioning to the creature to come and get him.

The *santark* hesitated. In the face of such odd behavior from prey, it was suddenly not sure what to do.

Traed's eyes narrowed to slits of glinting jade. "Will you disappoint me as well?"

The *santark* arched its back.

Traed stared him down.

With a hissing cry, the *santark* leapt aside, quickly disappearing into the undergrowth.

Traed's nostrils flared. Turning in disgust, he stormed back to the royal abode.

Hidden in the foliage, wizard's eyes, that were darker than the darkest night, watched his passage. They held more than a hint of concern.

On the planet Zarrain, where Traed had lived for a time, there was a plant native to its desert. It was called a *lutus*. The *lutus* grew strong out of the harsh sands and adverse conditions of the terrain around it.

Much like Traed.

When the *lutus* was opened, it was revealed to be full and hollow at the same time.

Much like Traed.

Yaniff stroked the feathers of Bojo as he considered the possibilities.

Late that night, Yaniff met with Gian in his private study.

Gian motioned the old wizard to sit as he poured him a cup of warmed *mir*. "Did you enjoy the celebration, my friend?"

Settling himself comfortably on the low cushion, Yaniff picked up the *mir*, sipping gratefully. "I am much too old for such wildness."

Gian gave him a disbelieving look. "Mmm-hmm."

Yaniff smiled into his cup. "Never mind that. It seems your festival went very well. Despite the sealing of the Tunnel."

Gian rubbed his jaw. "Yes, it did."

"Jenise has much to come to terms with—in her mind."

"I know. But I have the confidence she will."

"Ah, Familiar arrogance! How I miss it sometimes." The wizard grinned.

Gian snorted. "Now Yaniff, you have your own Familiar from what I hear. One who can give you all the arrogance you need to liven up your dull life."

Yaniff snickered into his cup. "He is not quite as arrogant as you were at his age, Gian. But then, few are."

"Mmm. Give him time."

Yaniff chuckled. Gian shook a finger at him. Wizards and their Familiars. Always a special bond.

Dara Joy

"Tell me, Yaniff, what transpires with Rejar?"

Yaniff paused in his drink. "What makes you think something has transpired?"

"Traed. He was completely stunned tonight during the celebration. He stopped as if he were thunderstruck. I noticed that his Cearix—or should I say *your* Cearix—was glowing. Now what was that about?"

"Rejar has come into his power." He placed his empty cup on the table. Gian refilled it. "It released earlier today for the first time."

"I see." Gian watched the ancient mystic with narrowed eyes. "And what was so miraculous about it? Is it not a normal occurrence for a Charl? A rite of passage?"

"Yes, it is." Yaniff returned his look. "This was somewhat different."

Gian exhaled slowly. "Then you were right all those years ago."

"Yes."

"Good."

Both men were silent in their own thoughts.

"I need you to do me a favor, Yaniff."

"What is it, Gian?"

"I would like you to open a signature arc, an image arc, onto Ganakari." As a high-level mystic, Yaniff had the ability to send a message, via an arc, through time and space and dimension.

Yaniff raised his eyebrows. "To what purpose?"

"I wish to pay Karpon a little visit . . . shall we say, once removed?"

Yaniff smiled wickedly. "Say when, my friend." He downed the last of his drink.

"You are not taxed from the sealing of the Tunnel?"

Yaniff scoffed at the ridiculous question.

Gian grinned. "Then *now,* I think."

The wizard inclined his head. A bolt of power was directed at the wall from his fingertip. It sizzled and snapped. Soon a tiny opening appeared, no bigger than a small stone. "Speak," Yaniff said. "He will see your image."

Gian crossed his arms insolently over his chest and propped his booted feet up on the table. He was going to enjoy this.

Karpon sat down in his favorite seat before the fire.

He was of a mind to go over his plans for his assault on the Familiar. A highly trained clandestine force would make the first attack on the morrow. This force had instructions to find and take as many Familiar as they could, using the special drug to render them malleable. Since the Familiar had a yen for adventure, many of them constantly traveled. In fact, Karpon had heard they couldn't bear not having their "adventures."

The beauty of the plan was that by the time the Familiar realized that a great many of their number were missing, it would be far too late. Such abductions were difficult if not impossible to trace.

The captives were already spoken for on the market.

Karpon had received a tidy sum for them, sight unseen; his coffers were bulging. He hadn't believed the price a prime male specimen brought on the illegal trade market! It was more than his greedy imagination had foreseen.

Suddenly a shimmer filled his vision. An image appeared before him. It was a man. His arms were crossed over his chest, his boots propped on a tabletop. He looked vaguely familiar. . . .

Familiar!

"You!" He jumped out of his seat to call the guards, but stopped when he realized the man was not actually there.

"What sorcery is this?" he sneered.

"You will not easily get another Familiar within your power, barbarian."

Karpon jeered at the image.

"The Tunnel on M'yan has been sealed forever— there is no entrance for you."

Karpon paled. The numerous stones he had already collected on account had come from some very dangerous beings. They would not take kindly the news that he could not deliver.

"Jenise is mine. She is with me here and here she will remain—forever out of your reach."

Karpon hissed at that piece of news. "Who are you?"

"In case you are wondering who I am," the image seemed to answer him, *"I am Guardian of the Mist. King of all Familiar. Is it not unfortunate that you did not know who I was when you had me chained to the wall like a beast? Just think what you could have done with that informat-*

ion . . . no telling how much you could have got-
ten for me in trade."

The image flickered and died out.

Karpon's fist crashed onto the arm of the
chair. He had had the King of the Familiar in his
power? And he had lost him! All because of Jenise. Now the Familiar had *her.*

A roar of outrage bellowed from him.

It was not over.

Not nearly over.

Jenise was fast asleep by the time Gian entered their bedchamber. It was almost dawn.
Disrobing, he slipped under the silken coverlet,
taking her in his arms. He had found a way to
thwart Karpon without harming the Ganakari
people. Exactly as his *tajan* had asked of him.

His retribution was only beginning, though.
Karpon would answer in the future for what had
been done to him in that cell; he would pay for
what had been done to Dariq.

A strong tremor shook him. Then another.

His time was approaching. He would not be
able to put it off much longer.

It complicated his task with her; if he had his
choice, the timing would be much different.
There was no way of knowing how a non-
Familiar woman would react to what was ahead.

The luxury of choice, however, was not his. He
would speak to Jenise on the morrow.

Then she would have to make her true choice.
For good or ill, Gian had run out of time.

Despite his discomfort, he tangled himself around her, as was his feline way.

The entire night he held her as the tremors continued to assail him.

Chapter Sixteen

Jenise sat by the edge of the lagoon.

Hidden by fronds and dense foliage, the choice spot allowed her privacy while still affording her a perfect view of the aqua water as it gently lapped the shore. Off to her right, a waterfall cascaded into a large pool; its flowing sound was a soothing balm to any troubled spirit seeking peace.

Idly, she tossed some pebbles into the water, watching concentric rings spread across the surface. The initial simple action of the stone hitting the water always caused more complex aftereffects. *An analogy to my life,* she thought.

The stone hitting the water was much like her first encounter with Gian. Their coming together had been a quick, decisive action. The ripples of consequence were still reverberating through both their lifelines.

She had never sought such complexity.

Yet it had found her.

In her quest for freedom and simplicity of spirit, somehow her life had become more layered. More entangled. *More enriched* . . .

Gian.

It always came back to Gian.

He would not easily release her, that she knew. Despite what he had said to her, a man like Guardian of the Mist would not give up his battle for her; it would go against his very nature to do so.

And what about her? *Did she not want him herself?* Want him. Crave him. Taste him. Even when he was apart from her she could still feel him inside her, part of her.

He had grown within her like another seed of herself.

Jenise had never been sure about destiny before; but now she wondered. Were they meant to be together? She could not deny the strange closeness between them; the way they came together like pieces of a puzzle made whole; the way they fit.

But if she embraced this concept of destiny, where was her self-determination? Her freedom? What future could she make for herself? Thoughts in turmoil, she tossed another stone into the water.

Hidden as she was, she was still not surprised to feel Gian's presence behind her. There was no place that the Familiar could not find her if he so desired, of that she was certain. If she left him, it would have to be with his complete agreement.

A condition that seemed highly unlikely.

She felt him sit down behind her silently. Allowing her the privacy of thought if not space. So like a cat . . .

Finally she spoke as she gazed out across the water. "I am a prisoner here."

"No," he answered her softly. "You are not."

"But you will not let me leave!"

"It is too dangerous." It was not the answer she wanted; it was not even an answer to her accusation. But then, she was learning that the Familiar were masters of subtlety; their words were often chosen to produce the outcome they sought.

She exhaled noisily, exasperated. In a strange sense, she was charmed as well. The dichotomous nature of the cat—ever alluring, ever frustrating.

Gian was well aware of her mood. "I only want you to come to know this land, this people, as I do." His voice dropped a register, becoming a soothing, coaxing purr. "Do you not think it a beautiful place?"

"Yes, it is. Very beautiful. But it is not my place."

He leaned forward so she could feel his heat at her back while he smoothed a section of her long hair over her shoulder in a caring gesture. "Yes, *taja*, it is."

Her shoulders stiffened. "Do not call me that."

"I have taken a bond for you." His breath feathered the curve of her throat. "For me there can be no other."

His lips pressed against her shoulder. "I want no other."

"Please do not, Gian!" She shrugged her shoulder away from his warm lips; his touch, as always, was confusing her.

Gian stayed the course. His strong arm came around her waist, embracing her, pulling her back close against him. "Why not? We both want each other and the need gets stronger each day that passes. Surely you feel it. I love you, Creamcat."

Jenise closed her eyes at his admission. A tear tracked its way down her face.

He nuzzled her neck. "Do you not love me, Jenise?" He purred against her delicate skin.

"*Yes,*" she breathed, admitting the truth to herself as well. "I love you, Gian."

His lips latched onto her throat, drawing gently on her, lovingly on her. "When this business with Karpon is settled, I will take you everywhere you wish to go, Jenise. I will show you the Alliance, tempt you with new worlds, gift you with all that I have to share."

Jenise was overwhelmed at his offer. She hadn't considered that he might be willing to go with her. "You would do this for me? Leave your people?"

He smiled slightly against her skin. "I would

never leave my people . . . it is not a question of that."

She turned in his arms, pulling slightly away to look up at him. "But you just said—"

His beautiful green/gold eyes captured hers. "It is the way of the Familiar to explore. I can give you what you want, Jenise. In time. If you trust me."

Maybe he could. Already, he had surprised her on many counts. At times, he had bent for her, changed direction. And he had the courage to attempt new pathways—as he had proven to her countless times on their journey.

She bit her lip.

Perhaps she had not seen the situation clearly? Gian was not simply a man who exerted power; he was a Familiar who *shaped* power. Did he not metamorphose himself? Would not this ability touch other parts of his life as well?

The revelation struck her.

Long ago, when they had met, she remembered thinking that the Familiar would set her free. Perhaps it was not a mere thought but a prophecy. . . .

Could Gian be the key to her heart's freedom?

Was he right when he had said that such love could unbind the soul? Her aqua eyes filled with emotion as she watched him, revelation upon revelation hitting her at once.

"I simply ask you to think on it." His fingers brushed her lips. A strong tremor hit him. Beads of sweat dotted his brow. He pulled back from her, almost doubling over.

Jenise put a hand on his arm, pulled from her thoughts by his ashen complexion. "What is it, Gian? Are you ill?"

He sucked in a deep breath, regaining his composure. "No; I am not ill. I have asked you to think on these issues, and yet I am afraid that there is one decision you need to make now, *taja*. A very important decision."

She gave him a worried look. "Wh-what is it?"

"There is something that Familiar men do not speak of to anyone outside the Mist. It has to do with our very natures. In the wrong hands such information could prove disastrous to my people. What I am about to tell you is one of the many reasons we keep to ourselves in matters of bonding; one of the reasons we cloak ourselves in secrecy."

Jenise was torn between his trust in her and wariness of a knowledge that perhaps she would be better off not knowing. Her courage as well as her concern for him won out. "Does it have to do with this trembling you are having?"

His eyes gleamed in appreciation; she would hear him out. "Yes. It has to do with what we call the Incarnation."

"*Incarnation?* What is it?"

Gian enfolded her in his arms, bringing her close against his chest despite the small tremors still racing through him. "Have you not noticed that most of the males here are of a certain age?"

Jenise's brow furrowed. She had noticed that the other night at the celebration. "Yes, but I thought . . . well, I am not sure what I thought.

Everyone knows Familiars are so . . . so . . . "
She faltered for words.

He chuckled. "Mmmm. One of the reasons we
are as we are is because of our Incarnation.
When a Familiar man reaches his peak level
somewhere between the age of thirty and forty
standard years—and for each of us it is an individual timing—we incarnate."

"What do you mean by incarnate?"

"There is a process we undergo that enables
the male Familiar to maintain the height of his
physical perfection throughout the majority of
his lifetime."

"I do not understand; are you saying you do
not age?"

"No, we age, but only within a ten-year span
after our first Incarnation is achieved. There are
nine Incarnations in the male Familiar's life,
each spanning approximately a decade of time."

"So you maintain that optimum level as you
call it"—her cheeks blushed—"for ninety standard years?"

He nodded. "Our productive years, in which
we indulge the physical part of our natures."

The concept was most alien to her. "What happens after you have completed these nine cy-
cles?"

"We begin to age naturally for the remainder
of our life span. My *utal*, H'riar, has completed
his Incarnations. It is just one reason he makes
so worthy an advisor; he has experienced much
in his days."

"Is it so vital then for you to remain perfect?"

Gian grinned broadly. "Thank you, *taja,* but you misunderstand. Our physical appearance has naught to do with this. What is important is for us to maintain the peak of our physical *stamina.*"

"Why?"

"It is our greatest strength and our greatest gift to our mates."

Jenise gave him a wary look. "Just how is this Incarnation achieved?"

Gian exhaled. "Well, you see, the man and the woman—"

Jenise's mouth dropped open. "Surely you jest?"

Gian winced. "I am afraid not, Creamcat."

"But . . . *how?*"

"I must explain to you how we Familiar view these things. We believe that within our sensuality lies a gate to true spirituality. When we are mated our sexual natures take on deeper levels. It is part of a lifelong exploration between the male and his mate. This process takes us higher within ourselves, both as individuals separately and as one together."

"It sounds beautiful. . . ."

"It is, Jenise, although I have yet to experience it with you."

"*With me?*"

"Yes."

She swallowed. "What would it involve?"

"For a male Familiar, release and completion are two separate things. We aspire to pleasure a woman by bringing her to numerous releases;

sometimes making love for days at a time. Each time the female reaches her peak, her energy releases to the male—which in turn raises his energy level. Eventually, if they are in harmony, they enter into the tiers of the Incarnation ceremony; what we call the Nine Hundred Strokes to Love. The energy will flow back and forth between them, raising them to a higher state of being. You have seen me metamorphose into my cat self."

She nodded shakily, stunned by what she was hearing.

"A similar event occurs, only the male will begin to take on an energy form, bringing his mate along with him until Incarnation is achieved. It is a rite of endurance, a trial and a passage and a blessing all at the same time, which brings about not only physical changes but spiritual fulfillment."

He watched her carefully. Jenise felt the weight of the stone in her hand. "Do both mates have to undergo this Incarnation?"

"The male must; the female has the right to choose."

There it was at last. So he had been telling her the truth all along. It would ultimately be her choice. "There has never been a non-Familiar woman who has gone through this?"

"No."

She sucked in her breath, "What if I cannot . . . I am not Familiar, Gian! I may not be able to . . ."

His hand cupped her cheek. "If I see you are having difficulties, I will disengage."

"What happens if you do that?"

He glanced away and would not speak.

Jenise clutched his arm. "It is too risky, Gian! What do the men do who are not mated? Surely there must be some alternative."

A muscle ticked in his jaw. "There is. There are priestesses who guide unmated males through this. Such an option is not open to me, nor would I take it if it were. I have taken an oath for you; I cannot break it."

Nor would she want him to—but if his life were in danger . . . ?

"No. I cannot," he said, seeming to read her thoughts.

"Is there no other way?"

"In certain unusual circumstances, a male can sometimes complete the Incarnation himself by entering a deep meditative trance. However, such a state is extremely difficult to achieve; it can be dangerous for him."

There did not seem to be much choice. Not if she cared for him.

"Have you done this before, Gian?"

"Just once. There is a small Incarnation line on my inner thigh that—"

"I have seen it." He cocked his brow at her.

She blushed. "I wondered how you had gotten such a marking, especially there."

A dimple curved the side of his mouth.

"You went to these priestesses the last time?" For some reason a wash of unreasonable jealousy gnawed at her insides.

"Yes . . . as we all do when not mated."

A dismal thought occurred to her. "So you retain your vibrancy as your mates age?" Her nostrils flared as she realized what that meant. "That does not seem very fair or desirable to your females."

Gian chuckled. His arm snagged around her neck, tugging her forward. "Ah, but that is why we keep it such a secret." His teeth grazed the side of her throat in a teasing manner.

Jenise sulked. He could afford to smile about it. He was not the one who would—

At her pitiful expression, Gian could not go on with the jest. "Age has its own beauty, *taja*. Even so, at the moment of Incarnation we can give life, Jenise."

She gasped. "You mean . . . ?"

"Yes. We can gift our mates with Incarnation as well."

Her mouth dropped open.

He closed it with the edge of his finger. "I will not be gifting you with such a thing until the next Incarnation."

Her mouth dropped open again.

He glanced down at her through his thick veil of black lashes. "You see now why this information must never get out."

"Yes," she whispered, still stunned by what he had told her. If the Familiar had been hunted before, she could not even imagine to what lengths some would go if it were known they could bestow youth with their love.

A tremor shook him anew. His dry lips

pressed her forehead. "I will await you in our chamber. Make your choice."

With that he released her and left as silently as he had come.

And while Jenise looked out across the water, trying to make the most important decision of her life, Gian Ren entered their chambers to decide whether or not he should wait to give her the most precious gift of all. . . .

A gift he could only attempt to bestow once every ten years.

She weighed the pebble in her hand.

No matter how careful she had been, no matter how she had tried to withhold herself from him, it did not matter in the end.

He had captured her.

Jenise knew Gian's nature; he could do no less. He had been honest with her about that.

She wanted back that part of herself that he had taken. She wanted him to have it forever. Gian Ren had seeped into her. He was in her heart, her mind, her soul.

He was the tidal wave and the lapping ripple. He had hunted her bit by bit, zealously guarding what he had seized until she dwelled completely inside him. Taken.

Then he simply offered her his heart.

How dangerous these Familiar were!

She squeezed her eyes shut even as she squeezed the stone in her palm. *She wanted that noble heart*. She wanted *him*. The significance of the Familiar exchange of breaths came home to her. To be whole together, to be alive in each other's arms, to share the same breath . . .

To find an exalted peace.

She did not pretend to understand the mystical ways of the Familiar; or how they recognized their mates. But she had come to believe in their ability to do so . . . for he had shown her the meaning of this infinite love they shared, a love that was ever-changing and ever-growing.

A love that was untamed. Unbound. *Free.*

She opened her palm and released the security of the stone.

She came to him as he knew she would.

He had prepared the chamber for them himself. First, he lit hundreds of scented tapers; their glow was soft and ambient like love that endures.

He removed all of his garments. Then he scattered *tasmin* blossoms in the pool along with fragrant oils, placing the aromatic vials next to the cushions and *krilli* cloths that spread across the floor and low bedding. The silken cloths were in colors of purple and red, arranged in mysterious patterns, patterns designed to evoke the senses. To evoke her "taste."

He scattered petals over the coverings, allowing their luscious scent to rise in the air, knowing the heat of their entwined bodies would soon release yet more of the fragrance.

He opened the doors to the balcony, letting in the muted tropical breeze, closing his eyes briefly as he listened to the sensual music of *lati* filaments as they hummed in the night wind.

His blood beat heavy in his veins, pulsing through him in an ancient, expectant rhythm.

The Incarnation was a mystical transformation to the Familiar. Their sensuality became a true physical expression of love. It was a journey of discovery and renewal, for body, heart, mind, and spirit.

The male gathered his Incarnations about him throughout his life, pivot points of remarkable change, growth, and if he was blessed, much more. His female would awaken him fully. She would become the catalyst for him to bring true power into passion.

He would share this with his Jenise.

He would give himself completely to her and, he hoped, she to him. He would surrender himself to her female energy. She would conquer him even as he took her. Her woman's sensuality would release him and rebirth him.

He would become older and newer in the embrace of her love.

Gian placed a bowl of fruit on the woven rug, straightening to look at her as she entered the chamber. Their eyes met. Aqua to green/gold. Both knew what this meant.

He held out his hand to her.

She took it.

Slowly he walked behind her, lifting the fall of her hair to place his lips against her nape. He unclasped her caftan, watching it slide down her body.

Lifting her in his arms, he stepped into the pool with her.

His fathomless eyes reflected the room's flames as he watched her, examining each of her features silently.

"What do I do, Gian?" she whispered.

He smiled slightly. "Incarnation is spontaneous and intimate. There are nine tiers; I will lead you through them to direct your energies."

Her hand cupped his strong face. "Then I trust you to do so, my *taj*."

He sucked in his breath at the simple words that said so much. She had called him her king and in so doing had acknowledged not only who he was, but who he was to her.

He turned his face to place a scorching kiss in the center of her palm.

"I have not made my ultimate decision yet," she said hoarsely.

"Yes, you have."

He lowered her until she stood in front of him. Scooping up a handful of water, he watched the scented stream trickle over her full breasts. The gentle bubbling of the water in the pool soothed as it stimulated.

Jenise listened to the filaments chime, a light echoing sound which seemed to overlie the wondrous scent of *tasmin* and *krinang. Tasmin* from the floating blossoms, *krinang* from Gian. From outside, she could hear the jungle calls of animals.

"M'yan," he whispered. "It speaks to us even now." He ladled more soft water over her skin.

"Once it is in your blood, it will never leave you, Creamcat."

Like him.

Her lids fluttered closed at the heady sensations washing over her, not the least of which was his skimming touch. Barely there. Yet unmistakable.

She swayed in the water as he poured the scented liquid into her hair, infusing the strands with wet warmth.

Smoothly, he dipped into the water before her, tossing his hair back when his head broke the surface. His fingers clasped her waist under the surface, bringing her closer to him.

Once more he dipped under the water. Soon, she felt the lick of his tongue on the curved rim of her navel. A warm flick surrounded by the cooler, lapping water.

A small sound issued from her lips.

{Which laps you better . . . me or the water?}

His voice purred in her mind as she felt another hot lick further down between her legs. Her fingers clutched his shoulders. *Him or the water?* It was not even close.

He broke free of the surface and gazed up at her, droplets of water dancing on his thick black lashes, catching the flames in the room. He smiled slowly at her. Too sexual to be sweet, she knew.

He shook his head, flinging a spray of droplets on her and laughing in a low tone when she jumped back.

His arm snagged her around her waist, bringing her wet, heated body in contact with his. He dipped his head to brush her lips in a satin caress. Light touches of water. Light touches of Gian's lips. Light touches of burning skin. All designed to tantalize and provoke.

She murmured something incoherent as she lightly nipped his chin.

He lifted her out of the water. Stood with her in the center of the pool, letting the fragrant water sheet off them before he carried her to the plump cushions on the floor. There he carefully placed her as if she were on an altar for him.

He blew on her body, the barest warm breeze, from her shoulders to her toes. His heated breath evaporated the clinging water droplets. Her skin tingled everywhere his breath touched.

"Gian—" She placed her palms against his upper chest, feeling the satin texture of his skin. "Hold me . . ." Gently, yet decidedly, he removed her hands from him, placing them by her sides. He did not want her touching him yet.

Taking a vial of *krinang* oil, he warmed it in his palms.

Pouring small amounts into his hands, he massaged the oil into her body with long, firm strokes. Everywhere his hands passed, her body rose to meet his touch. So he touched every part of her body with his moistened fingertips— from the curve of her lips to the curl of her foot.

The oil on her skin glistened in the light of the tiny flames. Gian's eyes glistened as well, embers of Familiar desire that Jenise recognized.

He reached over to a bowl of *gharta* fruit, carefully slicing the spiny exterior until the pink flesh within was revealed.

"Close your eyes, Creamcat," he murmured. Cutting a segment off, he took the succulent fruit and rubbed it along her lower lip, letting the juices trickle into her mouth.

"Mmmm . . ." She swallowed the sweet juice.

Gian leaned over her, his long hair brushing her breasts. Slowly, he licked the sticky-sweet residue from her lips. Jenise shivered.

He sat back on his haunches and as she opened her eyes, he placed one large palm on her heart, the other on her lower abdomen, feeling the rise and fall of her breath. He matched his breathing to hers.

Taking her hands, he placed one on his heart, the other low on his abdomen. She could feel their breath. Syncopated. *Harmonized.*

He watched her, observed her features, the tiniest nuances in her expression. His glance as potent as a touch.

Jenise knew what he was doing then. He was leading her into the Incarnation slowly, heightening all of her senses for him. Unfortunately, she did not possess as many senses as a Familiar woman. "I wish I had more to give you."

"I embrace that which you offer, Jenise, for it is my intention to gift you with the identical experience enjoyed by Familiar women, utilizing only the five senses you possess."

If she hadn't already adored him, these words alone would have done it. And there was that beloved feline arrogance of his! Her lips twitched as she teased him. "You are very confident that you can."

He shrugged disarmingly. "Of course. In fact, I am of the opinion that with my superior methods, your experience will surpass any other." He gave her a sexy wink.

"Your best trait is your humbleness, Guardian of the Mist."

He laughed, enjoying the sexual banter. He kissed her. A full, deep contact with his mouth. Then he sipped delicately at her upper lip, gently suckling on it.

And the bottom lip as well.

The tip of his tongue teased at the seam of her mouth, begging entrance. Jenise drew it inside, suckling on him. Gian held her close; he purred against her, stimulating her auditory sense as he rubbed and nuzzled, felinelike and playful.

In the same playful manner, he explored her with his mouth from head to toe—the soles of her feet, the rim of her navel, the crease behind her knee all knew the press of his velvet lips.

Their breathing became deeper.

He began the first tier of the ceremony by penetrating her deeply as she lay beneath him. He was dominant yet tender to her, the combination of his strength and sensitivity his true power. The depth of his strokes varied with the pace of his thrusts as he followed the ancient incremental pattern of eight shallow, one deep. Jenise was stunned by the highly stimulating movements.

He seamlessly brought her to the second tier. Seven thrusts shallow, two deep.

That was when he began to shift her position, as if performing the steps of an intricate, well-learned dance. In front of him. Over him. To the side of him.

By the time he reached the third tier, Jenise knew that the coming night would be more than she had imagined. The Incarnation picked up pace and rhythm, acquiring an almost trance-like quality. No matter how he tried to control his passion, with each tier, Gian was getting wilder.

He bit her shoulder and placed her under him so that she lay on her stomach. Sliding over her, he entered her from above and behind. "Raise your hips for me," he purred coaxingly in her ear. When she did; he bit the back of her nape.

Then he showed her how to move her body; how to open her inner muscles for him. He became hissing cat and sensual man; purring feline and demanding lover.

He was still.

He moved.

He captured her warmth.

He showered her with undulant waves.

He surrendered himself to the passion that he unleashed in her. Wild. Free. He rode the crest of her waves, holding back and yet not holding back.

Jenise wrapped him to her, held him, loved him.

But most important, she let him be Familiar.

She did not shrink from his feral thrusts, his untamed responses, his wild passion cries.

By the time he reached the sixth tier, she could not catch her breath. When he had spoken of the Nine Hundred Strokes to Love she thought he had been speaking figuratively. Now she was not so sure. What if she could not go on?

His white teeth grazed her throat and she forgot everything but his flawless touch.

By the seventh tier, she knew she was his to take. In whatever way he wanted.

As she tried to regain her own pacing by turning over onto her back, he sat on his knees before her, raising her legs to his shoulders. He clasped her ankles firmly, nipping the undersides of her heels as he pulled her up onto his lap and penetrated her fully. She cried out at the exquisite sensation.

Then screamed at the vibrational enhancement that followed.

"Gian! Gian, please!" she begged him.

He lightened his touch then, hearing her in his passion haze.

The palm of his hand came down flat on her feminine core even as he moved within her. He nudged the heel of his hand in on her and pressed sharply, sending her over the edge. As he had countless times already since he had started.

However, at this stage, the rapid vibrations of her release were a danger to him. During Incarnation, it was crucial that the male not achieve his own release until he reached the ninth level.

Growling something indecipherable, he placed her fingertip firmly beneath his manhood. *"Press,"* he commanded.

Shocked, she stared mutely at him.

{It will allow me to experience the pleasure without release, taja.*}* She did as he asked. He threw back his mane of hair and groaned long and low in his throat.

Withdrawing from her and placing his hand beneath her hips, he raised her to him. Then he loved her with his mouth. Jenise began sobbing. It was too much!

Gian was trying desperately to hold back, but he was in the grips of a ritualistic feral mating. He changed their positions. Lying on his side while enjoined to her, he tried to stop for a moment—an unheard-of thing for a Familiar man to do in the midst of Incarnation.

"You must surrender yourself to each moment, *taja,*" he said brokenly. "Each touch . . . each breath . . . it is the only way. . . ."

She nodded shakily.

His thrusts continued in the incremental pattern. Now his special enhancements strummed in syncopated pulse. It occurred to Jenise that the legendary enhancer of the Familiar was so much more than a simple sexual augmentation. While they occasionally used the technique to magnify pleasure, she now knew that the ability was intricately connected to this ritual of Incarnation.

When he reached the eighth tier, she knew he

was holding back for her. Beads of moisture dotted his forehead, his beautiful dual-colored eyes were passion-glazed, his hands shook. "I must stop for your sake," he croaked. "I—"

A strong tremor rocked his body. And hers. He groaned in pain.

He cannot stop the Incarnation, she realized. He would not survive it.

"No!" Weak as she was from the wild lovemaking, she clutched him to her, refusing to let him stop. She was not a Familiar woman, but she *was* a woman who could fight for what she loved! She knew the strength was in her. She would show this Familiar *the power of a woman's heart.*

"No, Gian! I want you to continue! Do you hear me? I will not let you stop!"

A burst of energy and longing seized her with her resolve.

She rolled with him, bringing him beneath her. He grabbed her hips, bringing her flush against him as he surged up into her with a dynamic penetration. Her hands rested on his chest as she leaned over him, moving her hips, showing him that she was a match for any Familiar woman!

Gian's eyes narrowed in approval as he watched her.

A soughing purr rolled from his chest.

There was only a moment to wonder if the cat in him had been testing her all along. . . .

With a mighty effort, his arms encircled her and he sat up with her in his lap. Still pulsing within her. Not getting weaker but stronger and stronger.

With their arms around each other, holding each other tightly, he sharply nipped her shoulder, using the *Sting of Honey* bite. A highly provocative and skilled maneuver designed to elevate sexual fervor.

It worked.

Jenise cried out, losing herself in the expertise of his lips, hands, teeth, and strokes.

He entered into the ninth level.

Nine sharp pulses of enhancement.

Nine strokes, all deep.

Jenise moaned into his mouth. He hissed into her throat.

Photons of light began to circle him, rising from his core, pulsing and glowing with his movements as the sexual energy between them rose higher and higher into something new.

Her feminine strength seemed to be lifting within her. A glow lit his form, blinking on and off as parts of him throbbed, humming as if he were in the process of metamorphosing. Only he was not transforming. . . . Something else was happening.

Pulses were skittering along her; she looked down at her own arms, shocked to see the glow around them as well!

He took her mouth in a blazing kiss. Uttering a fierce yell, he opened himself entirely to her, releasing everything to her. Surrendering his strength, his power, his love.

Both of them cried out at the sheer beauty of the moment.

Holding each other fast.

As the spasms and pulsations went on and on.

Until finally they sagged against each other, heads resting on each other's shoulders.

Jenise blinked. *She had done it!* She had brought Gian through his Incarnation! And she was not a Familiar woman. She cuddled her cheek against his shoulder in a loving gesture as she tried to regain her breath.

A small tickle *itched* in the palm of her hand, trying to get her attention. Uncurling her fingers, she gasped as a tiny yellow sphere of light rose upward.

"Look, Gian," she whispered in awe.

Spent, still breathing raggedly himself, Guardian of the Mist gazed up at the free-floating ball of light. Sudden moisture filled his green and gold eyes; an expression of unbound happiness lit his handsome features.

"What *is* it, Gian?" she uttered softly, awed by what she was seeing as well as what they had recently done together. They were still intimately joined.

The tiny light bounced over Gian, almost lovingly, before darting around her. "It is our son, *taja.*"

Jenise gasped. *"Our son?"*

"Yes, and he is Familiar!" His face glowed with pride.

Gian held out his palm and the little light flitted to rest on the surface of his palm. "Will you take him, Jenise?" he asked reverently.

Jenise was stunned. Familiar procreation was much different than Frensi. While she hesitated out of shock, the tiny light began to fade. "What is happening to it?" she cried, alarmed. "Why is he fading?"

When Gian spoke, his tone was sorrowful. "You have not accepted him. I understand that it is too soon—"

"I do accept him!" she called out urgently, afraid that with her ignorance of Familiar ways she had somehow harmed their child. She had not thought to have a child, but now that he was here . . . well, that was different!

Gian gave her such a look of love that Jenise knew she would never forget it. Cupping the tiny light, he solemnly placed his palm over her lower belly. With a strange ZIP! the light was gone.

"Where did it go?" she gasped.

Gian chuckled at her expression. "In you, *taja*. His physical body came to being within you this eve, but it is the spirit we created together that gives him his true life."

Her hand covered her stomach, hardly believing that their child was now residing there. *Gian's child.* Her eyes filled with tears. "Did you know of this before we started?"

He shook his head. "I knew there was a possibility, but that was all. A Familiar man can only bestow such a gift during Incarnation, but even then the energies must be exactly right for conception to occur. Although I had the ability to prevent it, Jenise, I could not bring myself to. So rare will be the opportunity for us . . ." He brought her hand to his mouth. "I decided it would be your choice."

Her fingers brushed his lips. "*Decided* it was my choice, hmmm?" The never-ending subtlety of the Familiar.

His eyes sparkled at her. "I see you begin to understand us."

She laughed. "Hardly."

"Good. I prefer to remain a surprise to you, my Creamcat." He grinned engagingly at her.

For the first time she noticed he appeared more vibrant and somewhat more youthful. Her strength had given this to him. A feeling of *power* rose up in her. "The Tan-Shi Mother was right then."

"What did she say?"

Jenise gave him a coy look as she ran her little finger lightly over the small second line that had appeared on his upper inner thigh. "Never mind, Guardian of the Mist, you have gotten me into quite enough trouble for one day."

He laughed, hugging her to him. "Ah, but I have *nine* lifetimes of trouble for you."

She smiled against his throat. "Yes, I believe you do."

He purred huskily.

Chapter Seventeen

Lorgin sat on the grassy knoll, bouncing his infant daughter on his knee. His father, Krue, scrutinized his every move as if he were about to commit an unspeakable blunder in the care of his daughter.

Lorgin sighed mournfully.

When it came to his first *nearchild* Krue was worse than . . . well, he was just worse! Who could have guessed that such a fierce warrior would get so *overtaken* by a mere babe?

Lorgin cocked his blond head to the side and stared at his daughter as if he were trying to see what strange command the tiny thing wielded. She gazed up at him with her enormous amethyst eyes and gave him a foolish little grin.

His heart melted as it always did. Well, yes, he

could see she was exceptional! He gave her a gentle hug.

"I vow Lilac and I shall wait a long while before we have a babe." His brother Rejar had sauntered over.

Most likely to cause trouble.

Rejar confirmed Lorgin's opinion when he gave his brother an evil grin. "After all, I would not want to do anything to interfere with this fine *rapport* you are building with Father."

Lorgin's nostrils flared. It was unusual for Rejar not to be under the watchful eye of Krue. Somehow, since Rejar had returned with a wife from Ree Gen Cee Ing Land everything had turned upside down! Including the fact that his brother was entering the Charl—a thing he had sworn he would never do.

Rejar casually tickled Melody under her chin. The babe reacted as most females did around the half-Familiar; she gave him a dreamy look of complete adoration.

Lorgin's amethyst eyes narrowed.

He lightly smoothed over his daughter's fuzzy red hair. "I am not too concerned, brother . . . knowing you, it should not be too long before you garner Father's *undivided* attention once again."

Rejar gave his brother his famous gamin grin. The smile that said, we shall see. Lorgin snorted.

The family had gathered on this hillside for Rejar's initiation ceremony. It was a secluded glade near the Towering Forest where most of the Lodarres line had been initiated. Lorgin, himself, was initiated in this very spot when he was but a young man. He noted that Traed and Gian and Jenise were making their way up the knoll to them.

"How many Charl does it take to don a cloak?" Adeeann, Lorgin's wife, cheerfully asked him.

Lorgin rolled his eyes. His wife had started these "how many Charl" jokes and they had taken Aviara by storm. "Will you cease these Charl jests!"

Adeeann gave him a smug look and waited.

Lorgin sighed. "How many?" he asked, resigned.

"Five."

"Five?" Rejar raised a black brow.

"One to don the cloak and four others to nod approvingly!" Adeeann grinned.

Rejar roared with laughter.

Lorgin gave her a reproving glance out of the corner of his eye, although his lips lifted at the corners.

Gian went over to greet Rejar. Jenise found herself alone with Yaniff. The old wizard congratulated her, his dark eyes twinkling.

"How do you know?" Jenise smiled at him, surprised.

"I am a mystic," he replied with a gleam. "I know many things."

Jenise shook her finger at him. "And what do you see of our child?" Her hand covered her abdomen protectively. "Only good things, I hope."

Yaniff grinned at her. "Could Guardian of the Mist sire anything less?"

Jenise laughed. "You do know him well!"

Yaniff chuckled. "I cannot tell you much, but the babe will be of golden hair—lighter than Gian's, darker than yours. His eyes will be aqua and gold and like his father's."

"Like his father's?" Jenise questioned, for Gian's eyes were green and gold.

"Yes . . . like his father's."

His meaning sank in. "The aqua eye . . . ?"

"Will have three tiny flecks of gold."

Jenise inhaled a deep breath. "He will rule M'yan then."

Yaniff stared at her silently.

"What else, Yaniff?"

The ancient mystic rubbed his chin. "He will inherit your Frensi gift."

She blinked at this. "The gift of the Dance?"

"Yes."

"But . . . that is impossible! It is only passed on to the females of my race."

"Why do you say that?"

"Because it has always been so!"

"Ah. Mayhap that it is because it has always been *believed* so."

She bit her lip as she pondered his words. "Perhaps . . . Then he will be able to—"

"Express his love through the Frensi Dance but only once in his life. To his perfect love, yes."

Jenise thanked Yaniff as she patted her stomach, praying that her son would not only recognize his perfect love, but also experience it throughout his lifetime. Her gaze went to her husband. Something Rejar had said had amused Gian, for he threw back his head in laughter, his perfect white teeth flashing. *He is so handsome. . . .*

So incredibly strong.

Her heart thudded in her chest. Gian was like a tidal wave. He rose up from nowhere, gathered strength and surged over her. And like the tidal wave, one could not assess what had occurred until after the wave had broken.

Gian had happened to her like this. While the track of his storm had always been clear to him, she had not realized the depth of the undertow until she had been pulled into his maelstrom.

She loved him so very much.

Loved him as Guardian of the Mist. Loved him as Gian Ren. Loved him as a Familiar. Loved him as a man.

She had found him on her way to escape; he had led her to freedom. Of body. Of spirit. Of being. Through Gian her Frensi nature had been released.

Walking over to him, she placed her hand lovingly on his lower back as he spoke to the sons of Krue.

While he spoke, he discreetly lifted into her touch, arching the curve of his back in blissful feline recognition. Jenise smiled to herself, stroking him softly.

"Are you ready to begin, Yaniff?" Krue took the old wizard aside.

"Yes, everyone is here."

"Mmmm." Krue's glance fell on Traed, a slight frown marring his face. "I had hoped for a double initiation."

"He will not come easy, Krue. There is too much within him from the past."

"Think you I do not know that? Nonetheless, he is a Lodarres, son-of-my-line. He needs to take his rightful place among his family."

Yaniff watched Traed speculatively. "Perhaps. Perhaps not."

Krue faced Yaniff, a fierce expression on his features. "There has been enough rebellion with him! He *will* join the Charl."

Yaniff appeared bemused. "Traed has inherited your stubbornness, Krue. There is much of you in him. It will be interesting to see the two of you 'discuss' this."

Krue narrowed his eyes. "Who said anything about discussion? He is my son, he will do as I bid him."

"Ho-ho!" Yaniff doubled over in laughter. "Much as your other sons have, hmmm?"

Krue hunched his shoulders. "Can I help it if I have raised independent sons who know how to think for themselves?" One amethyst eye glittered at the old wizard.

Yaniff chuckled. "Let us hope that Rejar can curb himself somewhat—at least for the duration of the ceremony." Both men caught Krue's youngest son in the act of running a suggestive palm over his wife's backside. They shook their heads.

Lilac shooed Rejar's hand away. Krue snickered.

"His frolicsome ways are a trial to me, Krue."

Krue knew that Yaniff jested by the look of pride the wizard gave his student. Rejar had done well.

Yaniff motioned the half-Familiar to him as the family members sat on the lawn in a semicircle before them. As Rejar turned to join his Charl master he happened to glance behind them.

From every pathway, mystics were converging on the knoll! They came from all directions, endless lines from every house on Aviara. And they were led by the Sages themselves.

They filled the fields around them and still they came.

"What is this?" Rejar murmured to his brother Lorgin.

Lorgin watched the procession coming towards them. "They come for you, Rejar."

"But why?" He was stunned.

"To witness your initiation."

Rejar's smooth brow furrowed. "I do not understand."

"Come, Rejar." Yaniff took the Familiar by the arm, instructing him to kneel before him.

In his hand, he held up a crystal point which dangled from a small gold circlet. The old wizard's voice rang out loud and true.

"The crystal is clear and hides no falsehood;
It is the window of vision and the veil of re-
flection.
Its being is pure as its nature is faceted."

Yaniff bent over Rejar, placing the golden circlet with the dangling point next to his ear. A glow came from his fingertips.

"This is the mark of a Charl.
Let it guide your actions in light throughout
your life.
Let it always remind you that wisdom is a
necessary mate to true power.
Thus the supplicant becomes the war-
rior. . . ."

The earring pierced Rejar's left ear cleanly. The crowd murmured its approval. Yaniff stood back.

"Thus the warrior becomes the mystic.
Arise Rejar ta'al Krue, knight of the Charl,
future holder of the true power!
THE TENTH POWER!"

The crowd began chanting his name. "Rejar! Rejar! Rejar!"

Rejar was staggered at Yaniff's words. *The tenth power?* The difference between power levels was exponential; a fourth level was not twice as powerful as a second—it was that power raised to the fourth level. Yaniff, the greatest power in the land, was a seventh-level mystic. Wizards such as Yaniff had the ability to see potential power levels. Tenth power? Impossible!

"What mean you, Yaniff?" he whispered hoarsely. "I have not such abilities—"

"Yes, Rejar, you do."

"But I . . . I do not . . ."

Yaniff placed a fatherly arm around his broad shoulders. "Think you I would cast you off without guidance? You have much to learn, Rejar. I will teach you all that I know; the rest you will teach yourself."

The second son of Krue was slightly pale around the mouth.

In truth he did not seem happy with what Yaniff had revealed that day. Rejar had never wanted such a destiny. But then destinies were not of one's choosing.

He cast a wary glance at his wife, Lilac. As he suspected, she was not overjoyed either. She took in the crowds with a wary eye, her concerned focus shifting back to her husband. They were both wondering what this new revelation would mean to them. To their lives.

Krue looked at his younger son, his speculative gaze shifting back to Yaniff. There were many questions in that warrior's eyes. Questions from his past. He looked then at his Familiar wife, Suleila, who was staring at her son in shock.

Krue's penetrating eyes returned to Yaniff. It was the glance of a seasoned warrior who had seen much in his life, a seasoned Charl who sensed there was more to this then met the eye.

Suddenly the crowd parted and the Tan-Shi Mother stepped through, followed by a hooded contingent of her personal disciples. The rumblings of the crowd grew as they passed by; it was so unheard of for the Tan-Shi to come to a Charl initiation.

This was a momentous day on Aviara, this day of·initiating Rejar ta'al Krue.

The Tan-Shi Mother approached Rejar, standing before him. She threw the hood of her cloak back. Long silvery hair blew in the light wind. "The Tan-Shi recognizes Rejar ta'al Krue!" She cupped the half-Familiar's hands in hers. Her entourage threw back their hoods, a sacred symbol of recognition and acceptance. A first in Aviaran history.

The Aviarans shouted the name of Rejar into the sky.

Rejar knew not how to deal with this. What did they expect from him? He was as he had always been; he did not feel any different whatsoever.

"Of course not," Yaniff murmured next to him. "For you have always been as you are. It is not in the being but in the recognizing."

Rejar viewed him cautiously. He shielded his thoughts from all Charl.

"Good." Yaniff nodded approvingly. "Begin to be very cautious, Rejar. It will serve you well."

The men of the houses lowered themselves on one knee before him. Each held out a Cearix to him as they bowed their heads in homage.

"What are they doing?" Rejar did not like this at all.

"They offer you their heritage." Yaniff motioned to Traed, who knelt, offering up Yaniff's Cearix as well. Even his own brother, Lorgin, had knelt before him, his hand outstretched with his father's Cearix.

"Why do they offer this to me?"

"Because you can see the 'truths' of their ancestors. You are the one, Rejar."

"No!" he hissed in an unsteady voice.

"It is so. You must choose one Cearix to be your first. Choose wisely." With that Yaniff went down on one knee before him, holding out a Cearix.

{You offer me Theardar's blade?} Rejar did not know whether to be insulted or not.

"It contains many truths, my student. The most painful lessons sometimes reveal the deepest knowledge."

Rejar stood on the hillside and let his blue/gold gaze scan the crowd kneeling before him. What should he do? Clearly, he would have to make a choice. He noticed that the elder wizard Gelfan had been very slow to bend a knee and offer his blade. He raised his black eyebrow.

Yaniff watched him closely.

Rejar reached out and took Gelfan's Cearix.

Sharp, he is . . . Yaniff smiled to himself. With Rejar's acceptance of Gelfan's Cearix, he had formed a powerful bond with Gelfan's house. Rejar had just made it much more difficult for Gelfan to undermine him in the future.

In the days to come Yaniff would advise him on which houses to align himself with and in what order. Such strategy was crucial, but Rejar had always excelled at games of strategy. Soon he would put his real skills to the actual test.

Ultimately, Rejar's passion would become his salvation or his trial. His kind heart would undergo the ordeal that always faced men of extreme power and conscience.

From all that was to come, the complete Rejar ta'al Krue would be forged.

Yaniff thought of the purity of the crystal he had placed in Rejar's ear and prayed that the half-Familiar Charl would always find its clear resonance within to lead him home.

At the end of the day Yaniff took Rejar aside privately and handed him a small, crooked staff upon which was tied a leather thong. "An initiation gift for you, my boy."

Rejar looked dubiously at the odd staff, which came only to his knee. "And what am I to do with it?"

"Why, nothing. It has already been done." Chuckling mysteriously, Yaniff walked away.

Rejar shook his head, shrugging his shoulders. Sometimes wizards were quite odd. His heated glance honed in on his wife. It was time they made their way home.

The crystal earring swirled as it hung from his lobe.

He wondered how ticklish such an earring would be on certain parts of his wife's anatomy.

A mischievous grin spread across his sultry features as he sought her out.

Taj Gian leaned back against the fluffy green and gold cushions of his bed as he waited for his wife to come to him.

What was taking her so long? She had told him she needed a few moments alone. Being feline in temperament, he understood such a need. But that had been some time ago!

He was just about to toss aside the silken coverlet and go in search of her when the door to their chamber opened. Jenise closed the door gently behind her.

Then she faced him.

With a motion of her hand, she unclasped her gown, letting it slither to the floor. Their eyes met.

Gian rested back against the bedrest behind him, waiting for her to come to him.

She did—but not in the manner he expected.

Her body began swaying slowly to a seductive tune she hummed. A tune that at once seeped into his senses, bringing him alive, awake to the present. Her hands twined in one intricate position and yet another, moving to the seductive rhythm with a grace of movement he had never witnessed before.

The long strands of her pale hair swung free as she undulated her body in a symbolic display of utter feminine beauty. Gian watched, spellbound.

As she slowly crossed the room to him, she

dipped and stretched and flowed to the erotic, mesmerizing tune. Her actions revealed her passion for him, spoke to him more eloquently than words ever could have done.

His firm lips parted as he realized it was the Frensi Dance of Love and that she was performing it for *him*.

For the first time in his life, Gian Ren let the tears flow freely down his face as he beheld her dance—a physical expression of her perfect love. He could understand why men spoke of it in hushed whispers, with longing. She became like a living work of art, her steps, her rolls, her sensual gyrations . . . the story she told with her body.

He would remember this for the rest of his life. In all that she was, in her dance, he saw the true power of the female. Endless. Enduring. Mutable.

Female power. Inner strength. Encompassing spirit. Its passion light released to be free when the male and female united on every level.

He opened his arms to her as her tune caressed his heart.

It came from the lips of his beauty, his creamcat. . . .

His soul love. Whose lips he licked.

Chapter Eighteen

Yaniff slowly climbed the highest peak in the mountains of the Sky Lands of Aviara, the birthplace of Traed's natural father.

It was said that the clearest visions visited some on these lofty peaks.

His winged companion, Bojo, dropped a uniquely designed black and silver pouch laden with clarified stones into Yaniff's hand. The wizard opened the string and scattered them over the mountaintop. Their source, and the way they had been attained, made them a perfect mystic's lens.

Strong gusts of wind tugged at his crimson robes as he looked across the land.

Clouds were building on the horizon, although in reality the day was clear. The roiling formations were dark, deep, and dangerous.

Yaniff watched the signs carefully.

There was a storm coming in. It rode the echoes of future history.

He listened closely—

The crest of the forewind whispered to him, *"Gifted . . ."*

AUTHOR'S NOTE

I hope you have enjoyed the story of *taj* Gian and his mate Jenise as much as I loved writing it. All of these Matrix of Destiny characters are very dear to me.

While these books are designed to be read on their own for the individual love story contained within, there are continuing underlying elements which connect all these books, forming the entire scope of the story. This epic adventure series spans many novels; so, yes, there are more to come!

I want to personally thank all of my readers for the wonderful cards, letters, and gifts you continue to send. A writer's life is by profession a solitary one. Your remarkable support is a powerful source of inspiration for me.

Haughty young Lady Kayln D'Arcy only wants what is best for her little sister, Celia, when she travels to the imposing fortress of Hawkhurst. For the brother of Hawkhurst's dark lord has wooed Celia, and Kayln is determined to make him do the honorable thing. Tall, arrogant and imperious, Hawk has the burning eyes of a bird of prey and a gentle touch that can make Kayln nearly forget why she is there. As for Hawk, never before has he encountered a woman like the proud, fiery Kayln. But can Hawk catch his prey? Can he make her...Hawk's lady?

___4312-2 $4.99 US/$5.99 CAN

Rejar

DARA JOY

Lord Byron thinks he's a scream, the fashionable matrons titter behind their fans at a glimpse of his hard form, and nobody knows where he came from. His startling eyes—one gold, one blue—promise a wicked passion, and his voice almost seems to purr. There is only one thing a woman thinks of when looking at a man like that. *Sex.* And there is only one woman he seems to want. *Lilac.* In her wildest dreams she never guesses that bringing a stray cat into her home will soon have her stroking the most wanted man in 1811 London....

__52178-4 $5.99 US/$6.99 CAN